# FIRE

## A MT. PROSPECT MYSTERY

# CORINNE MALCOLM IBELING & R.I. PARTRIDGE

Black Rose Writing | Texas

ISBN: 978-1-68513-294-1
LIBRARY OF CONGRESS CONTROL NUMBER:
PUBLISHED BY BLACK ROSE WRITING
www.blackrosewriting.com

Printed in the United States of America
Suggested Retail Price (SRP) $21.95

*Abby's Fire* is printed in Garamond Premier Pro

*As a planet-friendly publisher, Black Rose Writing does its best to eliminate unnecessary waste to reduce paper usage and energy costs, while never compromising the reading experience. As a result, the final word count vs. page count may not meet common expectations.

Cover Design by GetCovers

# Dedications

To my husband John, who supported me as a writer all these years.

—Corinne

To my husband Ernie, who encouraged me to never give up my dream.

—Rebecca

# ABBY'S FIRE

**A MT. PROSPECT MYSTERY**

# PROLOGUE

When I look back on the day that changed my life, I remember every detail. The thirty-minute ride home had passed in icy silence. With relief I saw our house come into view, tucked among the tall pines. Even at this distance it was homey, welcoming, with a thin column of smoke rising into the evening sky. Everything seemed peaceful.

Peaceful, that is, until I realized the smoke wasn't coming from the chimney. As we drew close, I could see that it was curling through the windows and snaking under the front door.

The deceptive quiet lasted just a moment longer. Then it was broken by the wails of fire trucks in the distance. I cried out in horrified disbelief, "Oh God! Brad, our house is on fire!"

Before the wheels had stopped turning, I jumped from the car and raced toward the door. By then, huge flames had appeared from nowhere. Black smoke enveloped me as the fire lapped at the wooden siding and burst into an inferno.

From behind me, Brad grabbed at my arm, trying to pull me away from the door. "Abby, no, it's too late! Don't—". But the rest of his words were drowned out by the roar of the fire as I plunged into the house in search of our boys.

# CHAPTER 1

ONE YEAR LATER...

Big trucks pack the double lanes of the Interstate as occasional gusts of wind rock the car. It's been a year since the fire, and my hands are clamped onto the steering wheel so tightly that even their white scars don't show. Dark clouds scud across a sky that's as dull as an old nickel.

My shoulders and neck are stiff after the drive from Des Moines, and I'm looking forward to reaching Mt. Prospect. It's been years since I've driven this stretch of I-80, so I'm surprised to see the giant restaurant-motel-gas station that appears at my exit. With tall poles showering golden light, it's about as alien as a space-station dropped onto fields dotted with dirty snow and the wet remains of harvested corn and soybeans.

It looks like a busy place on this late March afternoon, and I'm tempted to stop since I haven't had anything to eat all day except a snack on the plane. But my sister Vernelle is expecting me, and she'll have some yummy food ready when I get there. Vernelle is a surprisingly good cook. I decide to wait and turn the car south onto the blacktop toward Mt. Prospect.

It's been a long day, one that started early this morning at the Sacramento Airport. A nice lady from the hospital, probably some kind of social worker, made all the flight arrangements for me.

Though I've flown many times before, I was anxious at first. But when I reached the huge, familiar "artwork" consisting of pillars of suitcases (which never looked much like art to me), excitement and happiness bubbled up from my very soul. Pulling my wheeled suitcase, I wove my way through the concourse crowded with people and shops, carefree as a child.

Somehow I managed to ignore the sweet, wafting fragrance of the Cinnabon stand, handled my suitcase on the escalator with ease, and negotiated security without embarrassing myself. The others, would-be passengers and hopeful greeters, all looked stressed about one thing or another, but I wasn't.

It's amazing how free I felt after a year in and out (but mostly in) various hospitals. I've been through so many operations that only someone who's had that kind of experience can begin to understand. But maybe the freedom I felt was more like someone getting out of jail. I could finally say good-bye to cold rooms overlooking graveled roofs, lukewarm food on divided trays, and watchful—ever watchful—eyes.

I was aware that I was attracting some attention in the airport, and that's from people used to ignoring everyone except celebrities and possible terrorists. Even if they couldn't see my face, most people would notice the cadence of my left foot didn't match my right. But those people didn't know me, so it didn't matter. It didn't matter during my layover in Denver, where I bought a couple of postcards for my boys, and it didn't matter when I reached the Des Moines airport. It didn't even matter when I picked up the car that Vernelle had arranged for me there. But it would matter soon.

Still, I managed to get through the flight from Sac and the layover in Denver all by myself. I hadn't gotten lost or misplaced any of my things, and no one had bothered me, at least, not much. In fact, only two people, apart from airline employees, had spoken to me on the entire trip.

I was sitting in the Denver airport, waiting for my connecting flight to Des Moines, when a woman came into the departure area. Like everyone around me, I couldn't look away from her. As tall as a man, she had frizzy, blond hair and masculine features. At first, I wondered if she *was* a woman, but her tanned arms and legs looked feminine even with all the tattoos.

With a guitar slung over one shoulder, she wore a black leather vest with a pink T-shirt and cut-off denim shorts. Shiny dream-catcher earrings dangled from her ears, while matching silver bracelets circled her arms. Neon pink Nikes made a nice finishing touch.

She pulled along a small wheeled suitcase with an even smaller one attached that weaved behind it like the tail of an alligator. When the woman plopped herself down in the chair beside me, she gave a sigh like air wheezing out of a cushion.

One hand with long pink nails touched my arm, and I turned toward her, wondering what she wanted. "Sweetie," she said in a deep, fruity voice, "could you keep an eye on my stuff while I go to the little girls' room?"

I nodded, and she sauntered majestically away. I watched after her (so did everyone else), wondering who she could be. Surely she's a member of some famous rock band? Or maybe a star on a reality TV show?

In a few minutes, she came back and sat down, stretching her long legs out in front of her. I was trying to think of something friendly to say when I felt someone tapping my shoulder from behind. I turned to see a little boy standing there. He was blue-eyed and blond, and reminded me for a moment of my son, Hunter. I started to smile when he said in a nasty voice, "Hey lady, what happened to your face?"

I froze, unable to answer. But my new acquaintance swiveled around. With her mouth about an inch from the boy's face, she said in a low voice, "The lady's a Hollywood actress, kid. See that guy standing over there?"

We both looked at the man she was pointing to. Wearing a sharp gray suit, he stood against one wall, hands clasped behind him. He was very big, VERY big. I'd previously dismissed him as some kind of Homeland Security guy. When he saw us looking toward him, he nodded his shaved head, eyes unreadable behind dark glasses.

"That's this lady's bodyguard," the woman hissed. "And if you bother her one more time, he'll throw your scraggly little butt right out the door. You got that?"

The boy nodded, speechless.

"Good. Now, scram!"

The boy scooted across to his mother and whispered in her ear as she glared at us. Then her eyes flickered toward the man, and she looked away, arm held protectively around her son.

"You'd think she'd be a *little* embarrassed," I observed shakily.

"Nah, she probably sent him over, the bitch."

I managed a smile. "Thanks for helping me out. I had no idea what to say. How did you come up with that story so fast?"

She shrugged her wide shoulders. "It's what I tell shitty little kids when they bother *me*. Sometimes adults, too. You can't believe how rude people can be."

I said I was finding that out and asked if the man was by chance *her* bodyguard.

She smiled, revealing startlingly white teeth. "Maybe." She paused a moment then touched my arm. "Listen, sweetie, you are what you are--never try to hide from that. It's the one lesson I've learned in life."

I smiled my thanks. Then her flight was announced, and she stood up, towering over me as she gathered her things. She paused, pulling a card from her pocket. She scribbled something on it and handed it to me before striding away.

Surprised, I looked down at the card in my hand. On one side, in flowing script, was the name Zandra Marxx, which meant nothing to me. On the other was a caricature--just a few strokes of my hair and profile--but it was *me*. Beside it, the words, "You are strong."

I lost sight of my new friend as the crowd surged forward. But I think of her—the Woman at the Airport—with a smile and vow to remember her sensible advice: I am what I am. And I am strong.

And the boy's comment? I'll have to learn to deal with that kind of thing. As Vernelle would say, with a few expletives thrown in, "Toughen up, buttercup."

After all, his question was what everyone else in the room was thinking: *"Hey lady, what happened to your face?"*

# CHAPTER 2

The sky has turned from steel gray to charcoal, and tiredness floods over me. The euphoria I'd felt as I traveled is gone, and I just want to get to Vernelle's. I decide to watch for the shortcut. It's a curvy stretch of road that isn't traveled much but leads to the side of town where my parents' house—rather, Vernelle's house now—is located.

Suddenly, a big spatter of rain hits the windshield. "Damn!" I yelp. I don't need rain added to the mix of tired and dark. I keep saying damn with every drop that hits the windshield until I'm damned out and have to turn on the wipers. But it only gets worse as the drops of rain turn into flakes of snow.

Snow this late in March? Seriously? But, as anyone in Iowa will tell you, one week during March can be in the 80's, and the next can bring a blizzard. Brad used to say that Iowans are strangely proud of their unpredictable weather. I wish he was here beside me, with the boys bickering as usual in the back seat about who touched who first. But, no, it's just me alone in the dark.

I let up on the gas to focus more carefully on the wet road. It's shiny as a piece of black licorice in the glare of my headlights; already its edges are lined by patches of white. I peer out the side window, but with the darkness and blowing snow I can't see much. Farm buildings and fields are out there, but they've been gobbled up by the mini-blizzard.

I slow down even more and consider the situation. Of course, the various "ologists"–all those the so-called experts at the hospital—would tell me, "Draw on your inner strength, Abby. Think positive."

Okay, I'm only a few miles from town, I have a new car with plenty of gas, and there's a fancy GPS that can tell me—nothing, except that it lost its buddy, Mr. Satellite. Unbelievable. I try scolding it a couple of times, but the miniature car on the pretty, midnight-blue miniature screen refuses to budge. So much for technology. A dog with a sense of direction would be more help than that.

The short-cut—where is it? (Or, as one of my little boys used to say, "Where it is?") Could it be a mile or two farther? Or did I already miss it somehow? A light display on the dash tells me helpfully that I'm going west—but west of what? The map in my brain is all skewed, and I don't have a clue where I am.

Things had been going so right this morning, and now they're going so wrong. Vernelle hadn't wanted me to drive from Des Moines to Mt. Prospect by myself, but I said I've done it a thousand times before; what could happen? Well, this is what could happen— I'm lost in a snowstorm, and a glance at the car's clock tells me that now I'm not only lost, I'm late. Vernelle will definitely be getting worried.

With snow settling over the car like a downy blanket, modern technology fails me again—my cell phone can't find any service. No service? How can that be? I stare at the phone's screen in disbelief, resisting the urge to hurl it out the window to fend for itself in the snow. With the car barely moving, I wipe my sweaty palms on my shirt. I just want to stop the car and sit here. It would be so easy, so very easy, to do just that until either my phone works or someone drives by and rescues me.

But then, looming out of the darkness on the right side of the road is a house with light shining from a couple of windows. It shields the car slightly from the wind, and I pull into the driveway and stop. Now I can ask for directions to Mt. Prospect.

Getting out of this warm car is the last thing I want to do, but it makes the most sense. Freezing to death in the driveway doesn't seem like a good option. At my funeral, I can just picture Vernelle, standing over my coffin, hands on her hips, and scolding, "Abby, what the hell were you thinking?!!"

Swearing under my breath (I blame that on Vernelle's influence), I put on my jacket. As I pull my gloves from my jacket pocket, I feel the card the Woman at the Airport gave me. I get it out. In the greenish light from the dash, I can barely make out the words, but it's enough. "I am strong," it reminds me.

With new resolve, I step into the snow. That's when my leg gives out. If I weren't still hanging onto the door handle, I'd be flat on my back. My stupid left leg—it's weak and gets completely uncooperative at the worst possible moments. Somehow I manage to right myself and hobble to the sidewalk where the footing is more solid.

The sidewalk leads up some steps to an open porch across the front of the house. Here, out of the swirling snow, I can see a front door flanked by a pair of windows. The windows are covered with curtains, but a bar of light escapes between them on one side. When I'm close enough, I can't resist a cautious peek into the room.

Even though my line of vision is a little blurred--perhaps by moisture on the glass--the room inside is lit like the stage of a play. Near the center of the room, in front of a fireplace, is a small table with five people gathered around it. One is an older woman, clearly a motherly type, and next to her are two small, tow-headed boys.

The other two, nearly hidden by a pile of books and papers, are a teen-aged girl, also blond, and a dark-headed boy.

I smile then, because I can see that they're holding hands under the papers. It's a happy scene; they all look so contented that I feel a sharp pang of envy, especially since the little boys remind me of my own sons, Hunter and Grayson. After a moment, before they can see me, I step away and go to the door.

Surely, on such a snowy night, the mother would ask me in for a moment, and I could sit with them by the fire. Maybe I would pull the little boys onto my lap and rub my cold face against their silky blond hair. At the mere thought, my empty arms ache with longing.

I'm poised to give a sharp rap on the wood, then lose my nerve. After a slight hesitation, my hand drops to my side. My hair is long, and if I lean just right, I can keep the left side of my face hidden. But in the firelight, it will be clearly visible. It—my Halloween face. Half normal—the other half a scary mask.

The boys would be shocked and maybe even cry. The mother would grab them from me, while the others would stare in fright. Of course, I'd have to leave. With sagging shoulders, I return to the car.

Once inside, I turn up the heater until it's blasting out heat and my shivers stop. Opening my purse, I pull out my photos of Hunter and Grayson. Faded and almost worn through, they are the only ones I have. I hold the pictures a moment then put them away, wishing I had some recent ones. The boys will have changed so much by now, and I wonder when I'll see them again.

All the lights in the house go dark, and I'm afraid that I've scared the family. Did they see me and mistake me for a peeping Tom? With a sigh, I turn on my headlights and the windshield wipers. The snow has let up, and now I can see the house more clearly. It's just a little white Iowa farmhouse—nothing unusual. Yet there's something oddly familiar about it... And then I have it. This is "the old Miller place," as it's always been called. And it's owned, by one of those strange coincidences in life, by my sister. She inherited it from our parents (I got money instead, since I lived in California), and she uses it as rental property. I hadn't thought of the place for years.

The map in my mind straightens around, and I know exactly where I am. After backing the car onto the road, I head unerringly for Mt. Prospect, which is, indeed, only a couple of miles away. Not that I'm conceited, mind you—but who needs a GPS, anyway?

# CHAPTER 3

It's completely dark by the time I reach the big, red brick house where I grew up. After I put the car away in the garage, I follow the sidewalk through skiffs of snow to the back porch. I'm just reflecting on the fact that Iowans usually use the back door, except for strangers, when the kitchen door flies open.

Vernelle screeches, "Abby! Why the hell are you so late? I've been worried sick!"

I run up the steps, glad to be out of the cold wind that's whistling around the corner of the house. Good things—light and warmth and kitcheny smells--wash over me as I step into the room. "Sorry, I took the back way into town and ran into this crazy little blizzard that messed me up," I explain breathlessly. "I tried to call you, but there wasn't any phone service."

Vernelle gives me a fierce hug of welcome. As she pulls away, she says with a frown, "There are still some dead spots around here. People complain about it all the time. Anyway, that wasn't a blizzard you were in—that idiot weatherman on Channel 6 likes to call them 'snow events' these days."

I pull off my wet jacket and hang it on the rack by the door. "You could have fooled me—there were times I couldn't even see the road. It's been years since I've driven through anything like that!"

There's a brief silence. When I turn around, Vernelle says tremulously, "I just can't believe you're really here."

"Well, I am, Sis. It's good to be home." And it is. The kitchen, with its bright red curtains and red-and-white enamelware on the walls, is heaven compared to the bland rooms where I've spent the last year. I take a deep breath. "In fact, it's more than good—it's wonderful."

Vernelle's eyes are glistening. "Oh, Abby!" And suddenly there are tears running down her cheeks.

I don't mean to cry. In fact, I had promised myself that I wouldn't, but it's too much when I see Vernelle. Before I know it, I'm crying too, and we're hugging each other again and weeping. My tears are mostly happy ones, but there are sad ones mixed in, too. Maybe it's the same with my sister. We grew up in this home with loving parents; now, there are just the two of us.

Vernelle gives me a last pat on the back and wipes her eyes. "I'm all right. It's just that there were so many times that I wanted to bring you back home from California, and here you are. Finally."

"Believe me, I'm glad to be here, too. I never want to see another hospital, but I suppose I'll have to, sometime. Dr. Scott—remember him, the one who looks about twelve?—always has one more operation in mind, but I finally said that was enough for now. I have to get back to some kind of life."

Then a little waft of culinary heaven drifts by. "What is that bubbling away on the stove? It smells great!"

Vernelle shrugs modestly. "Just some soup I made. I figured that would be easy since I wasn't sure when you'd get here. But first, I want to show you the house."

There's something uneasy in Vernelle's tone. She takes my arm and leads me past the dining room (it's dark, so I don't see anything different there) and into the living room. Now there's definitely something different.

For as long as I can remember, this room has been the same: pale blue carpet and walls, a couch and chairs upholstered in pastel florals and placed just so in front of the brick fireplace. There were satiny blue drapes at the windows, and (daringly for Mom) a pair of raspberry-velvet occasional chairs, looking like new because no one ever sat on them. Small tables, big floral pictures, and lamps with frilly shades multiplied through the years. Definitely a feminine room--no wonder Dad spent most of his time in his den.

Now when I walk into the room, I think (but luckily don't say) "My God, I must be in a blizzard again!" Because all I can see is a snowstorm of white. Gone are the blues and pastels, the floral and the raspberry. Everything is shades of white—except for the floor. It's pale wood, with fluffy rugs scattered here and there.

I plop down on Mom's couch, which now has a cotton slip-cover, and stare around in wonder. I can barely recognize the ugly brick fireplace, since it's been painted faux white marble and filled with fake, white electric logs.

Vernelle walks around the room, pointing out the curtains, which are bleached-white panels, and the accents she particularly likes--beaded lamp shades, an old door leaning artistically against one wall, and pale green glass vases on odd shelves. I suppose you would call her décor "shabby chic," an effect I couldn't make look right in a thousand years, but it looks right now.

When I don't comment for a moment because I can't, Vernelle eyes me anxiously. "I hope you don't mind what I've done."

"Why would I mind? This is your place now, Sis. Just for the record, I think it looks like a page from *House Beautiful*. Anyway, you know my taste in decoration—anything I put together always looked more like what *not* to do with a room."

Vernelle laughs a little and relaxes. "Well, I wasn't sure what you'd think. I love going to flea markets and garage sales—I get things that I like and then paint them or repurpose them. I don't have much extra money, but I'm having fun decorating when I can."

I run my hand over the smooth, white cotton slipcover. "Doesn't that lawyer you work for pay you enough?"

She shrugs. "Clarence pays me what he can. There aren't that many clients right now; he has a shitty reputation around town, plus I think he gambles. I'll start looking for another job one of these days."

Her tone informs me it's a closed subject. Vernelle used to work for a big law firm in Omaha before she came back to Mt. Prospect to take care of our parents when they started having health problems. I'll always be grateful to her, since it meant giving up part of her life. But after Mom and Dad died within a few months of each other, she never returned to Omaha; I've often wondered about that.

"Anyway," she continues as she pulls me up from the couch, "I don't know about you, but I'm starved, and the soup is ready to go."

While I settle myself at the small table in the corner of the kitchen, Vernelle starts reheating the soup and sandwiches. "How was your flight?" she asks, checking the burners.

"No problem at all, Sis, though my layover in Denver was pretty interesting." When Vernelle looks up curiously, I tell her about my new airport friend and give a humorous twist to my description of how she rescued me.

"Zandra Marxx?" she repeats as she puts the food on the table. "Funny name for a guardian angel." I couldn't agree more.

I'm suddenly famished at the sight of the big bowls of fragrant tomato-basil soup and cheese sandwiches. ("Fontina, gorgonzola and provolone cheeses on sourdough bread with fresh tomato slices," Vernelle informs me.) As I said, cheese sandwiches.

A companionable silence settles over us as we eat. Between bites of my sandwich, I find myself really looking at Vernelle. Her short, dark curls and porcelain skin haven't changed much, and her lips are the usual candy apple red. But even her make-up can't hide the dark circles under her eyes. And she looks older than her thirty-one years. I can only hope she hasn't been too worried about me, though the last year can't have been easy for her, either.

"What?" she asks, catching my glance.

"Nothing. It's just that I'm so lucky to have you." I sip a spoonful of velvety tomato, and watch as she does the same, though her look is more critical. I'm sure she's judging something about its taste. Did it need a touch more basil? Less cream?

"Sis, this soup is *amazing*."

She nods with satisfaction. There are only two years between us, and I've missed her as the time has slipped away. Vernelle. She's always hated her name; Mom found it in some breathy romance she was reading. For a while, Vernelle tried to go by "Vern," but that didn't take. "Nelle" didn't work either, so she's stuck with it.

I smile at a sudden memory. "Sis, aren't you glad I don't call you 'Sissy' or 'Bee' for baby like I used to?"

She nods and smiles back at me; then her smile suddenly wavers. "Oh, Abby," she whispers, "your poor face! You used to be so beautiful--I just can't get used to--" Tears start to run down her cheeks again.

I reach across the table to squeeze her hand. "It's okay—truly it is. You know, I'm lucky that whatever fell on me—and I can't even remember what it was—burned only my left side. In fact," I add as I release her hand, "Dr. Scott used to tease me that if I'd been any worse, he could have found a new face for me. He's always wanted to do one of those whole-face transplants. Can you imagine waking up one morning and not even recognizing yourself in the mirror? At least I can recognize myself. I still have half of my old face—I guess you could say I'm still half pretty."

She sniffs. "I don't think your Dr. Scott is very funny."

"Humor in the hospital can be pretty bizarre, but it's better than crying all the time." I'm reminded again of the Woman in the Airport. "I am what I am; I have to accept that." I add firmly, "I've also decided not to hide away now that I'm back in Mt. Prospect."

Vernelle's impish grin is back. "You mean you're not going to emerge just at night, like a freaking vampire?"

"Exactly. It will take me awhile to get used to being here—after all, I've only visited a few times over the last fifteen years—but I'm going to act as if the fire never happened." If I can.

"As if Brad had never happened?"

"That, too," I agree. "You didn't like him, did you?" I've never asked Vernelle that question before, but I've always wondered.

She scowls. "No, there's something wrong with people who start every sentence with 'I.' What did you ever see in him?"

I think back to the early days with Brad. "When we first met in Des Moines, he was funny and charming—he always had a crowd of friends around. I was amazed that he paid any attention to little old me. I mean, there he was, this terrifically attractive airline pilot from New York, and I was just a kindergarten teacher from small-town Iowa. I really thought I was in love, but I'll admit I wasn't too thrilled about moving to California after we got married. I hated to leave you all; I remember being homesick for a long time."

"I know; it was pretty damn selfish of Brad! Why did Mr. Big-Deal Pilot want to move, anyway?"

I shrug. "I think he was just bored with Des Moines and wanted to go somewhere new. When we moved to Grass Valley, the old friends were dropped, just like he'd dropped his college and high school buddies—he said he'd outgrown them. He always found new ones; it was a pattern he had."

Even with our boys, he was crazy about Hunter until Grayson was born. And before long, he was tired of them both. "You know, the only thing that's been constant in Brad's life is his love of flying. I should have figured, sooner or later, he'd get tired of me."

Vernelle jumps up and ladles the last of the soup from the stove into our bowls as she sputters, "But to ask you for a divorce after the fire!"

"Well, he did mention it before the fire," I say fairly, trying to conceal the deep contempt I feel for him now. "And you know Brad would never have stayed with me through all this anyway. He was back flying a couple of weeks after the fire. He said it was his way of dealing with 'things.' Well, I sure wasn't one of those things. I just wish he hadn't taken Hunter and Grayson so far away."

For a second it looks like Vernelle might start to cry again. She turns away from me and her reply is muffled as she puts the ladle back into the soup kettle. "I don't think he had much choice."

"Okay, I'll give you that. But he wouldn't have won the Ex-Husband Award for Compassion through the whole thing, either. He hardly ever came to the hospital. His lawyer held my hand more than he did. Brad always disappeared when things got tough. I bet his new girlfriend will find that out soon enough."

As Vernelle sits down again, her pretty face takes on an ugly expression. "When I think of Brad going on with his life after what happened, and with a girlfriend yet! What a bastard! He makes me want to gag!"

"Hey, no gagging allowed--this soup is too good." I scoop up the last bit in my bowl and change the subject. "Anyways, I really appreciate you letting me stay here until I figure out what I'm going to do."

"What are sisters for," she says reassuringly, then adds, "And you take as long as you need. There's no rush."

Part of me wants to tell her that there is a rush—at least as far as I'm concerned. I want to petition for visitation rights with my boys. I'm giving myself ninety days to pull myself together and prove that I'm ready to be a parent again.

However, there's another part of me that refuses to say the words out loud, almost as if saying it might prevent it from happening. Besides, anything about Brad and the boys seems to genuinely upset Vernelle, so I decide to change the subject yet again. "Did I tell you that I got my directions mixed up tonight during the snowstorm and went by the old Miller house? It looks like you have some nice tenants."

She frowns, clearly puzzled. "You must have been off farther than you think—the house is empty now. In fact, the last family moved out in the middle of the night a couple weeks ago, and left the place in an absolutely freakin' mess! I don't know what I'm going to do. I really need that rent money coming in every month."

Now it's my turn to be puzzled. I'm pretty sure I recognized the house, so who did I see there? Ghosts, maybe? But the people weren't wispy and white, so that can't be it. Then I remind myself that I don't believe in ghosts. No, that's too strong. I don't know *what* I believe because I've never given it any thought.

Just as disturbing as the possibility of seeing ghosts is the possibility there was nothing there to see. What if I was really looking into an empty room and imagined the scene? Imagined holding two wriggling little boys on my lap because I miss Hunter and Grayson so much that my mind played some kind of trick on me? I know my face is a mess; maybe my mind is, too.

With hands that are not quite steady, I put my dishes into the dishwasher and somehow manage to steady myself. Vernelle is more familiar with her rental place than I am, so she must be right; I must have been at a different house. That has to be it.

Anyway, I'm home now, with Vernelle, and everything will be all right. I'm sure of it.

We spend the rest of the evening talking and relaxing. The snow has started again, and Vernelle turns on the electric fire. The fake logs flicker realistically, warming the white room. Still perched on the mantel are our graduation portraits, Mom's pride and joy.

The pictures are really nice: Vernelle and I are both smiling. And I still look like me.

# CHAPTER 4

When ten o'clock rolls around, we're both tired and ready for bed. Vernelle helps me get my stuff out of the car and carry it upstairs, where there are several bedrooms and two bathrooms. When we were young, Vernelle and I had our own rooms up here and shared a bathroom between us, though she points out that she sleeps downstairs in the master bedroom now.

There are changes here, too. The walls of my room are a pale sage instead of the sickly peach I'd talked Mother into years ago. The maple furniture is still the same, though, so it doesn't feel strange as Vernelle helps me unpack, which takes about five minutes. All I have are clothes, and not many of them.

As I hang a couple of things in the closet, Vernelle asks, "What are your plans for tomorrow?"

"I have a few errands to run, but my biggest priority is getting some new clothes." I notice in the back are some shelves with several cardboard boxes full of stuff from when I was growing up. Looking through my childhood souvenirs will give me something to do while my sister is at work. But shopping definitely comes first. "I'm sick of the things I bought after the fire—and besides, who wants to wear clothes that remind you of a time you'd rather forget? They're better than hospital garb, but not much. What's around besides Walmart?"

Vernelle slides my suitcases into the closet. "Sophie—remember her? She still has her shop downtown. I haven't been in there for a long time. She sells mostly old lady clothes now—you know, the matchy-matchy outfits with a lot of sparkles that little grandmas wear for a night out at bingo. She must do okay, though. She always has a bunch of new things in the window, and every now and again there's some pretty cute stuff, so it might be worth taking a look.

"When you're done shopping, how about meeting for lunch?" Her smile is much more relaxed now, so is her voice. "I always eat at the Main Street Café. It still looks like it did when we were in high school, but the food's pretty good."

Having such a mundane conversation about lunch plans makes me feel normal again. We agree to meet at the café at noon, and after a last hug, Vernelle disappears down the stairs. Once she leaves, I gather my night things and go into the bathroom. It takes just one look in the mirror, and I sink down, clutching the edge of the bathtub, my sense of normalcy gone.

In spite of the best efforts of the plastic surgeons, there are patches of skin that are stiff and puckered and my left eyelid still droops a little. My nose is the dividing line. The left side a disaster, on the other side, me.

Maybe it's because I'm tired, or maybe it's because I'm in my childhood home, but I can feel my throat tightening up. Unwanted tears fill my eyes. I know it's ridiculous, but I can't help it. Everyone says how brave I am, how wonderful it is that I can keep going, but it's pretty much a façade. In the privacy of my head, things are different.

I'm not brave. I keep going because I have to. In fact, the only thing that *does* keep me going is the knowledge that I have to get better—mentally and physically--to get my boys back. The thought of them makes me grab a Kleenex and dab my eyes—I will *not* cry.

What's frustrating is that, as far as the boys are concerned, Brad still has power over my life. A few months after the fire, he transferred to a job in New York, where he's originally from. He only visited me a few times in the hospital, though you could hardly call them "visits." No flowers, no magazines. No cutesy items from the hospital gift shop. Just Brad, perched on a chair, wishing he were somewhere—anywhere—else. It was pretty obvious the real purpose of his visits was to talk about the divorce.

What hurts even more is that Brad only brought the boys to see me once, and that was when I was still in a drug-induced fog. I remember seeing them standing at the foot of the bed. Hunter held his favorite toy airplane tucked under one arm. His other arm was across Grayson's shoulders. Grayson, as usual, had his teddy bear with him.

I'm sure I didn't look like myself (more like a creepy mummy), with the burn dressings and tubes running in and out of me. The boys were probably frightened, but they didn't cry. They didn't say anything, and I couldn't come out of my drug-induced fog enough to talk to them. Anyway, I fell back asleep, and when I woke, they were gone. Brad never brought them again. And when I asked about them, he said he had taken them to New York "to be taken care of."

Though he was suspiciously evasive (and I was too drugged to get the whole story), I'm convinced that Brad took the boys to live with his parents. I doubt that Chloe (the new girl-friend) would want to play "step-mommy" for more than five minutes with a couple of rambunctious little boys. Realistically, they're better off with his parents. Brad was proud of Hunter and Grayson, but he didn't actually enjoy spending time with them. You wouldn't guess it from the way he talked, though.

I'm reminded of the last time our family came to Iowa to visit. My parents were still alive. On our rare trips to Iowa, Brad was bored to death and not very good at hiding it. As usual, that day,

Dad took Brad golfing, the one thing he liked to do. Brad's an excellent golfer, and it gave him the opportunity to tell Dad's golfing buddies his favorite exploits as a pilot. Brad could be pretty entertaining when he chose to be.

While Brad and Dad golfed, Mom and I had gone uptown with the boys. She had been so proud of us, but I didn't realize then what it meant to her. Her friends had children and grandchildren they saw all the time, while Mom had daughters in Omaha and California, and grandchildren she rarely saw. She never complained, but I can still picture her striding along the sidewalk that day, pushing Grayson's stroller with one hand and hanging onto Hunter's hand with the other, nodding to her friends like a hen showing off her chicks.

When we visited, my parents always took us to the only "nice" restaurant in town, a dowdy kind of place called "The Mayflower," where everyone went to celebrate special occasions. Brad liked going out to eat because there were plenty of people to admire the handsome pilot and his attractive family. Hunter and Grayson were "my boys," when he introduced them to my parents' friends—as in: "Look what I produced." Trophies, maybe, like me.

Once all the attention died down, Brad would get bored and drink too much, leaving my father to pick up the tab, the cheap bastard (as Vernelle would say). But I knew Dad didn't care. He'd give me a wink when he paid the bill and I knew he was just happy to be with Mom and me and the boys.

The boys—my reason for living. Also my reason for not sitting here any longer, in a puddle of self-pity. I finish sniffling, feeling utterly drained, and get ready for bed. I avoid the mirror this time. Obviously, I'd lied to Vernelle. I'm not used to the way I look. How could I be? It's only half me.

As I climb into bed, I concentrate on how glad I am to finally be out of the hospital. And away from all the "ologists," including the doctor who counseled me on how to "deal with my situation." She wanted me to stay in the hospital for further treatment. But I finally made up my mind it was time to go, and Vernelle offered—wanted—me to come back home.

So here I am. And while my face is a mess (okay, only half of it), the one thing I do have is plenty of money, mostly from a huge insurance settlement. That's something Brad's big-deal lawyer explained to me there in the hospital as I scratched my name on a stack of documents. He said Brad was being "very, very generous" (his term) because he wanted me to "get on" with my life, as he was certainly getting on with his. Coming here is my first step.

One of the other "ologists" explained that the fire was a "cascading event"— something you don't expect but which affects everything in your life. *That* was certainly true. I never expected to be staying here with Vernelle, divorced and abandoned by my handsome (but scurvy) husband, and deprived of my children, home, and friends—and so much more—by a fire. My whole life had literally gone up in flames.

I click off the bed-side lamp, glad of the darkness that floods over me. Darkness is kind. It hides the discolored, puckered skin that covers the left side of my body and my left hand which used to resemble nothing so much as a claw, though after several surgeries it's a lot better now.

Darkness. I laugh when I remember Vernelle saying something about going out only at night like a vampire. I wish I could.

Being around strangers with my Halloween face was one thing; being around people who've known me all my life—former classmates, even—is another. Oh, they'll be kind. But I can always spot the pity and sadness in the first quick look they give me and their determination not to show it.

Before drifting off asleep, I remember again the Woman at the Airport. She would be surprised to know that she's become an inspiration for me. "You are strong," she had told me.

During the last year, I've prayed a lot, and I am praying now for courage that will take me from the pathetic creature I was a few minutes ago—near to sobbing on the edge of the bathtub—to someone she'd be proud of.

# CHAPTER 5

I wake up to a silent house. Vernelle's already gone. By the time I'm showered and dressed, I've pretty much planned my day. A few tuneless whistles even escape my lips as I start to fix my hair. But seeing myself again in the bathroom mirror freezes me like an evil spell. This morning, I force myself to lean into the glass and confront the stranger that is now me, face to ugly face.

Of course, mirrors being tricky, my right side looks messed up, but actually it's my left side that is scarred and disfigured. I could dab on the make-up that another of the "ologists" showed me to use to cover my scars. She said that I'd feel "more comfortable around people." Comfortable? With makeup so thick it might crack if I smiled? Well, I'm not going to spend an hour every day plastering on gunk to feel "more comfortable" around people who have the choice of looking the other way when I walk by. I dig the sack of makeup bottles out of my suitcase and toss it into the waste-basket, where it makes a satisfying thump.

Under the sack are several bottles of pills. They, too, are supposed to make me "more comfortable." They, too, make a satisfying thump as they join the makeup in the wastebasket. Good riddance. If I'm going to deal with my life, I'd better start now.

Still, what can I do with a face like this? I'm thankful that Vernelle has welcomed me home, but I can't just sit around all day.

Normal people have jobs. Before I married Brad, I loved my job and was proud of my work as a kindergarten teacher. I certainly can't take up teaching again; I'd have to spend half the day on the floor, coaxing the little kids to come out from under their chairs. Not much learning going on there.

Any job that deals with the public is out, too. I couldn't take it, and neither could they. But I'll have to find something to do. Defiantly, I pull my hair back and tie it into a pony-tail. With a last, wry look in the mirror, I head downstairs.

Vernelle left a little note on the kitchen table saying, "The cook does not do breakfast," so my first meal of the day is a quick run-through at McDonald's. Then there's a stop at my new bank to draw out some of "Brad's" money. Brad already bankrolled the car Vernelle chose for me, but there are other things I need.

With a wad of cash tucked in my purse, my next stop is Walmart, where I buy jeans and tops as well as a heavier jacket. Then, remembering what Vernelle said about Sophie's, I head downtown. Maybe I can find a couple of dressier things there, though I can't imagine why I'll need something "dressier."

But first, I take a lap (as we used to say) around the town square with its big Romanesque courthouse. Downtown Mt. Prospect used to be bustling with shoppers; now there are too many tattoo parlors and nail salons, even some empty buildings. And where there were several nice clothing stores for women, "Sophie's On the Square" is the lone survivor.

Because my mother was a good friend of the owner, I remember coming here sometimes. At least from the outside, the store hasn't changed much, and Vernelle was right—the clothes in the window are the matchy-matchy outfits that the permed-and-styled set seems to like. But since I'm here, I may as well go in.

Time does stand still, apparently, at "Sophie's." The pale green carpeting and trellised wallpaper with coral roses that I remember from years ago look the same. So does the lone spindly chair in the corner by the front window, reserved for husbands brave enough to venture in.

Almost immediately, the woman at the back of the store comes bustling forward. "Abby!" she cries, "How wonderful to see you again!" Amazingly, it is Sophie herself. Time hasn't been kind to Sophie. Her face is traced with fine wrinkles, and her curly hair is now a cloud of white. Still, she's wearing a floaty yellow outfit that's bright as a beam of sunshine, and her blue eyes sparkle behind big black-framed glasses.

She looks so genuinely pleased to see me that it's easy to smile back. "Hello, Sophie, it's nice to see you, too. I didn't know you would be here today." Frankly, I thought by now she'd be tucked away in some ocean-side senior resort in Florida.

She wrinkles her nose. "Some days I wish I weren't here, but working in the store keeps me going. And I'm so glad you came in, Abby. How it takes me back! Your mother often brought you girls with her when you were little." Now she hesitates and her smile fades. "I was so sorry to hear about the fire and about your boys."

*Don't fall apart,* I tell myself. "Thank you. It was an awful loss. But at least I know I'll see them again soon."

Her expression turns to sympathy, but not pity. She takes my arm and pats my hand. "Of course, dearie. All in God's time." Then she brightens and says cheerfully. "Now, I doubt you came in just for a chat. What can I do for you?"

I glance around hesitantly. "I need some new clothes—you know, a step up from jeans and casual stuff."

Sophie gestures toward the circular racks that crowd the green carpeting. "My specialty! Why don't you take a look? It's still early, so you'll have the store to yourself for a while. Just call if you need help."

I move from rack to rack, each packed with clothes in coordinating groups. I manage to find a pair of pants and matching top in the right size and take them back to the dressing room. As I'm trying them on, Sophie asks to see what I've chosen. After she assures me that there still aren't any other customers in the store, I step out to stand in front of the floor-length three-sided mirror.

Arms folded, Sophie regards me pensively over her glasses.

I look uncertainly at the woman in the mirror wearing the brown outfit. "Don't you like it?"

Sophie's beringed hand waves dismissively. "Besides the color, it's too old for you."

"I'm afraid I didn't see a juniors' section," I say meekly.

"I gave up carrying a junior line when the girls started dressing like hookers." She pauses. "Are you planning to hide in the woods, dearie?" she finally asks. "Because that shade of taupe makes you fade into the background."

"I hadn't thought of that, but maybe I should." I move closer to the three-sided mirror. From certain angles, I can see a dozen versions of my ruined face, and my defiance from earlier this morning fades away. "Why should I care about clothes when I look like this?" I whisper.

Sophie leans her face next to mine, and we stare at our reflections in the mirror. "Yes, you were very pretty once. But so was I. Now look at that eighty-five-year-old face: the wrinkles, the age spots, the saggy skin. Beauty is transient. We all lose it one way or another, whether it's old age, disease, or an accident like you had. With my daughter, it was disease. She was only twenty, with no hair or eyebrows, a scarf around her bald head. She was bed-ridden, and her skin was so fragile that if you touched it, it would just tear away, like a strip of paper."

I am appalled at myself. "Oh, God, I'm so sorry, Sophie. I forgot about your daughter."

She pulls back from me and shakes her head. "I didn't mean for you to be sorry. It's just that life happens sometimes."

"I know." I frown at my reflection in the mirror. "But I guess I am trying to be inconspicuous."

"Forgive me for saying this, dearie—you're not going to be inconspicuous anymore. But maybe you should give people something to look at besides your face."

No one has ever said anything like that to me before, not even one of the "ologists." "What do you mean?"

Sophie pulls me to one of the racks I'd skipped over. "Look at these coordinates. My customers grab them up for cruises, but they're just what you need!"

Truly, the garments hanging on the rack are beautiful. They don't look like old-lady clothes. They look as if they were designed by a six-year-old with tropical-sunsets in mind: deep purple and lime green and turquoise and even a bright pink. The fabrics are silky, gauzy, or shimmery, trimmed with smocking, sparkles, or iridescent beads. One top has gauzy pink puffs sewn all over it; another is a wave of sea shades from blue to aquamarine. There are capris and pants and skirts with matching tops. They look more like art than clothes; I'm almost afraid to touch anything.

But Sophie isn't timid. She piles my arms full and sends me back to the dressing room with a dozen outfits. I'm cautious at first, but soon a wondrous joy takes over as I happily try on one thing after another. The last outfit I model, for Sophie's approval, has pants with a matching tunic shimmering with the shiny black and turquoise and green of peacock feathers. It's something I would never have chosen before, but my reflection in the mirror is so amazing that I can't resist.

Before I can put my old clothes back on, Sophie whisks them away and stuffs them into a sack.

As I'm paying (the price-tags make me gasp, but Brad doesn't care), Sophie wraps the new garments in orange tissue paper and tucks them into coral shopping bags. Her last advice as I'm leaving the store: "Don't wear these lovely clothes just for special occasions, dearie. Wear them everywhere you go. And when people ask where you got them, say, 'Why, at Sophie's On the Square, of course!'"

# CHAPTER 6

The inside of the Main Street Café is as plain as its name. Still, the front counter is lined with old guys perched on chrome stools, and most of the booths and tables are full. It's a busy place. Humming voices, clattering dishes, and a blaring TV (which no one is watching) combine for a noise level just short of a rock concert.

As if the noises weren't enough, the smell of hot hamburger grease and frying onions hits me like a wall when I pause in the doorway, looking for Vernelle. Conversation ceases for just a moment and then resumes as I cross the room and sit in a front booth, though I can still sense some curious looks directed my way. Since the décor in the place hasn't changed any more than Sophie's (and it was drab to begin with), I must look like a peacock in a henhouse in my new outfit.

By leaning into the big front window, I can see Vernelle hurrying along the sidewalk. Really, we don't look much like sisters.

Whereas I'm blond and thin and tall (I prefer "willowy"), Vernelle is short with frizzy brown curls and a compact figure. Beneath her coat, open and flapping in the wind, is a pantsuit of hot pink and black that looks pretty classy. Though I know Vernelle buys most of her clothes in consignment shops, she's picky enough that no one else could ever tell.

Her cheeks are a matching pink from the wind, but she looks more preoccupied than happy—considering she's meeting her older sister for lunch. As she passes my window, I rap sharply on the glass. She grins and waves. Soon she has hung up her coat and is sliding into the booth across from me, jamming a pink patent-leather purse into the corner. Her eyes widen as she takes in my outfit. "Where on earth did you find that? I love it!"

"Would you believe at Sophie's? Plus some other things— Sophie calls them 'cruise clothes,' and frankly, I don't know whether I have enough nerve to wear them."

"Why not? It'll give the natives something to talk about besides the weather and each other."

A waitress appears and tosses a couple of menus on our table with the casual attitude of someone dealing out cards. Vernelle doesn't bother to open hers and hands them both back before the waitress even has time to whip out her little tablet. "We'd like two plates of the Special, and glasses of water first, please."

As the waitress leaves with a resigned shrug, I look at Vernelle in surprise. She rolls her eyes. "Come on, Abby. Everyone knows you can never make up your mind what to order at a restaurant, and the lunch special today is really good." She points to a whiteboard. "Take a look." The whiteboard states (in multi-colored hand printing): "Baked Pork Chop, Potatoes and Gravy, Green Beans, Applesauce, and Roll & Butter. Drink Extra."

It does sound good, and I'm suddenly starving. I've barely started telling Vernelle about my other purchases when our food begins arriving in installments as the waitress makes her rounds like a busy mailman. First: glasses of water. Second: a basket of rolls and butter. Next: little dishes of applesauce and green beans. Last: platters of meat and potatoes swimming in brown gravy. The baked pork-chop is so tender that it almost falls apart when I take a bite, and the potatoes and gravy are real. After months of hospital fare and fast-food, a real Midwest meal fills a craving I hadn't even known existed.

Usually a slow eater, I manage to clean my plate faster than a hungry I-80 truck driver. When I finish dabbing up the last bit of gravy, I look up to see Vernelle watching me with amusement. "Hey, this food is almost as good as yours," I say defensively.

"I know it's good, but it's not what I'd serve if I ever opened a restaurant. Just look around. Is there anyone younger than us here? No," she goes on as I turn to look around, "the younger people in town are all eating fast-food sandwiches somewhere. What this town needs is a decent soup and sandwich place, right?"

"I have to agree, Sis." She nods with satisfaction, and I add, "So, did anything exciting happen at work today?"

Vernelle peers around then leans toward me, whispering confidentially. "Everyone in here knows that I work for Clarence, so I can't say much, but he gave me the afternoon off, so we can spend it together. He's at a c-a-s-i-n-o."

"I think most of the people in here can spell," I whisper back.

We push our dishes aside only half empty and ask for to-go boxes. One thing I'll say about portions in Iowa: they're still based on farmers who do intense physical labor for a living and need the calories.

After the waitress tosses to-go boxes on the table, I ask Vernelle, "What do you want to do?"

Before Vernelle can answer, there's a disturbance in the restaurant. I say 'disturbance' because it's hard to define. The door must have opened again; there's a sudden whoosh of cold air around our ankles. Conversation falls to a whisper and then continues more noisily than before. I'm facing the door, and I recognize the man coming in. His name is Tom Trimble.

"Thomas Trimble" might sound like a character in a cartoon, but that's about as far from the real Tom Trimble as you can get.

He's the president of the local bank, which means more when you know that the Trimble family has had the controlling interest in Mt. Prospect's only privately-owned bank since back in the days when the town was a couple of shacks in the middle of the Iowa prairie.

Tom's fiftyish and handsome, with a full head of silver hair and a meaty build. To me, his tan is too dark to be genuine, his teeth are too white, and his smile is too wide.

He advances through the place like a politician, smiling at some and waving or stopping to talk to others. It's interesting to watch the reactions of the customers. Many seem genuinely happy to see him, but there are others who look away or give him a downright dirty look—directed at his back.

He's headed toward a group of businessmen at the back but pauses by our table and leans down deferentially. "Ladies, nice to see you." He directs his warm smile (tempered by cold, colorless eyes) toward me. "Ms. Bennett, welcome back to town," he says with the assurance of someone with a flawless memory. Then he turns to Vernelle. "I had to give Garrett Tabor hell the other day, Vernelle, and it was your fault." Somehow he manages to emphasize her name with a faintly intimate tone.

Vernelle turns on a fake smile of her own. "Really, Mr. Trimble, and why would that be? I was just giving some business to your bank."

"That's not how I see it. Garrett approved your mortgage on the old Miller place. I told him that piece of crap doesn't deserve a penny of my bank's money."

Vernelle's smile stays determinedly in place. "As I'm sure you know, that's income property to me. Since Miss Bryant died, I need money to fix up the house. Nothing much has been done to it for years."

"And as I'm sure you know, that house should be bulldozed after what happened there. I'll do it myself if you don't want to. I have offered to buy it from you often enough."

"What happened there is ancient history, and anyway, the house has been in our family for years. Our grandfather grew up there, and I promised my dad that I wouldn't sell it."

She might as well not have spoken. "We Trimbles have always been very concerned about Mt. Prospect's reputation. Having that place around just keeps the story alive. In fact, I promised my dad I'd make sure it was destroyed someday." He leans down and hisses into Vernelle's ear, "Did you get that, honey? Destroyed!" And with a quick, fake smile, Tom Trimble walks away.

"What the hell?" I exclaim.

"Shit!" Vernelle says at the same time. Then she gives me a crooked grin. "Abby, dearest, I haven't heard you swear for years."

"I never swore around the boys, so I kind of got out of the habit. But what was all that about?"

Before she can answer, the waitress removes our now empty dishes and leaves the check. By that time, Vernelle's usual porcelain-white complexion has turned a pale pink. "If you remember, Miss Bryant rented the house for over thirty years, and Dad never had to do much to it. I think a new furnace was about it during all the years she lived there. So when she died, the house was really in bad shape. I don't mean it was falling down—she kept things repaired—but the appliances are old, and the carpets are shot. I figured it was the perfect time to do some needed updating, so that's when I went to the bank. Who would guess that Tom Trimble would even know—or care?"

"How much did you borrow?"

Her face goes a little pinker. "Twenty thousand, but I've spent ten already to replace the furnace Dad put in plus air conditioning. Then, while the house was still empty, a friend of mine asked me to rent it to this family she knew. They were desperate—their previous rental was sold out from under them—so I let them have it, and they moved in the next day. They paid the security deposit and seemed okay. Then, all of a sudden, they moved out a couple of days ago. No notice. Nothing. When I stopped by there yesterday, the place was a mess—not vandalized or anything, just a mess. I can't rent it out again like that."

What Vernelle says makes sense, but it's hard to forget the expression on Tom Trimble's face. "Listen, Sis, I'm going to give you the money to pay back the loan you got from Tom Trimbles's bank. Then I'll pay for anything the house needs myself."

Vernelle's eyebrows nearly hit the ceiling. "That's crazy! I can't let you do that."

I sit back, enjoying the feeling of being a big sister coming to the rescue. "Why not?"

"It's a freaking lot of money. That's why not."

"Come on, Vernelle. Let me do this for you." When she looks like she'll try to refuse, I add, "Please. I really want to do this."

"But why?"

"A couple of reasons come to mind: A, I have the money. B, I don't want you to have anything to do with Tom Trimble. He sets my teeth on edge."

"Mine, too, and I hate the way he says my name, the egotistical bastard." She considers for a moment then gives a reluctant nod. "Thanks." Then an evil smile escapes her lips. "Can I take the money in cash? Preferably all ones? I want to throw it right in his face."

I reach out and touch her hand. "I know you'd enjoy doing that, but I don't think it's a good idea to poke a stick at a poisonous snake."

She looks surprised. "Is that what you think he is?"

I nod. "That's exactly what I think he is."

# CHAPTER 7

It's a good thing we've eaten already, because neither of us would have been able to swallow a bite after that Tom T moment. As we're leaving the restaurant, I ask Vernelle what she would like to do the rest of the afternoon, since Clarence is at the c-a-s-i-n-o.

She rolls her eyes but doesn't hesitate. "Let's head out to the Miller place. I want to show you what I'm planning to use the money for."

I'm fine with that. In fact, I'm curious to see the place again myself, but I have something else to take care of first. While Vernelle waits in her car, I withdraw $20,000 in cash from "The Bank of Brad." At least, I try to withdraw that much money, but I have to go through about five people before I get to the head cashier. Thankfully, this isn't a Trimble bank—no chance of seeing Tom leering at me from some corner.

When I hand the money to Vernelle, she fans the packets of bills and grins. "I wish I could see Tom's face when he finds out I've given this shit-load of Ben Franklins to Garrett. I don't know how long the paperwork will take, but I'll pick you up at home. You don't want your new car out on those gravel roads any more than you have to."

Vernelle's business doesn't take long at all, and soon we're driving out into the country north of town. I should say that

Vernelle is driving while I alternate between hanging onto the dash and closing my eyes. Vernelle is one of those drivers who has the crazy impression that she's good, when I know for a fact that she flunked Driver Ed--twice. To take my mind off that topic (after the car bottomed out on the gravel a couple of times), I ask her how things went at the bank.

"It was okay." But she looks concerned. "I hope Garrett doesn't get into trouble over this. Tom Trimble can be a real ass-hole at times, and Garrett wants a good recommendation—he's looking for a different job."

"I take it you know Garrett pretty well?"

She glances at me, which is a concern in itself. "We just connected—you know?—when I applied for the mortgage. He's the loan officer at the bank. He's asked me out a few times, and we've had a great time. I told him—I had to tell him right up front—that I have a lousy reputation around Mt. Prospect."

"But that was years ago!" I protest. Vernelle was wild (that's the kindest word I can come up with) from the time she was in junior high.

"Maybe, but people around here have long memories. I don't want some shitty comment from one of my old boyfriends to get back to Garrett. You know, there are still a few of them around—the ones who aren't in jail, anyway." She's only half joking.

Back then, Vernelle was attracted to the "bad boys" in town—the losers. But who am I to talk? I married the biggest loser of them all.

The gravel road is soft from the spring rains, and the car slews around the final corner. Vernelle continues as if we hadn't nearly gone into the ditch. "I know what you're thinking, Abby, I do. But I've changed—I don't date guys like that anymore. I'm too old for that shit. Anyway, you know I had my standards even back in the old days."

This is interesting. "Really? And what were they?"

She misses the sarcasm in my voice. "I never used drugs or drank hard liquor, I made sure I never got pregnant, and I never came home drunk."

"You still upset Mom and Dad plenty of times. They were pretty much beside themselves trying to figure out what to do about you. You never made curfew once in six years."

She winces. "I know—I feel bad about that now. I'm just glad they didn't listen to Aunt Dorothy—she told them the only way to teach me a lesson would be to lock me in my room every night."

We pass a typical, old farmhouse. Across the flat field, I see a big red barn and silos that complete the picture. The familiar scene is almost as therapeutic as hanging out with my sister engaging in small talk. I keep the conversation going, "I don't know why Aunt Dorothy thought she should offer good parenting advice—Jean Ann was so mean that no one would even date her. And remember how Aunt Dorothy bragged that Jean Ann always had a date for Prom? Everyone at school knew she had to bribe freshman boys to take her. She bought her own corsage and drove, and the boys got free food and booze."

"Sex, too," Vernelle snickers. "And last time I heard, Jean Ann had dropped out of beauty school—again—and was living in Uncle Fred's basement with some biker."

"When you graduated from high school and business college with honors. Mom and Dad were very proud of you."

"I know. I'm glad about that. But here's what I really appreciated—you always accepted that I was choosing my own life. We never once had one of those "sister talks" where you tried to straighten me out. I don't know why, but I was different from you. I liked to drink and mess around. It was the excitement, I think. But sometimes my past haunts me. The guys I dated in high school still hit on me, and I get dirty looks from their wives. So I haven't dated much since I came back from Omaha."

"Maybe that will change with Garrett."

"Maybe," she allows. "I'm cautiously optimistic. Luckily, Garrett doesn't come from around here. He just got the bank job a couple of years ago, but he's already figured out Tom Trimble. He calls him "Tom the Bomb," because Tom acts like he's ready to explode sometimes. Garrett says the staff meetings are always tense. He thinks Tom is kind of nuts."

"That's nice to know."

"It's not good," Vernelle agrees, and slows as we pass an empty field. "That's where the Stockton house used to be—you know, where Ben Stockton, the murderer, lived. The Trimbles bought the place, and you can see what they did to it."

"It's gone," I say in surprise.

"It's gone," she repeats. "Totally."

\*\*\*

A half mile farther down the road, Vernelle turns into a muddy driveway and stops. We both sit in the car, staring through the mud-flecked windshield at the old house, which appears sad and dingy on a cloudy day like this. The snow from yesterday is mostly gone, but there are little drifts here and there in the yard, mixed in with dead grass and icy-edged puddles. A row of low yews straggles across the front of the porch, half dead and full of moldy leaves.

I'm guessing that Vernelle is looking things over in a landlord-kind of way, while my thoughts are completely different. Isn't this the place where I stopped last night? The location and the appearance of the house look right, though I don't remember those yews. And while this house is clearly empty, the one last night was not. In the light of day, I'm pretty sure of what I saw. There must be a similar house nearby—nothing else makes sense.

"It doesn't look like what you'd expect, does it?" Vernelle asks.

"What do you mean?" To me, it looks exactly like an empty house should look—blank and deserted. Even the windows are empty, except for a small one in the peak, which still shows a shred of raggedy curtain.

"I mean that you'd expect it to be some kind of creepy mansion, considering what happened here. But it's just a regular old house."

So, Vernelle wasn't thinking what I'd expected at all. And her words take me back to when we were growing up. We didn't talk much about what happened here, but when we did, it was always "the tragedy at the old Miller place."

I consider the white cottage dispassionately. "No, it looks pretty normal."

Vernelle sighs. "Might as well go in."

We scuttle along the cracked sidewalk toward the front door, heads down against a wind that is even more blustery than it was in town. I spot the tongue of a little red wagon, one wheel missing, that lies beneath one of the yews. The sight of it—or maybe it's the uneven sidewalk—causes me to stumble. Hunter had a little wagon just like that, and I wonder what happened to it. Was there anything left to salvage from the fire? The only things Brad brought to me were a few bits of charred jewelry—nothing much of any importance. He said our house was a complete loss, but still—

Even in the shelter of the front porch, dank brown leaves swirl in one corner, and an old porch swing rattles in a sudden gust of wind. Wherever I was last night, there wasn't a porch swing. That confirms I was indeed at a different house, which is a relief since the alternatives are either insanity or ghosts.

Vernelle produces a key from her pocket, unlocks the door, and we step into the living room. Pausing to frown now and then,

Vernelle walks around the room, and I follow her around like a shadow. It's fair-sized, with a nice open stairway along one wall, but the tan carpet has some nasty-colored patches. Vernelle rubs one with the toe of her shoe and swears under her breath.

On the end wall is a fireplace with a large mirror mounted above it. The mirror is cloudy around the edges and has a few spots in the corners, but isn't cracked or even chipped.

Vernelle joins me by the fireplace. "I love this mirror," she says, trailing a clear path across the dusty glass with her finger. "How amazing that it's survived all these years." She pauses thoughtfully.

Our eyes meet in the reflection. For once it's not the ruined side of my face that catches my attention. It's the good side. We have the same noses, jawlines and cheekbones. Despite having different color eyes and hair, we look like sisters.

Vernelle's thoughts have gone someplace else. "It's a good thing we can't see what this mirror must have shown the night of those murders," she says, catching me by surprise. "A whole family, wiped out in a matter of minutes. It gives me the chills."

As one, we shiver and turn away.

Through an open archway is the dining room with a built-in buffet, painted white like the rest of the woodwork. The bottom part has three wide drawers, and above it is an oblong window.

I'm leaning forward to touch one of the diamond-shaped panes of glass when I'm startled by Vernelle's sudden exclamation: "My God, this place is a freakin' mess!"

She's right. Obviously the former renters moved out in a hurry or just didn't care how they left things. There are fingerprints and crayon marks on the walls. Torn newspapers, old magazines, and broken toys lie scattered about on the dirty carpet. A couple of spindles on the stairway are even broken out, but at least someone left them at the bottom of the stairs.

Besides the dining and living room that we've already seen, there's a small bedroom and bath on the first floor. All of them need to be repainted. Even if the paint was clean, I doubt that anybody's idea of a good color scheme would include dirty beige.

We take a quick look at the three bedrooms and bathroom upstairs--again, dingy and dirty. Surprisingly, one of the bedrooms, is painted pink—a shade that anyone (except maybe a realtor) would instantly label "Pepto-Bismol," though it's faded in some areas.

Was this Miss Bryant's room? I can almost imagine pink frilly curtains and a matching flowered bedspread. I say almost, because it's a pretty big leap to think that the dignified Miss Bryant (a long-time Mt. Prospect teacher) would have picked that color. But maybe it was a "paint-chip" mistake; we've all made those.

Back downstairs, we move into the kitchen. I can't hear what Vernelle is muttering under her breath now, but I'm pretty sure I don't want to. Half-empty packages of food, a couple of broken dishes, wadded newspapers, and assorted plastic bags and containers clutter the counters. Vernelle slams shut a gaping cupboard door and looks discouraged.

I manage a perky tone. "It's not so bad, Sis. A good cleaning will work wonders. What's left to do is mostly cosmetic—painting for sure, and new appliances."

Vernelle gives me a scathing look. "What about this wallpaper? You can't paint that." She points an accusing finger at the "kitcheny print" (tiny turquoise eggbeaters and coffee grinders mixed with ivy leaves) that climbs up every vertical wall surface. Unfortunately, the wallpaper has come loose in places and is spattered with grease, bits of unidentifiable food, and the mortal remains of dead flies.

"No, I don't think you could paint over it—you'd see all those seams. It'll have to come off."

Vernelle wilts like a dying flower. "When they cleaned the house out, Miss Bryant's relatives left it spotless. I have to get this place rented, but I don't have time to redo everything, let alone take care of all the junk." She makes a sweeping gesture that takes in all the chaos surrounding us. "Even the garage—last time I looked, it was full of broken bikes and a lawn mower and plastic kiddy pools. What am I going to do?"

An idea is taking shape in my brain. "You might not have the time, but I do. I can't say that I want to do any cleaning, but I can definitely paint, and I can learn how to wallpaper."

Vernelle stares at me in surprise. "Better think that offer over carefully, Abby, because I'm tempted to take you up on it."

I mimic her earlier sweeping gesture. "Do you think you could hire someone to clean up the worst of this and haul it away? Do you know someone who does that?"

"Marge Hansen used to clean for Miss Bryant. I know she still works for some people around town. I'll call her tonight. As for hauling away trash, there are a couple of old guys who live in the trailer park that do odd jobs. I can give them a call, too."

"That'll work. If you can get this place cleaned out, I truly will take on the painting and wallpapering." Excitement begins building inside of me and I add, "It'll be fun."

Vernelle eyes me doubtfully. "It's a bigger project than you think, Abby. When's the last time you painted anything?"

She's right to be doubtful; I've never held a paintbrush in my life. "Okay, so I don't know much about painting, but it can't be that hard—the same with papering. I've always wanted to try wallpapering a room. I wish Aunt Dorothy was still around—now that woman knew how to hang wallpaper! Her house was full of it."

Vernelle giggles. "Remember her downstairs bathroom with the red-flocked paper? I'd hate it now, but I thought it was way cool back in the day. I used to pick at it when I was in there. One time I pulled off a whole little chunk from under the stool, just to keep."

I pretend to be shocked. "Vernelle!"

She doesn't look repentant. "I made a skirt out of it for one of my paper dolls. Still—all this painting and papering, Abby. Are you sure you want to take it on?"

"What else can I do while you're at work? Sit around all day watching TV? I want something useful to do, and I can't think of anything better than helping you. If you'll get the cleaning people lined up tonight, I'll start right away." I picture myself busily working away, full of purpose. "Won't you enjoy picking out paint colors and wallpaper? You're good at that kind of thing—just look what you've done with your house."

She's starting to look more cheerful. "And I can help you after work sometimes and on the weekends, though I have to admit I've always hired all my own painting projects done." She squares her shoulders and makes a show of being positive. "You're right. This will be fun, just the two of us. And it will take your mind off—"

Vernelle stops, looking stricken. "Oh, God, I didn't mean to say that, Abby. You seem to be doing pretty well. It's just that you went through so much, first with Brad the Bastard, and then that—that terrible fire!"

"It's all right." I reach out and give her a quick hug. "I don't want you to feel you have to walk on eggshells around me. I know I'm maybe a little fragile yet--that's partly why I came back here, to get better. I'm going to make a new life for myself, and this will help." Here I pause and add with determination, "I'm going to get my boys back, too."

"Abby," Vernelle starts with an edge in her voice. Then she turns away, dabbing at her eyes. Finally, she says, "As long as you think it would be good for you. And not too much. I don't want this to interfere with any of your doctor or therapy appointments."

I assure her it won't, but my mind is already on what needs to be done to the house. In fact, as we get into the car, I'm making a mental list of what we need to buy. I'm good at mental lists. Vernelle starts the car and pulls her coat more tightly around her as she cranks up the heater. "The place is like a wind tunnel," she complains.

For the first time I notice that the house, yard, and garage stand like a small island surrounded by plowed fields. "No wonder the wind whistles through like the Arctic. Didn't there used to be a big grove of pine trees around the house?"

"Oh, sure, but don't you remember? After what happened out there, Ed Miller kept the house, but sold Tom Trimble the farmland years ago. It was Tommy-T who bulldozed all those trees. Miss Bryant was still alive, and she was plenty mad. But he said they were on his land, and he could make more money raising corn than trees. These days, all the fieldwork is done by hired men, and I swear they plow in a few feet closer every year. Pretty soon there won't be any yard left at all."

"Tom must tell them to do that. Doesn't he know where the property lines are?"

"Probably he does. The problem is that I don't."

"Then we'll get this property surveyed and tell old Tommy-T to keep his freakin' plows off your land. Maybe we'll sue him for trespassing. Or maybe we could even confiscate his tractor! I bet he wouldn't like that one bit."

Vernelle looks uneasy. "Didn't you just say never poke a stick at a poisonous snake?"

# CHAPTER 8

As Vernelle and I head back to town, we're both thoughtful. Tom Trimble could as well be in the back seat. "He has nothing to do with us," I state with more courage than I feel. "I don't even know why we're worried about him. You don't owe his bank anything anymore, and I've got plenty of money to bankroll the remodeling. We don't have to have anything to do with 'Tom the bomb'."

"I guess." Vernelle smiles at my use of Garret's name for his boss. She perks up, which means her foot comes down more heavily on the accelerator. "Let's stop at the hardware store and pick up a bunch of paint chips. We might as well start making some plans."

"Do they have wallpaper, too?"

"Some. I think you can special order it if you don't like what they have. There are tons of those big wallpaper sample books. I like wallpaper, but I didn't use it in my house because painting is easier and usually a lot cheaper."

\*\*\*

Talbots Hardware store is located just off Main Street and is stocked with everything for home repair that you can think of. There's also a kitchen section, appliances, and garden stuff. When we walk in, a couple of clerks in their tan shirts with name badges are putting out picnic supplies and lawn ornaments. In the March hardware business, summer is right around the corner.

There's a big new section of electronic stuff that I don't remember, but everything else looks about the same. It's warm in the store. I take off my heavy jacket and fold it over my arm as I follow Vernelle, who's marching right down the main aisle. The clerks pause in their work. I swear I can feel them staring at my back as I'm walking by. I don't recognize them, but I'm sure they know who I am. Or maybe not—maybe they're just staring at my beautiful, peacock-bright outfit. I'm sure that's it.

An older man looks up from arranging pairs of gardening gloves on some shelves. "Good afternoon, Miss Miller," he says to Vernelle and gives me a nod and a smile. "What can we do for you two ladies today?"

"Hi, Stan. Abby and I just stopped by to get some paint samples."

"We have plenty of those," he gestures to the back corner of the store with a smile. "With all the paint you've bought here, I'm sure you know where to find them. We're even running a sale on our best paint right now."

"You always have good sales. That's why I buy all my paint here." Vernelle tosses out a friendly smile and continues to the back of the store.

I hurry to keep up with her and almost collide with a guy just coming out of the aisle. "Oh, excuse me!" I cry, nearly stumbling.

The man has on a baseball cap and dark glasses, so I can't read his expression. Can't tell if he's angry or not. But he reaches out a hand to steady me and says, "No problem," in a deep voice before going on his way.

When I reach Vernelle, I whisper, "Do you know that guy? What's the deal with the dark glasses?"

She whispers back, "I've seen him around town for a couple years. He never takes them off, even when he's eating at the café. Lots of gossip, but nobody seems to really know a thing about him. Just a guy that likes to keep to himself. Harmless enough—I guess."

Then she turns to a display that holds paint chips with more colors than I even imagined existed.

To me, the selection is overwhelming, but Vernelle's hand goes unerringly to the brown area, and she pulls out a sample card. "What do you think of this color for the living room and the dining room, since they're both together?"

She points at the palest color on a card with four shades of brown, "Chocolate Mist." "It's still pretty light, but it'll make that white woodwork pop, don't you think?"

"I think it's yummy." I smack my lips a couple times and add, "like painting chocolate malt on the walls."

Vernelle sticks her tongue out at me. "Gross!" She pulls out another paint sample. "Let's just do a neutral for the bedrooms— here's one, 'Subtle Sand.' This is good paint, but it still might take a couple of coats to cover that awful bubble-gum pink upstairs. I bet Miss Bryant had a Barbie-themed pink bedspread and everything to match."

I find myself cringing at the thought. "Come on, you're still sore because she always made you spit out your gum."

"So did the Spanish teacher, but at least I learned how to say, 'Spit out your gum' in Spanish. Escupe tu chicle," she recites with a respectable accent. Then with a laugh, she adds, "It's the *only* thing I learned in that class."

With the paint settled, it's on to the wallpaper section, where sample books fill three whole rows of shelves. We face each other with the same dismayed expressions; it would take us a week to go through all those books. Vernelle grabs one and checks the prices in back. "This stuff is really expensive, Abby. Let's see what they have in stock first."

A short aisle nearby is lined with bins of wallpaper, each with a small sample taped beside it. There are wallpaper patterns that look like wood, marble, and tile. There are designs for hunters, dog-lovers, and little kids, nurseries, laundries, and bathrooms (if your taste runs to shells), and lots of flowers and stripes for everything else. We don't see any that is specifically for kitchens; maybe people don't paper kitchens much anymore.

I look at the bins doubtfully. "Do you think any of these will work?"

Vernelle's face scrunches up as if she smells something bad. "No, let's try the clearance wallpaper. It couldn't be any worse than this crap." We start pawing through piles of miscellaneous paper and borders. The only thing they have in common is that nobody wanted them, and it's easy to see why. Finally, Vernelle holds up a roll that looks like textured plaster in variegated shades of pale yellow. "How about this?"

I'm perfectly happy to let my sister make all the decisions. She's the interior designer of the two of us, and it is *her* house after all. "I like it. It'll brighten up the kitchen, which seems kind of dark to me. But is there enough?"

She shrugs. "Let's get what there is. We can always paint one of the walls a coordinating color if we have to." The pile yields thirteen rolls. We have no idea if this will be enough; something tells me that you're supposed to measure before you buy wallpaper.

A helpful clerk piles a shopping cart full of the supplies we'll need for papering the kitchen. The only "fun" item is a utensil called a "PaperTiger," used to score holes in the old paper. Who could resist buying something called a Paper Tiger?

After hearing us talk, the clerk suggests watching some self-help videos on how to remove the old wallpaper and hang the new. I was afraid we'd have to buy a book; no doubt there's one called *The Dummies' Guide to Wallpapering*.

Once we're home and finish with supper, I spend the evening on Vernelle's computer. There's more to wallpapering than I would have thought. The do-it-yourself experts strongly recommend removing the old wallpaper first, particularly if it's greasy (ours is) or coming off (ours is). You can use the heat gun method or the soak-and-scrape method; various products are recommended, and I bet we have one of each in the trunk of Vernelle's car.

Vernelle makes the phone calls, managing to contact Marge Hansen and the old guys at the trailer court. By the time we go to bed, Marge has agreed to meet me out at the house later in the week, and the old guys will work a few days for us. Ace and Tuffy (Vernelle says a friend of hers always calls them "the geezers," though not to their faces) have assured Vernelle that they "know their way around trash."

And from the DIY videos on-line, I have a pretty good idea of the skill needed to wallpaper those four kitchen walls; I don't have it yet, but I will. The biggest job seems to be removing the old stuff. Though the experts say the heat-gun method is fastest, they caution that you can get burns from it. The mere thought of getting burned makes me shaky, and I decide that I won't use a heat gun, even if I have to scrape the wallpaper off with my fingernails.

# CHAPTER 9

Next morning I'm ready to head out to my new "place of employment." I'm so excited that I skip breakfast, but Vernelle has packed me a lunch big enough to feed a family reunion.

First, I make a quick stop at the hardware store, where I pick up a couple of buckets, garbage bags, rubber gloves, a stepladder, and even a "Bag of Rags," which we hadn't thought of yesterday. Who'd believe you could buy rags? And who would be stupid enough to buy them? Oh, that's right—me.

It doesn't take long to reach my destination. Soon I'll be able to drive to the old place blindfolded, considering the job I'm taking on. I would not, in my younger days, have even thought of painting a closet, much less a whole house. And wallpapering? Never!

As I head to the back door, keys in hand, something shiny embedded in the mud catches my eye—an old marble. After I pick it up and wipe it off, I can see that the marble's a clear blue-green with white streaks running through it like clouds in the sky. On impulse I tuck it into my pocket. A kid treasure. It's as if the house is giving me a little present.

When I get into the kitchen, its cold dampness goes straight to my bones. I turn up the heat and then take a moment to survey what needs to be done. Sadly, the nasty wallpaper hasn't disappeared overnight. I don't know why I thought it might. Maybe it's a delaying tactic, but I rinse out a pickle jar that's on the counter and drop in the marble. It lands with a satisfying plink.

The next step is carrying in all the stuff from the car, where it makes an intimidating pile in the center of the kitchen. I take a deep breath and get to work, starting in the corner by the cupboards. This involves scoring the paper with the toothy PaperTiger, spraying it with the removal solution, and letting the liquid work for the required time. Then, I tear off what I can and start scraping the rest. Some of the paper comes off in big strips, some in little bits, but it all goes into the garbage bags in sticky, sopping bunches.

It doesn't take long to figure out that this is hard, boring work. But it's also satisfying to uncover the green paint that used to live a quiet life under the busy wallpaper. And my already-aching right arm tells me that I won't need to work out at a gym; maybe I'll make an exercise video someday called "Wallpapering with Abby." Except for my scraping noises, the house is deeply silent. Tomorrow, I'll bring a radio to catch up on the local news.

By the time I'm ready for a break, there's no doubt I'm making progress. Most of one of the big walls is now bare of eggbeaters and ivy. It's good to be off my feet, even if I am perched awkwardly on the stepladder. A thermos of coffee and Vernelle's homemade gingerbread cookies are within easy reach on the counter beside me.

I'm just pouring myself some of the coffee when I hear a vehicle in the driveway. From the window I can see two men climbing out of a battered old pickup. One is chubby and bald, while the other has a head of thick gray hair and is spindly but neat in his bib overalls.

When I answer the door, they introduce themselves—Ace McKee and Tuffy von Muenster, reporting for work. The thinner one doesn't look like either a "Tuffy" or a "von Muenster," but he seems to be serious about his quirky name. Both men are old; in

Tuffy's case, he could be anywhere between sixty and eighty—it's hard to tell.

I introduce myself and invite them in. They carefully wipe their feet on the battered mat, not realizing that a few more muddy footprints won't hurt the dirty kitchen flooring. At first, their glances flicker toward my face, but if they're shocked, they don't show it. They probably already knew about me.

Their timing is perfect, and they agree in their courteous way to join me for coffee and cookies. As they lean on the counter, still crowded with junk, they sip coffee from steaming cups and survey the room. Tuffy is the first to make a comment. "Left the place in a hell of a mess, didn't they?"

I nod, swallowing a mouthful of cookie, then say, "For sure— and Vernelle says the basement and garage are worse. Maybe it's stuff that they didn't want, or they just left in a big hurry."

Tuffy and Ace exchange a guarded look. "Could be either," Ace says cautiously.

Tuffy adds, "I didn't know them people. They weren't from MP. Never saw 'em in town, neither." He pauses. "Your sister wasn't real clear on the phone. Just what is it you want us to do, Mrs.—?" He stops, apparently stumped about what to call me.

I manage a smile—or at least half a smile. "I'm not a 'Mrs.' anymore, so just call me Abby. We need you guys to haul away all the junk around here. Do you know someplace to get rid of it?"

Ace looks at Tuffy, who is clearly the leader of the pair, and expected to solve all problems.

Tuffy scratches his head. "I know a guy who has a pit out at his farm. We can haul some of it there. That way it won't cost you nothing, not like the Grant County dump—they've got real expensive lately. I got a pickup we can use." Ace is nodding like a bobblehead doll.

"Sounds great. When can you start?"

Now, Tuffy rubs his chin, giving the matter serious consideration. "We can be here tomorrow morning, late. We got another job lined up already." His eyes flick around the kitchen. "Looks like we better clean the counters off first. You ain't got hardly any room for your own stuff the way it is now."

After we agree on an hourly rate, Tuffy touches one of the dirty cupboard doors with a gnarled finger. "This used to be a real nice old house. It's a shame how those people left it. You know, we used to work for Miss Bryant sometimes."

That surprises me, but only because I'd forgotten how small towns work. "What kind of work did you do?"

"Oh, we spaded up the garden every spring, mowed the yard, raked leaves, that kind of thing. She was a real nice lady."

His comment makes me laugh out loud. "I was scared to death of her when I was in high school. She caught me daydreaming in English class one time; I was so embarrassed I just wanted to crawl under my desk."

Tuffy nods. "She was like that. I don't know if you remember my twin boys, but they was hellions in high school. Ma didn't think her week was right unless she got a call complaining about them boys from a couple of teachers or the principal. But they never messed around in Miss Bryant's class. I don't know why that was, but they never did."

I said I remembered his boys. I didn't say it aloud, but he was right—they were hellions. The substitute teacher who had them for P.E. when we were roller skating in the gym never came back again. She alternated sending the twins to the office, but it could have been the same one every time; they looked just alike. (Once, in the hot-lunch room, a kindergartener pointed at them and screeched, "Look—those two boys have the same head!") And I think Tuffy's twins even made the Home Ec. teacher cry a few times. There wasn't any real harm in them, but they were always in trouble.

Tuffy catches my eye and grins. "At graduation, every one of them teachers, except maybe Miss Bryant, stood up in the auditorium and cheered. Ma was mortified, but I thought it was damn funny."

After the "geezers" (it's hard to think of them as anything else) go on their way, I get busy again. Even with the stepladder, my neck is getting sore from reaching up so much, and my arms feel like I've never worked a day in my life, which is certainly true of the past year.

I'm more than ready when it's time to stop for lunch—turkey breast on marble rye sandwiches and corn chowder. There's enough for two. The soup is still warm, but I decide to buy a microwave for the future. I might grow old before this place is done, and that means a lot of soup.

I clear a spot on the counter for the sack Vernelle filled with stacks of foam plates, soup bowls and cups, plastic silverware, and napkins. As I take out what I need, something about these ordinary supplies tears at my heart. I was always the big sister, helping Vernelle cross the street, taking her into her Sunday School room, and walking with her to school. Now the little sister is taking care of the big one.

Around five, when my arms are too tired to move, I call it quits for the day. I clean up the bits of wallpaper stuck to the floor, rivulets of dirty water, and the piles of wet newspapers and rags. I'm pleased with what I've accomplished, but the excitement of this morning has worn off.

Outside, it's gray and rainy. For a moment I feel like the old, white cottage—forlorn and empty. My life shouldn't be like this; I should be in Grass Valley hugging Hunter and Grayson. Why had I let those precious moments slip through my fingers like sand? And Vernelle, though she seems to be getting her life together, is still marooned here in the town she always vowed to escape.

Talking about Miss Bryant with the geezers reminds me of a book we had to read in her 9th grade English class, *Of Mice and Men*. I hadn't liked it at the time because it was so sad. But while in the hospital I got sick of watching TV all the time, so I decided to read (or in this case reread) some of the classics. The message of *Of Mice and Men* is suddenly unmistakably clear to me now. We can have hopes and plans and dreams for the future—but sometimes life just slaps us down.

# CHAPTER 10

The next day, I buy a microwave and a little radio, and bulldoze a space for them on the counter. I tune in the Mt. Prospect radio station. Vernelle says, "Their music's crap, but nobody in town wants to miss the latest obituaries and funeral announcements." It will be a good way to get reacquainted with the local scene.

My arms are tired and sore from yesterday, but I keep squirting and scraping—except for the three minutes I spend hypnotized by a golden oldie called "I'm My Own Grandpa." If you listen carefully enough, the words actually make sense—who'd have thought?

By the time the geezers arrive, I'm proud of what I've accomplished—two of the walls are almost done. They've brought arm loads of boxes and sacks and begin clearing the cupboards and counters faster than two grocery store carry-out boys.

Around noon I break for lunch. I try inviting the geezers to join me, but Tuffy says, very nicely, that they always eat dinner at the Main Street Cafe. In the Midwest, the noon meal is usually the big meal of the day and referred to as dinner. Lunch is a snack break between dinner and supper. Somehow, the fact that I don't think of the noon meal like a Midwesterner anymore makes me feel even lonelier.

I'm guessing they have a group of old cronies they like to socialize with. They'd probably be uncomfortable eating with me anyway. Neither one has yet called me by my first name; they usually make these throat-clearing sounds if they want my attention.

After the pair heads for town, I take out my lunch determined to enjoy my meal and the break. My legs are now as tired as my arms, so I sit down in the cleanest corner of the floor to eat. Vernelle hasn't failed me again today—there's chicken noodle soup and ham sandwiches. It sounds ordinary, but the noodles are homemade. She made them last night while I watched TV. They're wide and chewy with a buttery taste and the soup tastes just like our mom's. The ham, sweet with some kind of mustard sauce, is piled high between slices of dark pumpernickel. Once again, there's way too much food for me. I can't imagine why Vernelle thinks I can eat this much.

It's a wonderful lunch, but I confess eating it by myself makes me feel a little lonely. Well, there's Jerry, the radio announcer, but he doesn't exactly interact with me. As I eat, I watch some wind-tossed branches through the kitchen window. There's a cardinal perched on one, its red feathers all ruffled up from the wind. When it opens its beak, I could swear it's yawning. Maybe cardinals get tired, too.

I'm PaperTigering like mad when there's a loud rap on the kitchen door. Grateful for the interruption, I stagger over the stuff on the floor (luckily without falling) and pull open the door.

Standing on the step is the woman who was the home economics teacher at the high school when I went there fifteen years ago--Mrs. Schwarz. She doesn't look much different now; I would have recognized her bird's nest of blond hair and wide smile anywhere. She has on a big necklace and matching terracotta earrings—metal rings connected with clay blobs. I can't decide if it's expensive jewelry or stuff made by her seventh grade Exploratory Class. But I'm more curious about why she's here.

She squeezes past me, bringing a wave of cold air into the room. "Abby Miller," she gushes, "it's so wonderful to see you again! I heard you were working out here and just had to stop by, since we have the day off, thank God. I'd go nuts if I didn't get a break from those little hooligans now and then. How are you doing?"

"My name is Abby Bennett now, Mrs. Schwarz," I say as I lay the PaperTiger on the counter. "I'm doing fine."

"Oh, don't be so formal! We're both adults now—call me Dickie."

"Dickie, then." I don't feel comfortable calling a former teacher by her first name, even now, especially one with a name like Dickie.

I never had Mrs. Schwarz as a teacher, but her high-pitched little-girl voice and knowing eyes make me feel self-conscious. It's as if she needs to look over my face and memorize every detail. Whenever she blinks, I can almost hear the little click of a camera. I manage a faint smile. "It was nice of you to stop by, but as you can see, I'm in the middle of . . ."

My hint that I'm busy doesn't faze Dickie a bit. She's peeking inside a cupboard before I can finish my sentence. Since politeness doesn't have much effect on someone that nervy—or that fast—I'm stuck with her for the moment.

Her smile is fake-friendly. "Well, Abby, it must feel real odd for you to be back here after so long. Are you living with Vernelle?"

I feel certain she knows I am. "For now." Then I add, "I'm afraid I can't stop for long."

Dickie gives a casual wave of her hand. "Oh, I'm sure you need a break about now. Anyway, I brought you a 'welcome home' gift." Three or four metal bracelets jingle on her wrist as she pulls an orange sack from her coat pocket and hands it to me. "You know us Home Ec. teachers—we always come prepared."

"Why, thank you." Dickie has such a bright, expectant look on her face that I'm forced to open the sack now, instead of putting it aside as I would have preferred. I'm beginning to feel that I'm following a script that Dickie has played many times before. Inside are a dozen cookies. "They look very good. I'll save them for later, but thanks." I lay the sack on the counter by the Paper Tiger.

Dickie frowns as she peers around with her bird-like flickery eyes. "I heard Vernelle was doing some remodeling out here. I hope she's not planning any structural changes. But I love that shade of green! I'll bet that's the kitchen's original color."

Which means either her eyes are bad, or she doesn't recognize ugly when she sees it. She goes on, "It's too bad you had to come back to Mt. Prospect under such horrible circumstances. Of course, the whole town was just so sorry to hear what happened to you out there in California. My condolences on—."

I interrupt before she can go further. "Is there something particular you wanted?"

Dickie's eyes widen innocently. "Well, now that you mention it, I actually came here with a proposition for you. As you probably know, I belong to the Grant County Historical Society."

"That's interesting." I'm wondering what on earth this has to do with me.

"I do hope you'll think so. The fact is that we'd like your cooperation on a project of ours. It's something we've been talking about for years, and now seems to be the time to put it into action. Mt. Prospect is a nice little town, but the guidebooks practically ignore it; the only thing they mention is that the biggest hailstone recorded in Iowa landed here in 1953. And no one had the sense to save it—can you believe it?

"And look at the motto on our big sign by the highway: 'Mt. Prospect, the height of friendliness.' Well, you can't market friendliness, either. It doesn't exactly bring people in."

"Bring people in" seems to do just that. There's the sound of someone outside. Ace and Tuffy step into the kitchen. They nod at Dickie, and she gives them a frozen expression in return.

Tuffy says, "We're going to take this load of stuff to the pit; we'll be back in a jiffy." They disappear out the door as quickly as two old elves.

Disapproval emanates from Dickie like strong perfume. "Those von Muenster twins—I'll never forget them! The year they took Home Ec.—we call it Family and Consumer Science now—was one of the worst ever. I think I called their mother every day."

"What did they do?" I ask.

"Surely you remember—weren't you in school then? They made my life hell. No matter how carefully I watched them--and watch them I did--they managed to do something to drive me crazy. The worst was the time their cookies exploded in the oven." She sees my expression and nods vigorously. "Yes, they did. I don't know what they put in those cookies, but they exploded like firecrackers. I made them clean out the oven, but I don't think they cared. They got the effect they wanted, and I got a few more gray hairs.

"Anyway, let me get back to why I'm here." She pauses, seeking words; I still can't imagine what this has to do with me. "As I said, the Historical Society wants something that will draw people into Mt. Prospect--a tourist attraction, if you will. We think this house could be just what we're looking for!"

"Really? Why would you want this old place?"

Dickie's voice lowers dramatically. "Haven't you ever heard of the Villisca Ax Murders? That whole family was killed—gruesomely--back in the early 1900's? The publicity about those murders put Villisca on the map. Tourists from all over Iowa still travel there to see the Ax Murder House. They spend tons of money, too, on souvenirs and such. We had a crime in Mt. Prospect almost that good, but the town's never made a dime from it."

"Okay, but what has that got to do with me?"

Here Dickie looks energized. "I'm glad you asked, because it has a lot to do with you—and Vernelle. You're family, so if you agree with us, this whole thing can happen."

"What, exactly, can happen?" Seriously, I don't like where this is going.

"Why, the Historical Society can restore this house to the way it was when the Miller family was murdered. They're all gone and even the murderer is dead, and his family has moved away long ago, so they won't care." She's walking in circles, gesturing wildly and seems to be talking to herself as much as to me. "Anyway, if we get enough publicity, maybe people will come to Mt. Prospect to visit the scene of that terrible crime. Someone could talk Ambrosia Swann into putting together a special edition for the newspaper." Here, Dickie pauses, looking thoughtful; everyone knows that Ambrosia Swann is notoriously unpredictable.

But she goes gamely on. "What do you think?"

"I don't think anyone would come here to look at an old empty house," I say, trying to discourage her.

"Are you kidding?" Her eyes are big and bright with excitement. "Just picture the crime—that Stockton boy got Mrs. Miller with one swipe of his knife through her neck when she opened the door. Then the girlfriend got it—stabbed a hundred times, they say—but he had to chase down the two little boys."

I feel the earth giving way beneath my feet, but Dickie seems oblivious to the effect her words are having. She goes on with a sickening kind of glee. "Can you imagine their frightened screams as they tried to get away? When he caught them, he slashed their hands and faces again and again. I've heard they were cut to ribbons. Blood must have been everywhere! Why, think of the scenes we could reenact right here in this house! Twice every day around Halloween. We could charge admission!" She comes to a breathless stop, her eyes shining with triumph.

The taste of bile coats my mouth, and I'd like to toss Dickie and her cookies right out the door. "Vernelle and I would never agree to that. This house will always be a home, not a sideshow! You and your Historical Society had better drop all your plans about that. Period." I pull open the door and add, "Thanks for the cookies, Dickie, but I need to get back to work now."

Dickie manages a faint smile and sweeps out the door.

I slam it behind her then lean on the counter. Some of Dickie's words keep echoing in my head about that awful night: the mother and daughter killed, those two sweet little boys, chased and stabbed to death. What kind of monster would do such a thing?

More bile rises in my throat. With shaking hands, I grab a foam cup from the counter and manage a few gulps of cold water. In a few minutes, after my stomach stops clenching, I wipe my face and sweaty forehead with a couple of the clean, wet rags.

I'm slumped in the corner on the floor, trying to get myself together, when the geezers walk in. Seeing me, they stop in astonishment. "Are you sick?" Ace asks with concern.

I sit up straighter. "No, something just happened that upset me. I'll be all right."

Tuffy eyes the sack of cookies on the counter, and his spindly body stiffens with anger. "That Schwarz woman's a damned busybody. Always was."

"She likes to spread gossip." Ace's jowls quiver as he shakes his head. "Don't you pay her no mind."

I manage a watery smile. "She wasn't gossiping. She was describing—in horrible detail—the murders that happened here. If you remember, the Millers were my relatives."

Tuffy bristles with contempt. "Dickie thinks she knows everything, but she doesn't know shit. Probably, nobody knows what really happened out here." There's a long pause as he studies my face. "Are you sure you're okay?" When I nod, he says, "Well, we're heading to the basement to see what we got down there."

I'm astonished that two old guys can create so many rattles and crashes. When they reappear, the geezers are lugging a decrepit card table and three folding chairs. The card table has one leg that won't stay up until Tuffy wraps it with some duct tape. It's a little shaky but holds. (Maybe I should try duct taping my leg.) They wipe off the dusty chairs (only a little wobbly) before setting them around the table.

I'm impressed, and they look proud of their accomplishment. "Thanks," I say. "It's just what I need for eating lunch—I mean dinner—when I'm here."

Ace and Tuffy look at each and give a nod. Then Tuffy clears his throat and announces, "Well, there's a lot more junk in the basement, best be getting to it," and back down they go.

I'm just getting back to work again when Vernelle comes in like a whoosh of fresh air. "Ta-da," she says, flinging her coat onto the chair. "Your new helper has arrived! Just show me what to do!" She's clearly dressed for the part, with a pink bandana tied perkily around her hair, a denim shirt, and jeans rolled up to her knees. Somewhere she's found long pink rubber gloves.

To match her mood, Vernelle turns on the radio, finds some music she likes, and gets to work. It seems a shame to even mention Dickie Schwarz, so I save that story for later.

Vernelle's a quick learner with a spray bottle--not so much with a scraper, but she's game to try.

While we're working, the geezers bring up boxes of old canning jars, a big blue enameled canning kettle, several more rusted card-table chairs, and a collection of miscellaneous flower pots.

It seems a shame that it's all destined for the pit. I urge Vernelle to take anything she wants, but her bewildered expression tells me she's not interested. So I suggest Tuffy and Ace sell anything they can and split the money among themselves and the "pit buddy." This seems fair to them, and they agree solemnly.

By now, we've finished most of the third wall, but have hit a tricky patch. I don't know what's going on, but the wall-paper seems a lot tougher to remove. Maybe somebody used additional paste (Gorilla Glue?), and we have to chip the stuff off with my trusty "broad or spackling knives." Frankly, I don't know what the hell spackling is, but I'm pretty sure I haven't yet spackled.

Vernelle's no longer looking so chipper. She has worked for ten minutes on a spot no bigger than a piece of toast, and the fingers of her pink gloves are shredded.

When the geezers invite us to join them for their "lunch" (aka mid-afternoon break) we call it quits for the day.

Vernelle gives a big sigh as she sits down, and it shows the extent of her exhaustion that she actually eats a Twinkie. I'm not really surprised when she admits that this kind of work is not for her. I suggest that she save her energy for kitchen pursuits, and she's quick to agree.

After they all leave, I clean up everything and then walk around outside for a few minutes. The air is fresh and cold and helps clear my head.

By the back porch, I can see some green spears poking their way through rotting leaves and the other detritus from winter. Spring bulbs, probably, though I can't remember whether daffodils or tulips appear first. In a patch of ground by the leaves, I find another marble. This one is small and looks like a million clear bubbles glued together. I add it to the jar in the kitchen then lock up, wondering if these marbles are some kind of message.

Sometimes, when you're desperate to find meaning, you'll find it anywhere. Even a jar of marbles.

# CHAPTER 11

I arrive home to find Vernelle waiting for me. She's not warm and welcoming. The bottles of pills I'd thrown away a few days ago are on the counter next to her. It's pretty obvious why she looks so upset.

She follows my gaze to the pill bottles. "Mind explaining what the hell you were thinking?"

I can feel my face flush. The last thing I want to do is fight with my sister. "I thought I didn't need them anymore. But maybe I was wrong. Thanks for rescuing them from the trash," I add in order to make peace.

Vernelle's not sure how to respond; it seems she was ready for a long, drawn-out argument. After a few calming breaths, she says, "Abby, from what I understand it's dangerous to go off some of those meds."

I don't reply. There's no point telling her that I don't like the way they make me feel, or that I really don't believe I need them anymore.

"Have you even made an appointment with your new doctor out here?" she goes on.

"Not yet," I admit. "But I will. I promise." *So much for my break from all the ologists.*

Vernelle's expression relaxes, along with her shoulders and rigid stance, and I can see how upset she must have been. Then she gives me a nod and a smile. "Okay." And with that she moves on to making dinner.

While we eat, I take one of my meds and explain, "This one is taken with food. The others I have to wait at least an hour."

She looks at the three bottles, then at me. "Abby, you said you'd stay on them, and I trust you. You don't have to worry. I'm not going to hover." She hesitates, then adds, "But let me know when you have your first doctor's appointment scheduled, so I can go with you."

"You don't have to do that," I say automatically.

Her expression borders between hurt and grief. "Abby, I couldn't be there with you much while you went through all those surgeries. The least I can do is drive you to your doctor's appointment."

I agree, but am eager to change the subject, so Vernelle gets an edited version of Dickie's visit. She's not as upset as I was, but she has a few choice words for Dickie, "damned freakin' busybody" being the kindest ones. Then she tells me about the time some mean girls got into Dickie's room at school and hung a bunch of tampons (colored red with magic markers) from the ceiling panels. Vernelle says she always felt sorry for Dickie after that, but she won't anymore.

I hope my sister wasn't involved, but frankly I don't care much.

Vernelle starts to work in the kitchen, while I clear off the dishes. Well, I shouldn't say "work" because she loves cooking; it seems to be her way of relaxing. She says that at night she often tries out new soup and sandwich recipes, her specialty.

She has the little kitchen TV turned to a decorating show, and I look up when I hear a familiar name. Pointing at the screen, I screech to Vernelle, "That's her, the woman at the airport!" We both stare in amazement as the host takes us through the beautifully decorated desert home of the "famous jewelry designer, Zandra Marxx."

When the program ends, Vernelle grins. "So she lives in Fountain Hills, Arizona, huh? I'm thinking road trip, someday!"

I doubt we'll ever actually do it, but her suggestion makes it clear she's not mad at me anymore. That makes me happy—the idea of starting the endless cycle of doctor's appointments again does not.

# CHAPTER 12

Sometime during the night, I awake to the wail of a fire truck, which comes toward the house and then fades off into the distance. Even as the sound disappears, my heart pounds so hard that I think it might explode. In a panic, I sit up and turn on the light. The sight of my room, familiar since childhood, calms me down. Still, the sound of the siren has opened a door into my past that I've tried to keep closed for a year.

The day of the fire started out as a seemingly ordinary day at our home in Grass Valley. The boys were playing outside on their swing set, and a work crew was remodeling the family room. I was in our bedroom, getting one of Brad's uniforms ready for the cleaners when I found the note in a pocket. I opened it without really thinking it was anything personal, but I was wrong.

It was VERY personal: all about a night spent together "making love love love!!!!" and how "wonderful!!! it was!!!" And as if all the exclamation points weren't bad enough, the note got worse; little hearts were drawn above some of the letters, as if it were written by a junior-high girl, only much more explicit. The signature was a bright pink lip-print at the bottom.

Shocked and horrified, I sank to the edge of the bed. I'd had suspicions about Brad in the past. But they were little whispers in the back of my mind. This was a GIANT SCREAM that my life—our life—was about to fall apart.

In sudden fury, I grabbed a wastebasket and started stuffing the uniform into it. That's when Hunter came into the room. He watched me dubiously. "Mommy, why are you throwing Daddy's pilot clothes away?"

I stopped, frozen, and stared at his puzzled little face. I finally managed to say, "It has a stain on it, hon. Mommy has to throw it away."

He came closer and patted my shoulder. "Don't cry. We can go to the store and get Daddy a new one, can't we?"

I hadn't realized I was crying, but I wiped the tears from my cheeks and managed to smile. "Of course we can, Buddy. How about if I go to town now and get Daddy a new uniform? Would you like Suzy to stay with you and Grayson?"

The concern faded from his face and he nodded happily. "Sure, she's fun." I gave him a hug, and he ran back to play, his errand to our room forgotten.

As I watched Hunter leave, I changed mentally from Mommy and Happy Homemaker to Spurned Wife. I was determined this time to find out what was going on. After asking the neighbor girl to come over to babysit, I left a message for Brad. He'd be landing in Sacramento around three. I asked him to meet me at a restaurant on his way home—one at the halfway point for us both.

I don't remember driving down the curvy road to the Valley Grille, but all of a sudden I was pulling up beside Brad's big Lexus SUV in the parking lot. When I went in, he was seated at a table with two mixed drinks in front of him and a menu in hand. A waitress was ready to take his order, and I could tell from her flushed face and guilty smile that Brad had been flirting with her. He always did, sometimes right in front of me; this was the first time I didn't care.

Brad added an appetizer (and a wink at the waitress) to the order as I sat down. An appetizer couldn't fix my appetite. In fact, the thought of food made me sick. I pulled the note from my pocket and shoved it across the table at Brad. He glanced at it and didn't even look embarrassed. "I'm sorry you found that, Abby, but maybe it's better if this all comes out in the open now."

"What comes out in the open--that you've been screwing one of your flight attendants?" The crude expression made me feel better, since it fit the situation perfectly.

I don't usually talk like that, and Brad was shocked. "Abby, someone might hear you!" He looked around the room, apparently concerned that there were some ten-year-olds with big ears nearby. "Anyway," he continued, leaning back and looking in total command of himself, "it's not what you think. Chloe and I are in love."

"When that woman called last year and said you were messing around with a flight attendant, you swore it was a lie—that she was just trying to cause you trouble. Was that Chloe then?"

"That was someone else," he said hurriedly. "Just a little joke that went too far. It didn't mean anything. You know I still love you on one level, Abby. It's just that Chloe and I are *soulmates*. You don't know what that feels like, because you've never experienced it. But with Chloe and me—well, it's just too strong for us to resist." Brad's handsome, boyish features radiated sincerity.

I took a sip of the drink in front of me, barely noticing the taste. I was trying not to gag over the idea of "soulmates." "So, you and Chloe are totally in love. Where does that leave us?"

"I hadn't meant to tell you yet, but since you brought it up, I want a divorce."

There was no US anymore. I felt as if someone had dumped a gallon of ice water on me. I was truly dumbfounded. "A divorce? Now?"

He shrugged. "Whenever. Chloe and I haven't exactly made plans yet."

The word "whenever" released my frozen brain. I leaned right into Brad's face, ignoring the waitress hovering around with some nauseating stuffed peppers—Brad's favorite. "Well, you and your *soulmate* Chloe better make plans, because you're moving out, like yesterday."

Brad put on his pouty face. "I want this divorce to be amicable, Abby. It will be better for all of us."

"Since when have you been concerned with 'all of us'? Maybe a divorce can be 'amicable' under certain situations. But not when you've been cheating, breaking your marriage vows, and totally disregarding the welfare of your two little boys! By the way, when you get home, you'll have to tell them you're leaving. They'll need time to adjust."

He was taken aback. "I thought you could tell them—I'm not very good at that kind of thing. You could get them used to the idea."

"They'll never get used to the idea. They idolize you. And don't tell them something stupid like 'Mommy doesn't love Daddy anymore.' Tell them the truth—that you've found some 'mommy' you like better."

Brad went white around the mouth. Reality was starting to set in. "Okay, I'll tell them. But I want you to know you'll have plenty of money. Dad will even help out. He likes Chloe."

"Your parents have met Chloe?" Beyond everything else, this was the ultimate betrayal. I drained the rest of my drink in one gulp.

"Just for a minute when we had a layover in New York." Brad's voice had taken on a defensive whine. When I didn't answer, he went on. "I want you to meet Chloe, Abby. You can't help but like her."

I decided to set him straight on that one right here and now. "I never, ever want to *meet* Chloe. Seeing her across the table in a lawyer's office will be punishment enough."

Brad sat up and frowned dramatically. "That's not acceptable. Chloe's going to be part of the family. After we get married, she'll be the boys' step-mom—think about that! You'd better find a way to treat her nice."

"This is a stupid argument. How I treat Chloe, the home-wrecker, is so not part of this discussion!"

"Well, I'm making it part of the discussion. You'd better listen to me, Abby: If you don't act nice to Chloe—if you say one mean thing or make her cry—there will be consequences." At my scoff and shaking head, his expression turned scary ugly. He leaned in and said with a snarl, "My dad can get a team of the best lawyers. They'll hang you out to dry. I might even go for full custody of the boys."

I wanted to wipe away the smug look on his face with a slap. "You are so full of shit, Brad. Even if—*if*—your imaginary lawyers could convince a court to take the boys away from their mother, you wouldn't want that! And Chloe sure wouldn't want them."

He looked even more smug. "No, but my parents would. You know my mother—she'd love to get hold of them."

Brad was right about that, and the thought terrified me. Monica had always treated me decently, if somewhat condescendingly (like a nobody from Iowa), but she was controlling and bossy to everyone around her, except Brad. She had always treated him like a god. She would, indeed, take the boys if she could get them. The possibility of a long drawn-out custody battle hit me hard.

I drained the second drink that had magically appeared in front of me; I still don't remember what it was. After a few more drinks and acrimonious comments, we argued our way out to the parking lot. When Brad started to get into his Lexus, I followed him. He turned around in surprise. "You drove your car, Abby."

I told him I wasn't comfortable driving. It wasn't that I wanted to be with Brad, but between the booze and the shock, I wasn't in any condition to drive the treacherous road (now becoming dark) that led to our home. The boys were already going to lose one parent; they didn't need to lose two.

Brad started to say something but finally shrugged and got into his SUV. And it was on the way home that we saw our house was on fire—a sight now etched permanently on my brain.

Though it's not easy, I take a deep breath and try to put the whole scene out of my mind by remembering the happy times with the boys. Eventually I'm able to go back to sleep.

And then the dream starts. As usual, I'm trapped in the burning house. The roar of the flames and the horrible crackling of blazing wood are all around me. The intense heat is searing my skin, and I can't catch my breath even to scream . . .

For the second time, I awake in a panic. This time I get out of bed and wipe my face with a cool washcloth as I wait for my heart to slow down.

Finally, I climb back in bed, and, though I try to go back to sleep, I just doze in spurts until pale sunlight replaces the moonlight streaming in my window.

Why do dreams have to seem so real?

# CHAPTER 13

I'm glad Vernelle left early, because I'm tired and out of sorts from my miserable night. The fire dream is one I've finally learned to live with; it's less frequent now, but no less disturbing. I scold my Cheerios for having such a happy name but nothing to improve a person's mood--like little blue marshmallows or fake strawberries. A big slug of chocolate syrup poured across my bowl makes me feel instantly better.

Drops of rain spatter the windshield as I drive to the house, but by the time I pull into the driveway, the sun is peeking through the clouds. I notice a hearty whiff of spring in the air when I get out of the car; I can identify the whiff because it smells like manure, and that's spring in Iowa.

Today, the prospective house cleaner, Marge Hansen, is coming, and I still don't know what questions to ask. My only idea, "Do you know how to clean?" seems a bit insulting, but I spend the next few hours chipping and scraping without coming up with anything better.

When I glance out the kitchen window for the fiftieth time, Marge, short and plump as a hen, is already headed to the back door. She has a purposeful, no-nonsense stride, and when she stumbles, she turns to glare at the offending concrete walk. I just hope she's not one of those people who sue over every little thing.

I hurry to let her in, but my comment on the beautiful spring morning doesn't sit well with her. She looks back outside as if she'd experienced a day different from mine. "I don't like a damp day like this. It sets off my arthritis no end," she says flatly.

When Marge takes off her black coat and scarf, I see that everything about her is faded: short, grayish-blond hair parted in the middle, pale blue eyes, and a powdery complexion. Still, she must have been pretty once, though she's older than I expected.

I invite Marge into the kitchen and pull out the least wobbly chair for her at the crooked table. "I was just ready to have a little break, Mrs. Hansen. Would you like some coffee and cookies while we talk?"

She surveys my little attempt at hostessing dispassionately. "Just coffee; I never snack between meals. I like to watch my weight." She settles heavily onto the chair and looks at me with a jaundiced eye. "It doesn't look like you have to worry, though. You could put on a few more pounds—you're like a stick. And that sister of yours could use a few, too. Maybe she'd get a man that way. Men don't like those 'skinny minnies' like you see on the TV these days."

I hand Marge a cup of coffee, and she peers down at it suspiciously. "I like my coffee black. I don't hold with that fancy stuff they sell at the Java Hut in Iowa City." It's distracting to picture Marge at anything called a Java Hut. When I sit down with my own coffee, I see that she has a couple of cookies in front of her. Maybe she doesn't count cookies as "snacks." Smart of her.

While Marge's strong jaws methodically crunch one of Vernelle's snickerdoodles, I describe our plans to rent the house again. She pauses between bites. "Did you know I worked for Miss Bryant for twenty years? I was the one who found her body. She didn't associate with hardly anyone after she retired from teaching. She said she was sick to death of people. She went to church, but not much else. The only neighbor she talked to was that man who lives back in the woods all alone. I told her he must be some kind of kook." She pauses then and says, as if her mouth can hardly form the words, "Miss Bryant said he was nice enough.

"Anyway, she was dead for a couple of days before I found her body. It was sad. Taught in this school district for forty years, and just a few people came to the funeral. They didn't even shut down school so the teachers could be there. Disgraceful, I call it. That superintendent has a heart like an iceberg. Of course, nobody around here really cared if she was a good teacher. She didn't hold with all this computer silliness—she made them kids write out their essays in cursive, like they should."

When Marge pauses to take a breath, I ask her if she could do some cleaning for us.

She takes another couple of cookies and looks around the kitchen with deep disapproval. The counters and cupboards are cleared off, but they're still dirty, and the floor is a sea of muddy tracks mixed with wallpaper scraps. "Them people who moved out were from Shueyville. I knew they'd trash the place."

"They didn't exactly trash the place," I interject, defending people I don't even know. "They just moved out in a hurry—didn't clean the cupboards and things like that. They did leave some stuff behind, but we'll take care of that. We just want you to clean."

She looks rebellious. "It's dirtier than you think. I know that kind. I don't do basements or attics—my legs can't take the stairs anymore. Or the top windows—too much reaching. Miss Bryant was tall, so she always did the top panes for me. She was real nice about not wanting my arthritis to flare up."

I assure her that we don't want her arthritis to flare up, either. "We'd just like you to clean the kitchen cupboards and counters, and wash the woodwork. No windows." I gather my nerve and continue. "The bathrooms could use a good cleaning, too. Vernelle is going to replace the appliances and carpet, so you don't have to worry about those. We'll get your cleaning supplies if you can give me a list."

My offer doesn't please Marge. "I bring my own," she says sharply. "When people furnish cleaning supplies, they always get them at the Dollar Store. I don't like that cheap stuff from Mexico. It don't clean worth a darn."

She pauses to eat another cookie. "How much are you paying? Miss Bryant made it worth my while to drive way out here, and gas prices have gone through the roof since she died."

"How about double your usual hourly wage? You can keep track of your time—work whenever it fits in with your schedule, and we'll pay you at the end of each week."

She allows that that would work just fine as she takes the last of the cookies. "I always liked this house. Miss Bryant wanted everything just so. In the spring after school let out, we'd clean every room—carpets, walls, curtains, everything. Then she said she could relax and read her books the rest of the summer. She was like that." Marge looks around again. "You'll be lucky to get any renters, after them other people moved out like they did."

"Why?" I ask in surprise. "Do you think people will be scared to live here?"

"Well, it does have a past. Miss Bryant didn't hold with all the rumors, though. The only thing was, she saw faces in that mirror in the living room sometimes. But she said they never scared her—she liked the company."

Faces in the mirror?

But Marge has already regretted mentioning the matter, and her face shuts down like a trap. "It prob'ly wasn't anything—just one of Miss Bryant's little jokes. She was such a kidder."

Miss Bryant a kidder? I've never heard that one.

Before she leaves, Marge arranges to come on Monday, Wednesday, and Friday afternoons. "And that's more time than I can spare" is her parting shot as she puts on her black coat and pushes open the door.

For me, it's back to removing wallpaper. I work steadily, but the living room is calling. "Faces in the mirror?" It sounds so strange that I wonder if Miss Bryant was "losing it" there at the end. Of course, she had lived nearly thirty years alone in a house where a multiple murder had taken place. Could such a terrible crime leave behind a kind of residue, like tendrils of smoke after a fire? I shiver at the thought.

The geezers are in and out the rest of the day, hauling trash from the basement, and I keep busy scoring, squirting, and scraping. On one of their passes through the kitchen, Tuffy stops and "harrumphs" in my direction (apparently his name for me).

"What?" I ask.

"Do you want us to move them appliances so you can get at the rest of the paper?"

I look at him blankly.

"The wallpaper," Ace adds helpfully. "There's still some behind the stove and fridge."

I groan. True, I'd forgotten those areas. After Tuffy and Ace pull the appliances from the wall, I send them home; they have to be worn out, though they look sprightly as ever. Maybe I'm the one who's worn out.

I finish up, putting the garbage bags in the corner for the guys to deal with tomorrow. Then, before leaving for home, I turn on the light in the living room and stand in front of the mirror. All I see is what I'd expected—me with the empty room behind me. I turn so that only my right side shows. It's a strange comfort--no burns, no scars. Nothing. And no one else. There are a few dark spots in one corner of the mirror, but even an active imagination can't turn them into faces. Fires in the night and faces in the mirror—Miss Bryant and I would have made quite a pair.

That night, I pull out the boxes of mementos from my closet. There's only one that goes back to my childhood—a box containing a couple of dolls and some old doll dishes wrapped in tissue paper. I think Grandpa and Grandma Miller gave me the miniature tea set, but I don't remember for sure. All the pieces are white with a bright blue rim; below the rim is a yellow band with pink roses. And, as if that wasn't quite enough decoration, there are garlands and curlicues of gold. I set the dishes out on the floor, charmed by their color and quaintness. There's a teapot and lid, a creamer, and four cups and saucers. The only piece missing is the sugar bowl.

The other boxes are things from school. I'm surprised and intrigued at what's there—report cards, class pictures, artwork, and "friendship pins" that were a big deal one year. I wasn't much of a saver like some girls, but from high school there are dried up corsages, a formerly silver-toned tiara, and several of the little souvenir Prom books given out each year. There's an envelope of college things, too, though not as large.

I sift through it all, bringing back memories I hadn't thought of for years and making me feel a little lonesome. Sadly, my friends from high school don't live around here anymore. Like me, they headed for Des Moines or other big Midwest cities after graduation to find work.

I set the tarnished tiara on my head and practice the "parade wave" I used the night I rode a Corvette convertible in the Homecoming parade. I thought my life couldn't get any better than that moment. And now I'm the only one who has returned to Mt. Prospect to live—me, Abby Miller, former Homecoming Queen—divorced, damaged, and alone.

# CHAPTER 14

It's Saturday, but Vernelle has errands to run and can't help me with the house. In what has become an almost automatic trip by now, I drive out there anyway. Along the sidewalk, green stalks have suddenly burst into golden daffodils. And there in the dirt by the flowers is another marble, one with tiny threads of red and blue glass that form a spiral down the center. I've never seen one like it, but it looks old, and I add it to the pickle jar. The marbles seem to be getting better, too. I can just see myself on *Antiques Roadshow* saying, "Oh my, I never imagined they were worth so much!" But I'll save them for the boys; they'll have a whole collection if this continues.

I miss my boys so much. A pang of sadness hits me so hard that I have to sit down as soon as I've let myself in. After taking several deep breaths, I work up the courage to call Brad in order to ask to speak to them. My anxiety rises with the first ring, but then a message tells me his number isn't any good anymore.

For a while I can't stop crying. Then a thought comes to me. *I'm their mother. Surely, I have to have some rights!*

The lawyer Vernelle works for might not be good for much. But maybe he can talk lawyer to lawyer with Brad's attorney and at least arrange a phone call once a week. That thought gives me enough hope to get me up from the table, but still not able to work. I need a solid goal. Something more than occasional phone calls. It's been a year and I need to *see* my boys. I'll get myself together, and petition for them to come visit me here in Mt. Prospect in say...three months. Ninety days. That seems like a reasonable goal. It gives me time to figure out what I'm doing and prove I'm recovered enough to at least get visitation rights.

Now I'm up and going, working at those spots of wallpaper I missed in the kitchen yesterday with enthusiasm. Although I really didn't expect them, the geezers come strolling in. Just seeing them lifts my mood. They tell me they have a buyer for an item in the basement and clump noisily down the stairs. Soon there are sounds of something heavy being carried—accompanied by colorful swearing and grunts. A few minutes later, the geezers heave a washing machine up the last of the stairs—an old wringer-washer like my grandmother used to have. It's a pink Maytag—probably the epitome of luxury back in the 1950's.

After getting their breaths back, Ace and Tuffy awkwardly maneuver the washer out the door. They say someone wants it for a yard decoration; I hope it's not Dickie.

After the guys leave, I grab one of the broken spindles that have been on the stairway in the living room since Vernelle and I first looked at the house. This would be a good day to stop by the lumberyard for replacements.

The mirror looks different today, and I stumble to an abrupt halt, my breath almost sucked out of my body. My face's reflection is there all right, but the living room behind isn't empty. In the misty background of the mirror is the unmistakable outline of a small table surrounded by a vague tableau of figures that I can't make out.

My heart starts doing double-time as I whirl around to look behind me. There is, of course, no one there. No one and no table. I turn back to the mirror, but it's empty now, too. Did I take Marge's words so much to heart that I created the scene in my imagination?

Surely I'm not that gullible, but it must be what happened. It has to be.

With shaking hands, I lock the doors and hurry to my car, head-down against the wind—and something else.

At the lumberyard, I ask a young clerk about some replacement spindles. He says they're not in stock, so we page through an online catalog of fancy "millwork" you can order. He points to a spindle. "This doesn't match the one you have, but it's probably the closest you'll get. Did you know these are unfinished?"

The spindle on the screen looks finished to me. "What does that mean, exactly?" I have to ask.

"It means you'll have to stain them to match the others."

I'd already noticed a whole aisle of stains and varnishes in the store and ask doubtfully. "Will that be hard?"

He glances again at the spindle I'm holding. "It'll be hard to get an exact match. But when they come in, I'll help you find a stain that will come pretty close. Then they'll need a couple coats of varnish or polyurethane. It's all easy, really."

Of course it will be easy—because he won't be doing it.

# CHAPTER 15

Vernelle's car pulls into the driveway just as I arrive home. As we carry in sacks of groceries, I can tell from Vernelle's suppressed excitement that something's going on. But she remains stubbornly secretive until everything is put away and we're sitting down for lunch—in this case, Chez McDonald's.

Vernelle dumps the take-out sack on the table and divides the food absently between us. Then, with sparkling eyes, she leans forward and says, "Guess what, Abby—Garrett found a new job!"

"I'm so glad for him! And judging from your face, I'd guess he's not leaving town any time soon."

With a happy grin, she unwraps her hamburger. "No, thank goodness! It's with an investment firm right here in town, an excellent company. Garrett is really happy—it's just what he's been looking for. And when he gave his two-week notice, Tom the Bomb told him to lock his office and get out. What do you think of that?"

I grin. "Well, at least Tom didn't explode."

"It didn't bother Garrett. He said he can start his new job sooner that way. The thing is, he wants to celebrate by taking us—you and me—out for dinner tonight."

I can feel myself cringing inside. "Don't be silly, Sis. That's something you two should do together. I'll just settle in for a quiet evening."

"Garrett wants to meet you," she says sternly, "and I want you to meet him. He made reservations for three at the Italian Garden, so you don't have a choice."

I give in gracefully. "Then I would love to go. But where's this Italian Garden—Iowa City?"

Vernelle giggles. "No, remember the Mayflower? Well, somebody bought it last year and did some remodeling. There's no garden, just a few green plastic plants and a mural that looks kind of like Roman ruins, but the food is good. You'll like it—it's worth dressing up for."

I had considered telling her about the figures in the mirror, but it doesn't seem right to ruin her mood. She deserves to enjoy a celebratory date with her boyfriend.

And it says a lot about Vernelle's feelings for Garrett that she takes the rest of the afternoon to get ready. When I join her in the living room just before Garrett is due to arrive, she has on a very short black dress with a sparkly red scarf around her neck. Red, six-inch heels match the devilish look in her eyes.

My shimmery navy outfit isn't the eye-catcher Vernelle's is, but I feel more glamorous than I thought I ever would again. Still, the idea of going out to a popular restaurant makes me nervous.

When Garrett comes to the door, he gives an appreciative whistle that includes us both. Vernelle grins and whistles back. Frankly, I'm pretty amazed myself. Garrett doesn't look like the type of guy Vernelle would date, much less whistle at. Garrett's tall and thin with short dark hair and thick, square glasses, but his kind smile and intelligent brown eyes give me a hint of what she sees in him.

Most of the tables are full at the Italian Garden—what you'd expect on a Saturday night at the only nice restaurant in Mt. Prospect. It's an older crowd, and the candlelight is kind to wrinkles and balding heads, even if it makes it hard to see the food. As we follow the hostess to our table, I notice a few familiar faces in the sea of strangers.

Among a group of older ladies in glitzy outfits and a forest of empty wine bottles is Sophie. She gives me a wave and a wink that tells me she's noticed my "Sophie" outfit. On impulse, I make a quick curtsey, and Sophie laughs and claps her hands.

With soft music and the tinkle of silver and crystal, everyone seems to be having a good time. Well, maybe not everyone. At a nearby table are Tom Trimble and his wife, Silvie. Awkward. They don't seem to have much to say to each other, unlike Garrett and Vernelle, who obviously have *lots* to say to each other.

Sylvie is a fake blonde who appears faintly drunk. She was beautiful in the past, but now, even in the candlelight, her wooden smile and carefully-preserved face look like a mask. I wonder what it is that she hides from the world.

Ambrosia Swann brushes by our table with her son, Burdett.

Burdett, who must be pushing fifty by now, is tall and attractive, with silver hair and a professional smile. At eighty-plus, Ambrosia's still the vinegary editor of the town newspaper and has a legendary feud simmering with Tom. When the hostess seats them at the table next to the Trimbles, Ambrosia refuses the chair Burdett holds out and sits with her back toward her old adversary.

Across the table, Sylvie's mask slips for a moment as her glance lingers hungrily on Burdett's face. But Burdett seems to turn pointedly toward his mother. What was that all about?

In a few moments, Tom and Sylvie rise to leave. When they pass our table, Tom gives Garrett an icy stare and looks right through Vernelle and me. Sylvie stumbles after him.

I'm impressed that Garrett maintains polite composure, in spite of the curious eyes in the room turned his way. News—especially hirings and firings—travels fast in a small town.

Though it's some kind of pasta the Italians have probably never heard of, our meal is lovely. When we've finished our meal, Garrett suggests stopping by the local sports bar for a drink, but I insist on being dropped off at home. I may be a third wheel, but at least I'm not a stupid third wheel.

# CHAPTER 16

Sunday in Mt. Prospect would usually include an hour at the Methodist Church, but I'm not quite ready to take that on yet. Vernelle doesn't have a hangover (she insists) but merely a headache, so we take it easy in the morning. She's still bubbly happy about last night, though. And most of her sentences start with "Garrett."

In the afternoon, Vernelle and I load up all the wallpaper supplies and head to the Miller house to check my progress. On the way into the front porch, I notice that the geezers have hauled away the little red wagon. But in the spot where it used to be, there's another marble in the mud, and it goes immediately into the pickle jar. This marble thing has gone from quirky to strange. Some little kid must have had a big hole in his pocket.

Vernelle is impressed with the kitchen, and why not? The counter and cupboards are cleaned off (if not exactly clean), and the room, now plain green, actually looks much bigger and neater.

What it will look like with yellow walls and new flooring I can't even imagine.

When we're ready to leave, we go back through the living room to the front door. It takes just one glance at the mirror to see that the scene has returned—still misty but clearer than yesterday. With a shock, I realize it's exactly what I saw the night I peeked in the window. The mother, the daughter, the children and the boyfriend are all there.

With bated breath, I ask Vernelle if she sees anything odd about the mirror today. She considers it critically. "Maybe spottier than before. I think it would look better with a black frame, don't you?"

I reach out and touch the mirror; the glass is cold and lifeless. I jerk my hand away, though not because the scene is frightening. In fact, the people in the mirror seem almost welcoming. I take a good look at the mother and daughter. Naturally, there's a family resemblance between them, but they seem familiar to me. That's when I notice that the girl looks a lot like me at that age. This is the Miller family. Somehow knowing who they are keeps them from being scary.

What is frightening, however, is that I can see them and my sister can't. Which means this is the house where I stopped on the night of the snowstorm. How can that be? Of course, there's only one logical answer, but I'm not ready to admit I've gone insane.

\*\*\*

On the way home, Vernelle chatters about the row of daffodils alongside the house—she loves daffodils—and how pretty the yellow kitchen will be. She doesn't notice my silence—or that I am clutching my hands in my lap to keep them from shaking.

"Vernelle," I ask, my voice wavering more than I want, "do I seem okay to you?"

She takes one quick glance at me and pulls the car over to the edge of the road. "What do you mean?"

"You know what I mean."

She blows out a loud breath and shrugs uncomfortably. "You're dealing with things pretty well, but of course I've been worried. Especially when I discovered you'd thrown out your meds."

At her expression, I feel bad for making her feel bad. "Sorry," I mutter.

"Don't be. I get it. But give yourself time. Make the appointments with the doctors in Iowa City that Dr. Scott referred you to and work with them. I just want you to take care of yourself."

I smile and nod to show her I know she really does care and wants the best for me, then I add, "I will, but I'm just not sure what good it will do to see yet another 'ologist. I'm so tired of them. They just want to keep going over the same thing—the fire. Why in the world would I want keep reliving that again and again?" My voice is becoming urgent, part of me hoping to make her understand. "Why should I, Vernelle? Sure it was tragic, but nobody *died*. I know what happened. They don't."

I can't read my sister's expression as she reaches over and takes my hand. "Abby, I know you *think* you know what happened. But there's stuff about the fire that you still don't—" she stops herself. "Things you haven't come to terms with, yet."

I'm about to argue, then my hand automatically touches the scars on my cheeks. "I'm trying, but it's a lot to get used to."

She nods. "That's why it's important you have the support you need."

"I promise. I'll call for an appointment tomorrow. I don't know what I'd do without you," I manage to say. We hug, say we love each other and then head home, both wiping away tears.

We spend a quiet evening watching *Pride and Prejudice* on the movie channel. I won't deny it: whether I'm staring at the screen or eating popcorn, in the back of my mind is THE MIRROR. No matter what spin I put on what I saw, there really are only two possibilities: either I'm nuts—or something bizarre is going on with that mirror. And I don't know which possibility terrifies me the most.

# CHAPTER 17

On Monday morning, I call the first primary care doctor in the area on my list and make a new-patient appointment. The very perky scheduler informs me they are booking three months out, which is fine by me. I can put my self and my life back together without the constant interruptions of one doctor appointment after another.

Vernelle's ready to head to work by the time I enter the kitchen. "Make sure to call the doctor, today," she says, trying to sound casual about it.

"Already did. Give you the details later," I assure her.

Relief eases some of her worry lines as she heads out.

\*\*\*

An hour later, I'm at the Miller house. For the sake of my sanity, I stay determinedly out of the living room. I can't bring myself to take a hammer to the mirror, but the thought lurks in my mind. On the other hand, if I just stay away from it . . .maybe the ghosts will go away.

So I tackle the mindlessly boring job of washing down the walls for the new wallpaper. When my arms begin to feel as if they're falling off, I literally throw in the sponge. Luckily, my cell phone rings at that moment; it's the lumberyard calling. With relief, I climb down from the shaky stepladder and grab my purse.

The clerk who helped me order the spindles is busy at the register, and the other, a girl who really ought to be sitting in an Algebra I class somewhere, is making keys for a tall blond guy. Even at this distance, I can see he's good-looking, really good-looking. Making keys with a noisy machine doesn't look like much fun to me, but they're both laughing. The only other customer is a man studying the selection of paint chips. Surprisingly, he's someone I recognize--it's the man I literally ran into here at the hardware store when Vernelle and I were looking at wallpaper.

The girl finishes with the key customer; now it's my turn. When I say what I'm here for, Wendy (her name tag informs me) hands me the new spindles wrapped together with twine.

After I'm done paying, it occurs to me that the spindles won't jump into their places in the stairway all by themselves, so I ask Wendy how to install them. "Honestly, if I were you, I'd get a carpenter. If the old spindles are broken off, someone would need to get the pieces out before you could replace them."

"Do you know anyone who can do that for me?"

"Sure, Drew's right over there. He's a carpenter, and he just told me he's winding up a job. Do you want me to ask him?"

"If you'd introduce him to me, I'll ask him myself. I expect he'll have some other questions. By the way, my name is Abby Bennett."

She doesn't waste any time. "Hey, Drew, can you come over here a minute?" Drew was the key guy, a carpenter god if there ever was one. He comes striding toward us, a friendly grin on his face; I'm thinking he might be fun to have around the house.

Wendy performs the introduction like a pro. "Drew, this is Abby Bennett. She needs some spindles replaced on her stairway. Do you think you could help her out?"

I am turned a little sideways from Drew—I think I always instinctively hide my left side when I meet someone new. Drew flicks a glance over me, one of those assessing looks that guys like him give any female younger than their grandmothers. Then he leans one hand casually on the counter.

"Well, now, Abby," he says with a slow, easy smile, "I'll see what I can do for you."

As I turn fully toward him, Drew's face freezes. When he doesn't say anything more, I try to fill in the awkward pause. "It's just a little job, but I'll pay whatever you want."

"Yeah, well, I just remembered I don't have time for that kind of job right now." Then he turns away and is gone, without even a "sorry."

Wendy looks embarrassed and apologizes in a generic kind of way.

"It's okay," I mutter. "I'll find someone else."

I walk mindlessly down one of the aisles, trying to collect myself. That look on Drew's face—disbelief, revulsion. . . If I've forgotten, for a time, what I look like, Drew just reminded me. And why did I think he might be "fun to have around"? Because he reminded me momentarily of Brad, that's why. Which is just plain stupid; Brad is gone from my life. And if Drew's reaction is anything to go by. . .

I give myself a mental shake. None of that is important—getting Vernelle's house ready to rent is. And standing in an aisle with bins of paintbrushes on one side and cans of stains and varnishes on the other, I feel overwhelmed with what I have taken on. Who was I to think I could fix up a house? I can't even replace a spindle in a stairway—and I scared away the guy who can.

Suddenly, there's someone at my elbow—the man with the ball cap and glasses who was standing by the paint chips. "Don't feel bad about Drew. You dodged a bullet there. I hired him one time, and his work was crap," he says in a deep, gravelly voice.

I'm caught by surprise. "Thanks," I stammer out. "It's just that I really need a carpenter; now I'll have to find someone else."

"What exactly do you need done?" The man doesn't ask the question willingly; it's more like it's torn out of him against his better judgment. He's about my height and broad-shouldered, wearing a heavy denim jacket and a baseball cap. Dark sunglasses shield his eyes (even here in the store), and his face is further hidden by a clipped mustache and beard. He looks like an uncover drug agent or maybe a serial killer; it could go either way.

But I'm desperate. I hold up the new spindles. "These have to be stained and put back into a railing, plus a couple of other repairs—holes in the plaster, things like that. They're not big things, but I can't do them myself. I guess I need a Jack-of-all-trades." I stop, suddenly embarrassed; where on earth did that old phrase come from?

A full minute goes by, and the man is still standing there. He riffles the paint samples in his hands and finally says, "I guess I could help you out. I'm not a flashy carpenter like our buddy Drew, but at least I know my way around a hammer."

It's probably the least gracious offer I've ever had in my life, but I don't have the luxury to turn anyone down. "Thanks, I'd appreciate your help. By the way, my name is Abby Bennett." I extend my hand. "My sister and I are fixing up an old house—the Miller house. It's north out of town a few miles. Will that be a problem?"

He reluctantly shakes my hand, but his lips twist in what is (possibly—I'm not sure) the shadow of a smile. "I guess you could call me a 'Jack-of-all-trades' for real. The name's Jack—Jack Allender. I know the place—I live just down the road, back in the timber."

It's disconcerting not to be able to see the man's eyes as he's (probably) looking at me. But all I see is my own reflection in his sunglasses. I can't help but wonder what exactly he means by "back in the timber." His tone is resigned when he says he'll drop by tomorrow to check things out. He doesn't seem concerned whether I pay him or not.

As the man makes his way out of the store, I notice that he limps slightly, but with his right leg, not left like mine. I figure we'd make a good couple in a sack race—if serial killers have time for sack races.

I ask Wendy if she knows the guy. When she nods, I tell her that I just hired him and wonder if he's okay, leaving out the part about thinking he looks like a serial killer.

She shrugs. "He's been coming here as long as I've been around. I asked my boss about him once, and he said he knows somebody who used to know this guy. He's okay. I usually wait on him, because I think he's kind of funny." She sees the question on my face. "No, I don't mean he's flirty or creepy or anything, just funny. My boss's wife says he's old enough to be my father. Do you think he's that old?"

"Since you look about fifteen, I wouldn't be surprised."

She starts laughing as if I've told the funniest joke she's ever heard. "Fifteen?!! I'm nineteen!"

"Well, he's still old enough to your father. If he started early enough, maybe even your grand-father."

She laughs again. "That's great! He always calls me 'Windy with an i'; when he comes in next time, I'll call him 'Gramps'."

Well, he's probably not that old, but a sweet young thing like Wendy shouldn't be joking around with a (possible) serial killer, no matter how "funny" she thinks he is.

# CHAPTER 18

There are a couple of guys in the yard walking around with tripods when I get back; Vernelle's property is being surveyed. She contacted somebody through Clarence's office who does surveying, but I didn't think she could make it happen this fast.

After lunch, it's time to hang the wallpaper; that's the right term, even if it does sound kind of mean. The wallpaper bible says to begin in an "inconspicuous" corner of the room. (It's like the author knows me.) I choose the area above the back door, since starting with short lengths of wallpaper seems to make sense. If nothing else, my mistakes will be smaller.

First, I make a plumb line with a level (as directed), measure the length (as directed), cut the strip of wallpaper (as directed), let it soak in warm water, and "book it" (as directed). Then I hang it upside-down—I know this because I cleverly marked the top with a penciled X. The strip comes off easily, though, and I reverse it. Next, using the wallpaper brush, I smooth the strip in place, and, taking the "broad or spackling knife" and sharp scissors (the wallpaper bible is adamant about the sharpness), trim the top and bottom edges. The first strip is done. Nothing to it, really. I figure the entire room should only take about a hundred hours at this rate.

When Marge arrives, I stop to help her carry in a box of cleaning supplies and mops and brooms, all to a litany of comments about her husband, Ike. I can't decide if she likes him or not (the comments indicate either/or) or even if he's alive or dead (ditto).

Once she has her black coat and scarf carefully hung over a folding chair, Marge puts on an apron. I'm impressed. Who would expect Marge to have a green polka-dotted apron with purple flowers embroidered on the pocket—and ruffles? With single-mindedefficiency, she runs a big sink of soapy water and starts scrubbing counter tops and cupboards.

Any hope that Marge will be cheerful company fades as we work. Our conversation goes like this:

Me: "So, did you have a relaxing weekend, Mrs. Hansen?"

Marge: "Oh, I don't relax on the week-ends. When do you think I do my own cleaning? But I did go to the school play Friday night with my sister-in-law."

Me: "That's nice. What play did you see?"

Marge: "They usually put on a musical in the spring—that's what I was expecting. You can't beat a nice musical like *Guys and Dolls*. I don't remember the name of this play—some silly mystery with people running in and out of doors all the time."

Me: "Did you know any of the kids in the play?"

Marge: "My sister-in-law's neighbor girl was in it, but don't ask me why. She couldn't act her way out of a paper bag."

Me (determinedly): "Well, I'm sure you had a pleasant evening."

Marge: "Not really. Nobody taught them kids how to speak up, so I couldn't make head nor tail of what was going on. No music, neither. Even if you can't understand the words, you can always enjoy the music. And they charged admission. If you ask me, we should've got paid just to sit there."

Me: silence.

Then, the silence becomes so disconcerting I measure (or possibly cut) the next piece of wallpaper incorrectly. I'm sure Marge notices, since I'm on top of the stepladder, foolishly holding onto a strip of paper that's six inches too short. I'm tempted to throw it away but decide I may need it later. A vision of the entire kitchen covered in short strips crosses my mind.

Still, I manage to measure, cut, and hang the next strip correctly. It's the one after that that looks like a challenge. It will have to go partly above the door and partly down along the side of it to the floor. I decide to wait on that one until I'm by myself and can concentrate.

Mumbling about something else I have to take care of, I disappear into the dining room with a paper and pencil. Before Jack-of-All-Trades gets here tomorrow, I need to make a list of repairs he can do. Judging from our short acquaintance, I'm guessing the man won't be any more company than Marge; maybe they can have some kind of "oppositional" contest.

First on the list, of course, is replacing the spindles. Next, I note the huge number of nails in the walls—and holes where others used to be. The walls are made of old-fashioned lathe-and-plaster, which is hard and nearly indestructible, but some of the nail holes are big enough to poke a finger through. I can't imagine what hung there. In one corner of the living room ceiling, there's even a place where a chunk of plaster is missing.

In the bathroom, which I normally try to avoid because it smells, there are cracked floor tiles and relentlessly dripping faucets in the sink and tub. Upstairs, the bedrooms and small hallway have the usual nail holes plus a few minor cracks in the plaster walls. Besides these things, I don't see much that needs repair. In my estimation, Jack should be able to finish everything in a couple of hours. And then leave.

When I go back downstairs, the mirror is doing its thing again, only clearer today, like a big-screen TV. It should frighten me. I know it should. But instead, I'm fascinated by the scene: Once again, the family is gathered around a table. Their names come easily to me now. There is Nancy Miller, the mother, busy with needlework of some kind; Audrey and Ben still doing homework; and the twin boys Davie and Dennis, are—well, it's kind of hard to see what they're doing. But the scene is clear enough that I notice something new. Amid the papers on the table is a little pot of daffodils.

Since I don't feel like I'm having a mental breakdown at the moment, I decide to entertain the possibility of the supernatural. The big question that comes to my mind is this: If there is any self-determination in the ghostly after-life, why would the four Millers return to this house where they were murdered?

But one look tells me why: they were happy here, before it happened. So happy, in fact, that I wish I could join them by the fire and chat about their lives back then—not the murders, just their everyday lives. Then it occurs to me that they don't even know who I am.

After checking to make sure Marge isn't around (and feeling totally foolish), I lean forward and whisper to the mirror, "I'm Abby Miller, some sort of cousin of yours. I'm fixing up your house, so I'll be here a lot. Just so you know."

But they don't pay any attention to me, which is a relief, really. I have enough going on in my life without forming a relationship with a family of ghosts living in a mirror. Still, they all look so contented and peaceful. . . . a lump forms in my throat, and I turn away.

# CHAPTER 19

The next morning Jack-of-All-Trades arrives. I'm relieved to see he drives a big gray pickup instead of a white van with black tinted windows. Still limping slightly, he walks toward the house and glances around, eyes unreadable behind those dark glasses. I'm glad the geezers are here, cleaning out the basement. I wouldn't want to be alone with this guy.

When he steps into the house, Jack pulls off his glasses and tucks them into his pocket, but the baseball cap stays on. He has nicer features than I remembered, but I don't see any sign of the humor that captivated Wendy. To me, he seems, though not exactly threatening, then, well, intimidating. And if this guy has a pet out there in his woodsy hideout, I'll bet it's some kind of vicious pit bull.

When Jack looks at me, his eyes are as brown and hard as pebbles. Somewhat nervously, I lead him on a tour of the rooms, pointing out the plethora of nails and nail holes that dot the plaster like a bad rash. I catch myself apologizing for nails and nail holes I certainly had nothing to do with.

Jack pulls out a small notebook and pencil from his pocket and begins taking notes. In addition to the nail holes, he notices the huge hole in the ceiling that needs to be repaired. He doesn't say much else until we get to the bathroom, which he surveys with a deep

CORINNE MALCOLM IBELING / R.I.PARTRIDGE 103

frown. After he steps in to look at the broken tiles, he stamps one boot heavily on the floor. "Yeah, this isn't good."

I look at the floor, trying to guess what he means. "The tiles are ugly and cracked, but what else?"

He kneels down and examines the floor around the toilet more closely. "Haven't you noticed how squishy the floor is here?"

"That and the nasty smell. What does it mean?"

"At a guess, I'd say the seal under the stool is bad, and water has been leaking into the subfloor. That would account for the softness and the smell."

"Oh, no. Will that be expensive to fix?"

He shrugs his wide shoulders and stands up. "Depends on how bad it is. You need to have someone else look at it. They'll say you need a new subfloor and tile, but don't let them sock you for a new stool. This one probably just needs a seal. I'll fix those dripping faucets for you, though you should replace them sometime. And after the new flooring is in, you should add a new vanity." He jerks his head at the offending vanity. "The sink in that one looks like crap."

Vernelle is not going to like the news one bit. Neither will the banker—oops, that's me. But for the first time, I have someone here who can give us an honest appraisal for what needs to be done. "Vernelle needs to get this house rented soon." I sweep my hand in the direction of the kitchen and living room. "Would you mind looking around to see what else needs to be done?"

He nods, though he's quick to point out that he's not an expert. The rest isn't too bad—more nail holes upstairs and a couple of cracked windows. When he's done, Jack says, "I'll take a look around outside to see if there are any obvious problems, but you should have the roof inspected. All these repairs won't do much good if you have a leaky roof."

Great—the thought of a shingling crew skittering around on the roof like monkeys makes me shudder. I'm not discouraged so much by the money all this will cost as much as from the time it's going to take.

Then Jack surprises me by saying he'll get his tools from his truck so he can get something done today. He doesn't exactly sound enthused.

Glad to be alone again in the kitchen, I go back to my wallpaper, starting with the long strip I'd skipped that runs along the top of the door and then down one side. It's hard to measure and harder to cut. I finally get it in place then notice the woodwork is now dripping with sticky paste from where the strip kept flapping against it. With a sigh, I get a rag and wash it off.

The next strip goes from ceiling to floor. I get it cut and hung all right and have turned to start on the next when something falls right across my head and down my back. Something big. Something wet and big, namely my newly—hung strip of wallpaper, which has fallen completely from the wall.

I give a yelp of surprise. "Damn, damn, damn!" How could this have happened?!! I'm still trying to get the wallpaper off without getting covered in wet paste when I hear someone laughing.

One of the geezers must have come in. "Hey!" I screech, "would you stop laughing and help?"

From my vantage point under the paper, I see a pair of blue jeans and boots approach, and someone lifts the wallpaper off. Jack is holding the wallpaper and still chuckling, and I finally give in and laugh reluctantly with him. "I could have sworn that strip would stay up! And for God's sake, don't let it tear. I have that piece measured and trimmed already."

"You look like you could use some help." He's still chuckling as he climbs up the stepladder. He lines up the top of the strip and smoothes it on with the brush in quick, efficient swipes, even giving the wallpaper a few whacks along the edges. When he steps down and hands me the brush, I finish the length of the strip. It stays on this time.

I survey it with satisfaction and some frustration. "What went wrong?"

At least Jack has stopped laughing. "You didn't get the top part on tight enough. When that came loose, the whole thing went. I'll help you with a couple more of these long pieces, and then you're on your own."

I don't have any objection to that. I cut, soak, and book, and he hangs and trims. The papering goes much faster with Jack's help. He either has done this before, or he paid more attention to the self-help videos than I did. Amazingly, nothing falls down.

Once, we accidentally touch, his hand against mine, and I'm surprised by the shock of it. As I cut and soak the next strip, I try to remember the last time I've been touched by a man, even though Jack obviously didn't mean to.

Well, I've been poked and prodded on nearly every square inch of my body by male nurses and doctors over the last year, but I don't count that. That real man's touch—and I use the term "real man" loosely—was, of course, Brad's. I think back to the last time we made love. Oh, yeah, it was a week before the fire when Brad said, "I hate to tell you this, Abby, but you must be redistributing your weight lately. Your boobs are smaller and you're packing it in around your hips." No amount of foreplay was going to bring back romance after a comment like that.

He must have been thinking of Chloe's body—Brad just got his bodies mixed up. Not that Brad did much foreplay, as Chloe has learned by now. Still, to notice a man's touch—it's a sign that I'm coming back to life, though what's the point? What man is going to love me when I look like this?

One of my counselors said there's someone out there for me, "Someone like you, Abby." So, is there a dating site for disfigured people? Maybe I can find someone burned on the right side of his body; we'd make a matched set. Or someone blind—yeah, that's even better. In one movement, I yank the strip of wallpaper out of the water and shove it toward Jack, making darn sure our hands don't touch this time.

The next several strips go up rapidly, and Jack disappears into the living room. With a sigh, I decide it's time for lunch.

Sitting at the table, I take a moment to admire the wall of cheerful yellow wallpaper that's done. As I take my first spoonful of soup, I can imagine a little bouquet of daffodils on the counter. The soup, as usual, is delicious—baked potato, with a big glob of cheese melted in and a sprinkling of bacon on top. The sandwich today is (and I quote from Vernelle) "mesquite-smoked chicken with mushrooms and Monterey jack on whole wheat bread. Sour cream and salsa on the side." I've just taken a bite when I hear the words, "What the hell is that smell?"

Jack is standing in the doorway, and I nearly drop my sandwich as I turn toward him in alarm. "What? I don't smell anything!"

"Then you don't have a nose, woman. Whatever you're eating—what is it?"

"Baked potato soup and chicken sandwiches—my sister always makes me lunch. Would you like some?" The soup carton on the table is still half full, and there's an entire sandwich left.

He shakes his head regretfully. "No, thanks, I couldn't take any of your lunch."

Well, I'm sure not going to force it on him; I don't need the company that badly. "Okay," I agree, and go on eating. But he doesn't leave the doorway.

"Yes?"

"You're supposed to say, 'Oh, please, there's plenty here for two' and invite me to sit down—if there *is* plenty."

"Oh, please, there is plenty here for two. Bowls and spoons are in the sack on the counter. But be careful of that chair—it's a bit wobbly."

After filling a bowl, Jack eases himself onto the chair, which fortunately doesn't collapse under his weight. He's taken off his heavy jacket and is wearing a denim shirt with his sleeves rolled up. His brawny arms are what you'd expect, but his hands are finer, not scarred and rough anyway.

Still somewhat nervous, I ask him, "Do you want to warm up the soup? There's a microwave on the counter."

"No, thanks, it's warm enough, and I'm starved. I didn't think I'd be working here this long, so I didn't bring anything to eat."

At least this gives me a topic of conversation; you can't very well ask someone if he's on parole or how he spends his time back in the timber, so I ask what he usually has for lunch when he's working.

"Not that much—lunch meat sandwiches or something. I'm a lousy cook. If Hy-Vee didn't have a good deli and frozen food section, I'd starve to death."

I offer Jack the other sandwich, and he takes that, too. We eat in companionable silence for a while with Jack clearly enjoying Vernelle's food. On impulse I say, "I think I should tell you—well, obviously, you can see there's an elephant in the room."

He looks up from his soup blankly. "There is?"

"Me! I mean me." Is the man an idiot?

He regards me with raised brows. "I don't think you look like an elephant."

I'm not sure if he's joking or not and take a deep breath. "That's just an expression—surely you've heard it before! I mean what happened to my face."

"Well, it's obvious that something happened to you, but that's your business."

I bite my lip and try again. "Since you're working here for a while at least, I want to get it out of the way, because you've probably heard the stories around town."

He shrugs. "Tell me whatever you feel comfortable with, but keep in mind I can deal with it if you don't."

I don't feel comfortable telling my story to strangers, and he's not making it any easier. "It was a house fire, that's all, an accident—Brad and I weren't drunk, our meth lab didn't explode, and we didn't set the house on fire to collect the insurance. Those are just some of the rumors you'll hear around town. A burning beam or something fell on my left side. I've had a lot of operations, plastic surgeries, mostly, but this is pretty much how it will always be—my face, I mean."

Jack nods and sticks his right leg out from under the table. "Car wreck," he says. "I've had a bunch of operations, too, and this is pretty much how it will always be."

I find myself relaxing from tension I didn't even know I felt. "Then you understand what it's like."

The hard brown eyes regard me dispassionately. "I can only guess what it's been like for you, but I know one thing for sure—we've both been through hell."

# CHAPTER 20

After lunch, Jack has gone to the hardware store, and I'm slapping wallpaper up like a pro when there's a knock on the kitchen door. It's Dickie Schwarz, and I give a groan that's probably audible when I open the door.

Her usual wide smile is not in place. In fact, she looks distinctly uncomfortable as she clutches another orange sack. "More 'welcome-back' cookies?" I ask, probably sounding more sarcastic than I meant to.

Her flickery eyes dart at my face and then away. "They're apology cookies, Abby. I didn't realize until I left how rude I must have sounded last time I was here. I just want to say I'm sorry if I came across kind of pushy." Then, with a faint smile, she shoves the sack at me and is gone.

I peek in the sack; it's full of chocolate chip cookies. I'm still standing there, bemused, when Jack walks in the door. "Who the hell was that? She damned near put an ugly green stripe down the side of my truck when she backed out!"

"Her name's Dickie Schwarz. She's a teacher at the high school- -has been for years, even when I went there. She gave me these cookies, as an apology. When she dropped by a few days ago, she was really nosy about Vernelle's plans for the house."

"I remember her." He tucks his dark glasses into a pocket, then leans against the door-frame, a sack from the hardware store dangling from his hand. "She came by my place when I first moved here. I didn't invite her in, but the cookies she gave me were good—figured she was some kind of cookie Avon Lady."

I choke back a giggle. "Not exactly; she teaches Home Ec., and she has her students make cookies when she hears there's someone new in town—or old, like me."

"Her students make the cookies?" Jack has an odd expression on his face. "Where I taught, when the kids in Home Ec. made cookies for any adults—especially teachers—they always spit in the dough or something."

Interesting. I open the sack. "Have one. They're chocolate chip, and they've been baked. I don't suppose anything too dangerous can get through 350 degrees in the oven."

Jack takes one—doubtfully. "So what's her interest in your house? Does she want to rent it or something?"

"If you'd like to join me for a cup of coffee, I'll tell you about it." Jack sits down and tosses his baseball cap on the floor; his hair is a thick mixture of black and gray. I wonder how old he really is—not exactly a grandfather-type, but not all that young, either. Mid-forties, maybe?

I slide into the other chair and pour us each a cup of coffee. "She and her Historical Society buddies think this house would make a good tourist attraction. I wouldn't be surprised if there are rumors going around that it's haunted—the last renters certainly moved out in a hurry."

Jack is examining his cookie. When he's satisfied (apparently) that there's nothing identifiably foreign on it, he dunks it into the steaming coffee and takes a bite. "They never said anything about it to me. I stopped a couple of times while they lived here—once to help one of the kids fix his bike and another when they couldn't get their car started. The only odd thing I saw was . . ."

And here he pauses. "What?" I ask.

"The day before they moved out, that banker's car was in the driveway—you know, the guy with the funny name."

"Tom Trimble?"

"That's the one. I wondered what the hell he was doing here. As a matter of fact, I've noticed he's been driving around a lot lately. Getting back to Dickie, it'll take more than ghosts to make this house into a big-deal tourist place. Anyway, I wouldn't trust the judgment of anyone whose name sounds like a parakeet's."

I almost choke on my cookie. "She thinks it could be advertised as a "murder house" like the one in Villisca. Have you ever heard of that? I don't know much about it."

He takes another cookie. "You don't want to know the details, believe me—it was pretty gruesome. A crazy guy with an ax wiped out a whole family during the night, back around 1900, I think it was. Lots of accusations, but the case was never officially solved. So what happened here? I've heard some stuff, but it sounded farfetched to me."

I lean back in my chair. "A family was murdered here, too, in the 1960's. They were relatives of my dad, so I guess I know about as much as anyone. The Millers and their three children lived in this house--a teen-aged daughter named Audrey and twin boys, who were younger. The accepted story—and believe me, nobody really knows—is that Audrey had a fight with her boyfriend, a kid named Ben Stockton who lived on a farm just down the road. He got so mad that he came here with a knife one night—seeking revenge, they say—and killed them all.

"Well, except for the father, Ed. This was a big farm back then, but Ed worked at a bank in town—the Trimbles' bank, I think. He was at a meeting and came home to find the place full of cops and ambulances. Ben was here, too—he was just a high school kid. He must have been caught with the knife in his hand or something. Anyway, it was a no-brainer for the sheriff. Ben was arrested and taken to jail that night."

I pause to sip my coffee. "That's when the story gets even sadder. Sometime during the night, Ben committed suicide. He was found hanging in his cell. End of story."

"What happened to Ed Miller? That had to be pretty devastating, to have your whole family wiped out." I catch a note of sympathy in Jack's voice, but his hard features don't alter much.

"It had to be," I agree. "After that, Ed lived alone here for years. He got fired from the bank before he finally drank himself to death. I've always heard that he wasn't a very nice man, but what happened to his family wrecked his life. When he died, my Grandpa Miller inherited the place—he was Ed's brother. And then it passed on to my dad Dad. That's why Vernelle owns it now."

Jack swishes another cookie around in his coffee. "No wonder the Historical Society wants in. But they better have their ducks in a row if they want to make a tourist trap out of this place. Since the murders happened in the 1960's, there could still be family of the Stockton kid's around."

"Supposedly not. You know, I've always wondered how one person—a boy like that—could kill a whole family. It wasn't like he had an ax. You'd think someone would have gotten away."

Jack shrugs. "At a guess, I'd say the victims tried to protect each other, but the guy with the knife always wins."

"Maybe." Jack's dark eyebrows rise quizzically, but he doesn't say anything. I'm glad, because I don't want to think of that innocent-faced kid in the mirror as "the guy with the knife."

I shiver and decide to change the subject. After taking a bite of my third cookie (they're actually very good), I ask casually, "So, you used to be a teacher?"

CORINNE MALCOLM IBELING / R.I.PARTRIDGE 113

He's frowning. "If you want to know stuff about me, just ask."

"Okay, so you used to be a teacher?"

He rolls his eyes but answers readily enough. "It's ancient history now, but I taught for years at East Cedar High School up by Tipton. That was my second career—before that I was in the Navy for ten years. When I got out, I went to UNI and got a teaching degree in Industrial Arts. My classes were woodworking, small engine repair, classes like that. Loved it, loved the kids. Didn't love some of the stuff that went on. I saw good teachers getting out of teaching because of what they have to deal with—disruptive students, lousy parents, spineless administrators. I didn't have trouble with the kids, but there are some who don't come to school to learn. Sometimes, it's not their fault, sometimes it is."

"Is that why you got out of teaching?" I regret the question as soon as I ask it. "Sorry, that's not any of my business."

There's a long silence. Jack contemplates his cup of coffee as if he could will it to speak. "It's okay. I can talk about it now. Seven years ago, I was in a car accident. I spent most of the school year in the hospital and then in therapy—you know the kind of thing.

"I came back with a month of school left. It took me that month to realize I couldn't do it. It wasn't fair to my students, and it wasn't fair to me—I couldn't be the teacher I used to be. My speech was pretty good by then, but sometimes I'd forget where I was in a lesson, or whether I'd already made an assignment. I could tell by the kids' faces—even the good ones—that things weren't going well, so I didn't sign my next year's contract. The school board said they'd hold my job for me. They even offered to get a long-term sub until I got better, but that wasn't fair to the kids, either. So I quit and moved here."

"To do what—carpentry?"

"At first I did carpentry work for other people. Then I started making furniture and selling it on my own. It's something I'd always wanted to do; I just never had time before."

"What kind of furniture do you make?"

"Have you ever seen Stickley furniture?"

I nod.

"I don't copy their designs, but I like the Craftsman style—simple lines, nice wood." He pauses. "What about you?" His mouth quirks a little. "I'm guessing you aren't a professional paper hanger."

"God, no. I was a teacher, too, but just for a while. I taught kindergarten for two years in Des Moines. Then Brad and I got married, and we moved to California. I quit teaching, but I still miss the kids." I can't continue; that thought leads to a road I don't want to travel. Instead, I jump up and start putting the snack things away.

Jack is still sitting there, drinking his coffee. I manage to get myself together enough to say, "That's interesting—what you said about Tom Trimble. He doesn't want Vernelle to rent this house. I wonder if he did something to make those people move out? I can't imagine what, though."

Jack takes a last sip of his coffee and stands up. "I can. I've heard he really throws his weight around this town. He probably came up with some kind of threat. He looks like the type."

His words haunt me the rest of the day. Tom Trimble and threats—the words seem to go together.

# CHAPTER 21

It's been exactly one week since I started my "Vernelle's House Project," and set the goal of obtaining visitation rights in three months. And I'm feeling good about both, though I thought I'd have more done on the house by now. At least I've made a good start, and the geezers have been working like troopers, cleaning out the basement. It occurs to me that I've never been down there. I didn't even think to have Jack-of-All-Trades check it out; we don't want any more surprises like the bathroom.

With some hesitation (and a quick prayer that my left leg won't give out), I tread with care down the steep wooden stairs to the clammy basement. It's old and damp and gloomy but bare of everything now except some empty shelves and festoons of cobwebs—and another marble. It's destined for the pickle jar, but I'm beginning to wonder if these marbles are somehow being left for me to find. And if so, why?

When I return to the kitchen, Jack leans around the corner to tell me that the spindles are back where they belong in the stairway, and the hole in the ceiling has been patched.

Once again, Jack's hat and dark glasses are in place, and he seems more distant than yesterday. Maybe he wishes he hadn't told me what happened to him; I doubt that he's normally a talkative guy. On the other hand, who does he talk to, back there in the timber?

The kitchen is definitely showing progress. Two walls are papered, with two to go. The yellow walls positively glow, like waves of sunshine. I'm glowing, too, with satisfaction, because the strips of paper all stayed up. I was worried that they'd run down the walls during the night like big drips of butter.

Then it's back to my routine of measuring and cutting and hanging, with the radio tuned to the usual MP station for company. When my new pal DJ Jerry gives the day's birthdays, Marge's is among them. I don't pay much attention to what he says after that, but before the next commercial, he announces that Marge Hansen is the lucky winner in a drawing for $25 in Mt. Prospect "bucks." She can spend them in any store in town, and I wonder what she'll buy with her $25—Flowers? Perfume? Sexy lingerie to tempt Ike?

When the third wall is finished, I figure it's time for lunch. Setting my usual place at the table, I check out the food. The soup's still steaming hot, and there are two big sandwiches.

The question is, do I ask Jack if he'd like to share my lunch, or not? Maybe he brought his own lunch today, and it would seem pushy. But he liked the food yesterday, and oddly enough I enjoyed his company. It's hard to explain why, since I haven't really got the guy figured out yet. The hard eyes are difficult to get past, but I like his deep voice and quick laugh. And while I'm often in a turmoil of worries, he's a pool of calm and common sense.

Jack's not in the living room, but the spindles look perfect; had I not known which ones they were, I wouldn't have been able to tell the difference. All nails are gone from the walls, and the plaster is smooth and bare. It's like magic.

As I'm looking around in amazement, Jack comes down the stairs and hands me a tin can full of nails. "Jesus, I think those people decorated with these things. In some rooms it looks like a 'connect-the-dots' game. I'll fill the nail holes this afternoon. After lunch."

At least the dark glasses are gone and I look him in the eyes. "The spindles look nice, Jack. What do you fill nail holes with? I always used toothpaste."

"I won't even comment on that." Jack opens a sack that's on the floor and pulls out a plastic container. "Bought this yesterday—it's called 'spackling.'" As if I didn't know.

I give him a sideways look. "I don't have the faintest idea of how you 'spackle,' but I have a 'broad or spackling knife' if you want to borrow it."

He starts to laugh. "Well, then, get your 'broad or spackling' knife, and I'll show you how to fill nail holes. It's a skill no one should be without—particularly someone who used toothpaste."

But when I bring my knife to him, Jack says it's too big and gets one of his own; he calls it a "putty knife." I'm not sure of the difference between putty and spackle, but I'm not going to ask. Jack opens the spackling (it looks like marshmallow crème), puts some on his knife, and presses it against the hole. Then, turning his knife over, he takes a swipe that clears off the excess in one quick, seamless movement.

Now there is a tiny white dot instead of a black nail hole. "That's it?" I ask.

"It might have to be sanded down so it's smooth enough for paint, but yeah, that's basically it. Do you want to try?"

I take the putty knife and try to do exactly what Jack did. Though I get the nail-hole full, I leave a ridge of the stuff on the wall. "Here," he says, and guides my hand with his. I'm conscious of how close he's standing to me. Jack might not be able to fly a 747 across the country, but he can spackle nail holes like a wizard—and smells nice, too.

After I fill a couple more holes by myself, I return the can of spackling and putty knife to Jack with a flourish. "I don't know about you, but I'm hungry. Did you bring your lunch?"

"Sure."

"Would you like to eat with me?"

His long pause makes me uncomfortable, and I say hurriedly, "That's okay; you don't have to."

I turn around, but he follows me into the kitchen. "I have to get my cooler out of the truck first," he says gruffly.

After pouring my soup into a bowl, I take a carton of milk and packet of sandwiches out of my own cooler. When Jack sits down, he eyes the steaming gold liquid in front of me. "What's that stuff?"

"Butternut squash and apple soup. The sandwich of the day is roast beef with Swiss cheese, lettuce, tomato and onion, with mayo on rye. What do you have?"

He puts a can of beer on the table and takes a sandwich out of a baggie. "Essence of olive loaf on Sara Lee—sounds erotic, doesn't it?"

After a glimpse of his sandwich, I grin and say, "Change that to 'pathetic.'" The piece of lunch-meat hanging out of the sandwich is curled around the edges as if it's given up hope of being used. Even worse, I point out that there's mold on his bread.

"There is?" He looks genuinely surprised and lays it down. "It's not that old."

I repress a giggle. "Well, I think that's what that green stuff is. Honestly, Jack, I have plenty for us both, and Vernelle was thrilled that all the food disappeared yesterday. You'd be helping me out."

Jack doesn't need another invitation and helps himself to soup and a sandwich. We eat in silence for a few minutes. Jack has an absent look on his face as if he's trying to make up his mind about something. Finally, he seems to come to a decision. "I basically lied to you yesterday, Abby. It was a sin of omission. I've thought about it all night, and I need to come clean."

It's a shock to hear Jack say my name for the first time; this must be serious. I watch his face, unable to guess his next words. What's Jack's story? Alcoholism? Drug abuse?

"I got hurt in a car wreck, like I said. My wife, Steph, and I were taking our daughter to Iowa City for an allergy appointment when we were involved in a huge pile-up on I-80 and got T-boned by a semi. To be honest, I don't remember any of it. Lily—our daughter—was killed. She was eight."

"Oh, my God. I'm so sorry," I whisper, blinking back sudden tears. A dead child; I hadn't expected something like that.

Jack nods and looks away. "Steph came out okay, but I didn't. My leg was crushed, and I had some head injuries. Just so you know." There's a long pause. "Steph and I couldn't get along after that. We got divorced, and that's when I moved here. Steph's remarried and has a couple of little girls now. I'm happy for her."

"A cascading event."

His dark eyes regard me questioningly.

"A 'cascading event'—that's what my doctor called what happened to me. An event that's like tipping the first in a row of dominoes. It goes on and on. It takes just a few minutes—or seconds—and your life is changed forever. You can never go back."

Our eyes meet, and he gives a nod of understanding. "Yeah, five seconds on the Interstate, and my life was never the same." He pauses thoughtfully. "My brain was pretty much scrambled for a while. It's still frustrating when I stutter, or have an idea and just can't get it out. And I stumble sometimes, like you, but it's because my brain doesn't always get my balance right. With you, I expect the burns did some damage besides your face."

I find it disconcerting that Jack has been analyzing me like that, but I shrug and smile. "Some. I'm better, now." I want to tell him that I'm hoping to get my boys back soon, but after hearing about the loss of his daughter, it just doesn't seem right. "I think all this climbing up and down the ladder hanging wallpaper has been good for me. Maybe I'll become a professional decorator."

After what he's seen of my "decorating" skills, I expect to hear a hearty guffaw from Jack.

Instead, he gets up and leans both hands on the back of his chair. "Maybe you should. There's something satisfying about taking an old house and making it nice again. You're willing to learn, so I think you'd do just fine." Then, saying he has a million more holes to fill (and that's a rough estimate), he leaves the room.

With Jack's unexpected encouragement, I resume wallpapering. I'm starting the next wall when Marge walks into the room. "Whose old pickup is that out front?" she asks as she takes off her coat.

I pull a strip of dripping wallpaper out of the soaking tray and carefully 'book it'. "It belongs to Jack Allender. He's doing some carpentry work for me."

"I hear he does good work," Marge allows grudgingly. "But you be careful, Miz Bennett. You know he lives all by hisself back in them woods, like a hermit. You got to watch out for that kind."

With a last glare toward Jack, wherever he might be, she gets a bucket of soapy water and sets to work washing down the woodwork in the dining room. When I step around the corner later, she's washing the top of the built-in buffet. Giving the wood a last swipe, she pauses reminiscently. "Miss Bryant was real proud of the dishes she used to keep here—'Candlewick' it was she collected. And she kept tablecloths and napkins in these drawers—real linen ones, from Ireland." She frowns. "They was hell to iron, though."

She turns toward me, her jowls quivering indignantly. "And you know what them relatives of hers did with her stuff? Sold everything at a tag sale right in this house! Even put out her clothes—they laid all her slips and brassieres across the bed with price stickers on them. Why, she would have been mortified!"

"That's terrible, Mrs. Hansen! But if they wanted money so much, I'm surprised they left all that old stuff in the basement."

"I told them it was there, but those two cousins of hers are fat as a couple of hippos. They was just too lazy to carry anything up the stairs. Why, they didn't even look in the attic—stairs again! They wanted easy money—it all comes down to that. They said it was moldy in the basement, and they have allergies. Well, they sure aren't allergic to food!"

She seems destined to continue if I don't head her off. "I didn't know there was an attic in this house."

She gives me a look. "Of course there's an attic! Haven't you ever noticed that little window at the top of the house?"

I just nod and say hurriedly, "By the way, Mrs. Hansen, happy birthday! What will you buy with the $25 you won on the radio?"

She gathers up the sponges and pail of dirty water. "Oh, you heard that, did you? My sister-in-law always sends my name in on my birthday. Kind of silly, I think. But I've had my eye on a new can opener at Talbot's. There's nothing like a new can-opener to cheer a person up."

"No, indeed," I agree. I glance at the living room mirror; it's totally blank. I'm guessing that even ghosts wouldn't mess around with someone who's thrilled at the thought of a new can opener.

# CHAPTER 22

By the time Jack and Marge leave, the kitchen is almost done, so I stay later than usual to finish up. Fortunately, we had just enough to finish all the walls. I'm standing in the dining room doorway, admiring my beautiful sunshiny kitchen, when a voice from behind says, "That's real pretty, Ms. Bennett."

I whirl, my heart in my throat, to find Tom Trimble standing right behind me. Instinctively I move a couple of steps away. "What are you doing here?" Surprise—and anger—makes my voice shaky.

"Don't get your panties in a wad, honey. I was just passing by— saw your car and wondered who was messing around out here." Dressed in blue jeans and a leather jacket, Tom looks tanned and fit, like an L. L. Bean catalog ad for older men. He also has a bland smile, which I don't trust for a minute.

"I'm not messing around; I'm working here."

"Is that right?" he asks gently. "You know, I offered that sister of yours..." (and his tone somehow implies something dirty) "...a considerable chunk of money for this old place."

"It's income property for Vernelle. She told you that."

Tom's eyes wander around the room; I can see that he's not really impressed with what I've done. "She might want to sell it to me someday. For example, if she can't find a renter or if she loses her job—then she might be glad to take whatever I'd give for it."

"She's a good legal secretary; I doubt she'd lose her job."

His smile widens unpleasantly, and his eyes seem to linger on the damaged side of my face. "I'm sure your sister is a very good secretary. But Clarence isn't a very good lawyer, is he? He's also a gambler—been one for years. And not very good at that, either. His mother used to bail him out when he lost too much. But she's dead now."

"So, you bail him out?"

"Let's just say he's got everything he owns mortgaged to me."

When I don't reply, because the implication is all too obvious, Tom goes on. "You can't bankroll your sister forever. You can't even afford to keep her in those sexy clothes and high-heeled shoes she's always wearing."

"You don't know what I can afford." My left leg—my weak leg—suddenly wavers, and I touch the doorway for support.

"I can guess," he says easily. "Ms. Bennett, you're probably wondering why I care about this place so much. As you may know, I own a lot of property around here, so I drive by every few days. I like things clean and neat. It was fine when Miss Bryant lived here. She always kept everything nice. But that last bunch didn't— broken toys and bikes laying around, trash blowing all over the place. Next, you'll have Mexicans living out here. And you know what that means."

I straighten up—anger giving me strength. "I don't know what that means, but I know what trespassing means. You need to get out—now."

His colorless eyes sweep over me. He's still smiling, but I can sense that he's deeply angry. "I don't think you get what I'm trying to tell you."

Behind Tom, a figure appears out of the shadows, and a voice says, "The lady asked you to leave."

Tom turns slowly around. "Hey, aren't you that guy who lives in that shack down on Coonhunters Road?" His leering glance shifts between us. "Should have known you two cripples would find each other."

Jack is still partly in shadows—a stocky figure in a baseball cap and dark glasses. "The name's Jack Allender. Abby doesn't want you here. So get in your piece-of-crap SUV and get off her property."

"It's a Cadillac Escalade XZT," Tom says frigidly, "but you probably wouldn't know that."

"I know chicken-shit tan when I see it, and you've got one minute to get your butt into it."

Tom's back is toward me, but I can see that he stiffens and clenches his fists.

Jack sees it, too. "Go ahead—start something, Trimble. I'm sure Ambrosia Swann would be only too happy to print that you got beat up by a guy who lives in a shack and drives an old Silverado."

For a moment, I'm not sure which Tom Trimble will win out: the big guy who's used to throwing his weight around, or the banker who's conscious of his reputation. Finally, he says, "I'm leaving, but only because Abby asked. I always do what a lady asks." He turns a nasty look my way. "And the lady, if she's smart, always does what I ask her."

When Jack takes a step toward him, Tom brushes by and goes out the front door.

I can't move until I hear Tom drive away.

Jack pulls off his glasses; his eyes are flat and hard. "You're lucky I came back for my cooler. What the hell was that all about?"

Sinking into a chair, I give him the short version, and Jack whistles. "Jesus, the guy must be a nut-case."

My heart has finally slowed down. "I'm sorry you walked into that, but thanks for your help, Jack."

"You shouldn't be out here this late alone. Next time Trimble shows up, I might not be around."

"Sometimes I have to stay late to get things done."

Jack frowns. "Then make sure you lock the doors." He pulls a card from his pocket and hands it to me. "My cell number's on that. Put it in your phone, okay?"

I nod. He takes my hand and pulls me up from the chair. "Come on, it's time to go home. I'll wait outside for you."

After Jack leaves, I go through the living room to lock the front door, and there they are, my people in the mirror. I clutch the mantel, entranced. It's such a warm, loving scene—I wish I could step through the glass to join them, to meet these cousins that I never knew. I'd give Nancy and Audrey big hugs, and the little boys . . . well, the little boys I would hold in my arms and never let go.

Late that evening, I perch at the kitchen table while Vernelle paints her toenails a shade of red on the brighter side of crimson. "That shit!" she sputters. "So now he's chasing away my renters and threatening my job!" She takes a deep breath. "I know Clarence gambles too much—he's been gone a lot lately. If Tom threatened Clarence, he'd let me go in a heartbeat. He wouldn't want to, but he would."

"Couldn't you get a job with another lawyer in town?"

Vernelle bites her lower lip, concentrating on a delicate little toe. "Doubtful. Tom has more power than you'd think. But I'll never sell that house to him. Never." She looks up with a smile. "Let's not worry about that right now, Abby—let's make fudge instead. I have Dad's old recipe—remember how he always made us beat the hot fudge with a wooden spoon until our arms almost fell off?"

"Yeah, we'd do anything to lick the pan! It was great stuff." While I line up the ingredients, I mention, very casually, that the new carpenter got rid of Tom for me. Vernelle is impressed. If she knew that Jack looks like a serial killer, she'd probably try to hire him to get rid of Tom permanently.

# CHAPTER 23

An hour before I figure Jack-of-All-Trades will show up, I'm at the house on Thursday morning, eager to start painting. After the wallpaper fiasco, I don't want to look like an idiot again; an hour should give me enough time to get the basics of painting down, or at least look like I've got the basics down.

In the middle of the dining room floor, I've piled all the painting supplies I bought this morning, starting with a gallon of paint. Besides the color, Vernelle reminded me to get latex paint, which cleans up with water. There's no need to remind me about the time Dad almost burned down the garage cleaning paint brushes with gasoline.

Then, there's a paint-can opener, brushes of various sizes, paint rollers (large and small), the fuzzy rolls that fit on them (large and small), paint trays (large and small), a cup-like thing I can hold in my hand (but don't know why I'd want to), rolls of blue tape, more rags, latex gloves, and big sheets of plastic. It's a formidable pile.

I survey my canvas (metaphorically speaking). With one coat of magic paint, the room will go from dirty beige to "Chocolate Mist." You tape and you paint—what could possibly go wrong?

I decide to start on the wall closest the living room, which, because of the archway, isn't very large. First, I tape the woodwork along the edges. Next, I spread the big sheets of plastic over the floor, with newspapers on top of that, not so much to protect the carpet as to avoid tracking paint all over the place.

Then I put the stepladder in place, open a gallon of paint and pour some into the large tray. Next, I put a fuzzy pad onto the big roller, roll it in the paint, and climb to the top of the stepladder. The first "roll" is a big thrill, as it changes a whole swath of ugly into a satisfying shade of chocolate. I paint as close as I can to the ceiling, with enough care (and common sense) not to touch the white ceiling with chocolate, which would create a whole new problem to deal with.

I'm having enough problems already. The old plaster wall, with its rough texture, is taking a lot of paint. I don't want to put the paint tray up on the ladder, so I'm continually climbing down the stepladder to reload the roller and then climbing up again. This is definitely not going as fast as I'd planned.

To my great embarrassment, I sense someone watching me. In the midst of my upping and downing, I hadn't seen Jack come in. Stepping off the ladder, my drippy roller clutched in one plastic-gloved hand, I give him a resigned look. "This is wrong, isn't it?"

Truly, I think Jack's trying not to smile, but his brown eyes are crinkling around corners. He tips his baseball cap back on his head. "Woman, haven't you ever painted before?"

"From the look on your face—obviously not."

"Do you have a handle extension in that big pile of crap?" While I'm searching around, Jack adds, "A long stick?" This is said gently, but with the excessive patience of someone talking to an idiot.

Light dawns. "I remember Mr. Talbot carrying something like that to the car, but I don't know what happened to it. Just a minute."

I put down the roller and race out to the car. By the time I come back with the long stick from the trunk, Jack is pouring a slurp of paint into the mystery cup. Then he chooses a paint-brush from my expensive "pile of crap" and climbs the ladder. As I watch, he trims along the ceiling in one long sweep using the paint in the cup; then he paints downward until he meets my roller swipes. Suddenly, the wall starts to look amazing.

"Wow!" is all I can say.

Jack climbs down from the ladder, takes the stick, and screws it into the handle of the roller I was using. Then he hands it to me and gestures toward the wall. It's easy to dip the roller into paint and roll the paint across the wall as high as I want. "Wow, again!"

Jack stands there with his arms crossed, now openly smiling. "And so simple."

I'm properly humble. "Thanks. This will save me a lot of time. That wallpaper already took days more than I figured, and I still have to do the other rooms."

He looks around skeptically. "You took on a big job, especially for someone who's never painted before. Plus, you have paint on your nose."

"I do?" I walk over to the mirror. Then I forget about the paint on my face because the usual scene is there. There's nothing new going on, though—must be a day for reruns. I turn to Jack. "Do you see anything strange about this mirror?"

He comes closer and surveys it critically, then runs his hand around the edges. "No, just that it's pretty spotty, like old mirrors get. Probably original to the house, which is impressive."

All Jack can see are the spots? Disappointment floods through me, but there must be some reason—

"And you still have paint on your nose." Jack reaches over and, with his thumb, gently wipes the paint off. It's not, by any means, an intimate gesture, but it catches me by surprise.

He turns away and says abruptly, "Do you have a deadline to get this all done?"

"ASAP—Vernelle needs the money."

Jack studies each wall for a moment; I sense that he's measuring the square footage somehow. "If I trim and you paint, we can have this room done by noon. And forget taping. I can trim faster than it takes to tape. Don't get me wrong," (he adds this while he flicks a warning glance my way, as if I might start some kind of anti-tape rebellion) "taping's a good idea, but it takes a hell of a lot of time, which you don't have. Deal?"

It's a deal I can't turn down. We don't talk much, just paint. The dining room is done by the time lunch rolls around. Four whole walls of beautiful "Chocolate Mist" —which reminds me that I'm hungry.

***

The soup of the day is creamy cauliflower-and-artichoke-hearts with bacon, accompanied by a roast beef sandwich on rye— horseradish sauce on the side. Jack gives me a thumbs-up when I ask him to share my lunch and doesn't even try to fake me out with a moldy sandwich.

Once the food is served—and with a beer from his cooler—Jack concentrates on eating. My sudden feeling of happiness isn't entirely due to the delicious soup or the cheery yellow kitchen walls. It's not even that I can look into the dining room with its fresh coat of paint and imagine how the finished walls will look. Mostly it's because I have someone—a guy I barely know—to share these things with me. How pathetic is that?

Having finished his soup, Jack gives a grunt of satisfaction and leans back. "You couldn't have paid me to order cauliflower soup at a restaurant, but that was superb." Then he spreads his sandwich liberally with horseradish. "Why do you suppose it's called 'horseradish'? I can't imagine a horse would touch this stuff."

When I shrug at my lack of knowledge regarding horseradish, he adds, "If your sister doesn't work in a restaurant, it's a crime."

"Cooking's just her hobby. Vernelle is Clarence McAfee's legal secretary." I repeat Tom Trimble's threat about her; I hadn't mentioned that part the night before.

Jack looks concerned. "I wouldn't put it past him to get her fired. You'd better watch out—Trimble really has it in for you both."

I sip my last spoonful of velvety soup. "It's not us personally—it's the house that he hates. I'm worried that he'll try to burn it down or something because we won't sell it to him." I find myself cringing at the thought of Tom Trimble with a match in hand.

Jack smirks. "I doubt he'd try a stunt like that. Grant County has a good sheriff, from what I hear, and arson would get your banker buddy in some real deep shit—plus a day-glow orange suit."

He leans back, stretches out his legs, takes the ball cap off, and gives his hair a scratch before putting it back on. After considering for a moment, he adds, "On the other hand, it's not that hard to set a house on fire and get away with it. An empty house on my brother's farm burned down 'mysteriously' a couple of years ago. They never caught who did it—maybe just kids out for a thrill, but maybe not."

"So, your brother's a farmer?"

Jack takes a sip of his beer. "If you want to know something about me, just ask."

"So, your brother's a farmer?"

He laughs. "You got me there again, Abby. Yeah, my brother farms with my folks near Waterloo. They're always on my case about living alone out in the sticks. They worry that people'll think I'm one of those nutters with an arsenal of guns. What kind of idiot would think that?"

I answer that I can't imagine why anyone would think that and immediately feel guilty. Afterall, I'd thought he looked like a serial killer when we first met. That's worse than your everyday nutter. And who was I to judge? Me, who sees ghostly people in a mirror. "You apparently get out of the sticks once in a while," I murmur, hoping he'll miss my embarrassment.

"More than they think. In fact, I had dinner at the Italian Garden the other night. My dog likes their steak—has to be medium-rare, though." He considers me. "I remember seeing you there. Was that your sister you were with? She doesn't look much like you."

"Yes, that was Vernelle, and no, she doesn't look like me. Her boyfriend took us out for dinner. He used to work for the Trimble bank, but he changed jobs, so we went out to celebrate."

Jack turns suddenly serious. "I don't usually comment on women's clothes, but that was a real nice color you had on."

I thank him and then ask, "Why don't you comment on women's clothes?"

"I learned you can get into trouble, so I'd do it this way with Steph: if she was just trying on something and asked my opinion, I'd tell her honestly, good or bad. But if she'd already bought it, I always said it was very nice, no matter what."

"And how long did it take Steph to catch onto your little game?"

He takes another sip of his beer and grins. "She never did. She was tall, like you, so she looked pretty good in whatever she wore. I always thought that Lily would have grown up to look just like her, but—" his voice softens. "Lily used to slug me when I told her how cute she was."

"My boys are funny like that, too."

He looks surprised. "I didn't know you have kids."

"Two boys, Hunter and Grayson; they're seven and five now." I take a bite of my sandwich then put it down, not hungry anymore.

"They're with their father, because I couldn't take care of them--I was in the hospital so much after the fire."

Jack finishes one half of his sandwich, down to the last crumb, and starts on the other. "So what caused the fire?"

"We were remodeling our family room, and the construction guys were making an awful lot of dust. The smoke-alarm system was always going off, so they finally shut it down."

He pauses between bites. "Let me guess—someone forgot to turn it back on."

"Yes, and that's when the house caught on fire. The investigators said the fire had probably been smoldering for hours before the flames actually broke out. Brad and I were away from home, and the boys were with a babysitter.

"When we got to the house, fire was everywhere—smoke was even pouring out the front door. The fire department couldn't do much to save it. My first thought was for the boys, and somehow I managed to get into their room. Their beds were empty, and that's how I knew they were safe, thank goodness."

At the edge of my mind, I can see the roaring flames, feel the intense heat. I take a deep breath and go on. "I was trying to get out when something fell on me and trapped me inside. I don't remember anything after that—really, not for days. I've been in the hospital a lot this last year. Then Vernelle asked me to come back to Mt. Prospect to live with her."

I'm pleased that I can tell the story so factually. Jack nods. He'd stopped eating again somewhere in the midst of my story, but now he takes a last bite of his sandwich. I don't know how much detail to go into. "You may be wondering about my family—and the babysitter. She was overcome by smoke, but she was okay. My husband was smart enough not to go into the burning house in the first place, so he didn't get hurt. We're divorced now."

Jack takes another long sip of beer. "Why does your husband have custody of your kids? It doesn't seem right somehow."

"Ex-husband," I correct automatically. "And that part's easy. Brad's lawyers were always at the hospital with papers for me to sign, and I must have signed some custody papers. After just a couple of months, Brad moved out East with the new girlfriend—Chloe— and took the boys with him. She wouldn't want them, but his parents would." I'm careful to keep any bitterness from my voice. "Brad's mother pretty much said as much once."

I pause before my voice can get that pathetic waver I hate so much. "I'm going to get them back someday, but it will take time. Before I can even try, I have to get my life back together." I've said this so often that I ought to have it tattooed across my forehead.

As Jack finishes his beer, my mind goes back to a time when Alan and Monica, Brad's parents, were visiting us. Monica asked whether Brad and I had made provisions for the boys' guardianship if something happened to us. We'd always meant to, but never had. "We'd love to take them," she said. "And who else is there? Your parents are elderly and live in Iowa, for God's sake—and I can't think of anyone who would want your sister to raise them! So we're the logical choice. You know we'd give them everything, plus they'd have the advantage of living in New York City, where there's at least some culture."

Jack's voice brings me abruptly back to the present. "I don't like your ex's girlfriend."

"I don't either, but then I have a reason. You don't know anything about her."

" 'Chloe' sounds like a dog's name. That's worse than a parakeet's."

"Believe me, she's not a dog. I don't doubt for a minute that she's beautiful. Brad's nice looking too. When they're together, they probably look like Ken and Barbie."

Jack considers that. "Then I don't like either of them." He pushes away his empty beer can. "I hope it all comes out okay for you. I appreciate your telling me." There's a long pause as Jack stares out the window.

"Well, I'm glad we got that out of the way," I say with relief. "It's not something I tell everyone, but I know people wonder why I came back to Mt. Prospect alone.

"And the way I got burned is why my face looks kind of half and half. My doctor said it was great, because that way he could tell what I'm supposed to look like."

Jack's gaze comes back to me. "It's not that hard to see what you looked like before the fire. I'm getting kind of used to it, if you want the truth."

More to myself than him, I whisper, "I'll never get used to it."

Jack gets up from the table and starts clearing off all the dishes. "I need to go into town for some plumbing stuff. I'll replace those faucets in the bathroom this afternoon. Then I'll do some of the grunt work for you—pull up a couple tiles and see what's going on under there."

"Thanks. I really appreciate it."

"By the way, tell your sister thanks for the great meals. She ought to open a sandwich place in MP. I'd keep her in business."

Jack throws away the foam dishes and then turns toward me. "Abby, here's just a thought. I've spent the last several years living in my own little world. I don't like getting into people's personal lives, and I don't want them in mine. But I have to tell you this: Those scars on your face? You got them trying to save your boys. I can't think of anything more noble than that. You should be proud of the scars you have. I wish I could say the same for myself."

He slams the door with a bang and is gone.

# CHAPTER 24

In the afternoon, I feel a great sense of accomplishment as I begin painting the living room, and I'm making good progress by the time Jack returns. He watches for a moment then asks if I told Vernelle what happened last night and if I'll be careful when I'm out here by myself. When I tell him that I did and I will, he disappears into the bathroom. It's not long before I can hear loud metal noises and Jack swearing at something, presumably the recalcitrant faucets.

My surprise visitors of the day are Vernelle and Garrett. Clarence has given her the afternoon off (she thinks he's going to the c-a-s-i-n-o), and they're heading to Iowa City to comb through Vernelle's favorite donation/consignment stores. Her next make-over project is her dining room. She's planning to paint Mom and Dad's maple dining set and hutch black or white (she hasn't decided), so she's on the look-out for some needed accessories.

Vernelle is appropriately impressed by the kitchen and oohs and aahs over the dining room. Garrett surveys everything in his serious way and then asks me a few questions about painting. I warm up to him even more when he mentions that he's never painted anything before, but he's hoping that will change. I'm pretty sure he's not thinking about helping me; Vernelle is in his sights.

Jack can't help but hear us. I've previously mentioned him as the carpenter I hired for a few jobs, so he won't be a complete surprise to Vernelle if he joins us, though I doubt that he will.

But I'm wrong. With a cracked tile in one hand and a rusty faucet in the other, Jack comes over and introduces himself. He's very business-like as he takes Vernelle and Garrett into the bathroom to show them what's being done. I stop painting so that I can listen to them. He's advising Vernelle on the type of tile she should get and who would be good to install it, and she murmurs something in agreement.

As the happy couple leave, Vernelle whispers to me, "Your carpenter seems like a nice guy—he'd be welcome in my bathroom anytime." And she winks at me—winks!

Still pondering Vernelle's remark, I begin trimming along the woodwork in the living room, using the little cuppy-thing to hold paint. That's when I notice there's something new in the shimmering glass of the mirror.

For the first time, I can see what one of the little boys is doing. He has a small bag near his hands, and in front of him on the table is a circle—a circle of marbles. The sight startles me so much I gasp out a loud, "Oh, my God!" and drop my paint-brush and the cuppy-thing to the floor.

Jack comes shooting out of the bathroom. "What happened?"

I stare at him blankly and say that nothing happened.

Jack's mouth hardens into a straight line. "I still have my teacher ears, young lady—yeah, something definitely happened out here."

I kneel to wipe up the mess of paint with some rags. "Really, nothing—I just dropped my paintbrush." Jack looks suspicious, as any teacher would. Then, with a shake of his head, he stalks from the room.

I'm just lucky he didn't give me an after-school detention.

The spell is broken; the mirror is blank again. But those marbles. What in the world do they mean?

When I resume painting, I have some—actually a lot—of thinking to do.

Jack joins me for an afternoon break. I can't lie—these times with him have become the highlight of my day, and I worry that what I plan to tell him might scare him away for good. But I have to tell SOMEBODY about my idea before I explode.

I pour us coffee and put a pile of Vernelle's raspberry-white-chocolate bars on a plate. When I pass the bars to Jack, only my shaky hand betrays my excitement. "Jack, I finally figured out what's going on in this house. I haven't told anyone else; I can't."

He takes a couple of bars but looks wary. "Not even your sister?"

I hesitate. There are two reasons why I can't tell Vernelle. The first is she believes I still have some "mental issues" I haven't "fully resolved." If I tell her about seeing ghosts, she'll freak out. But I can't tell Jack that.

So I give him the second reason against telling Vernelle. "If my sister learns about this, she won't let me come out here anymore. Period."

Jack gives me a dark look. "Does this have anything to do with Tom Trimble?"

"No, it's totally different." I pause, trying to find words that won't sound crazy—until I realize there aren't any. "Jack, sometimes when I'm working here, I see faces in the living room mirror. It happened again a little while ago—that's why I dropped my paint brush."

Jack looks up from dunking a raspberry bar into his coffee; his hand is still in mid-air. "You see what?"

"Faces that appear in the mirror—the faces of the family that used to live here, the murdered ones. And before you say anything, I want you to know that Miss Bryant saw them, too."

He takes a bite of the bar, chews, and swallows before he says slowly, "So, you think there are ghosts in this house?"

"Well, there aren't white wisps floating around or mysterious moans, if that's what you mean, but there's definitely something going on in this house."

"And that's it?" he asks cautiously. "Ghosts in the mirror?"

"That's only part of it. The other part is that I've found some old marbles around the house. The marbles belonged to the kids that lived here—the ghosts in the mirror."

He pushes his coffee cup away. "Abby, I have to tell you, I don't believe in ghosts. I loved Lily, but I hope her spirit is in a happy, peaceful place, not floating around like she's some kind of lost soul."

"That's what I'm trying to tell you—the ghosts in the mirror have a purpose for being there."

He leans back in his chair. "Okay, I can see why you have an affinity for the people that lived in this house. After all, they were your relatives, and the two little boys—"

"It's not that. My little boys are alive; these boys are dead. I know the difference."

His dark eyes regard me for a long, thoughtful moment. "Abby..." He lets whatever he was going to say go and shifts in his chair. After a silent minute, he asks, "And what purpose do you think these ghosts have?"

I run my finger around the rim of my coffee cup. "While I've been working, I've been thinking. When I see the mirror, it's always the mother and the children with Ben Stockton. So I must be seeing what took place on the night of the murders, because the father is never there."

He rubs a hand across his stubbly chin. "But the murderer is? That makes no sense—if anything you're telling me could possibly make sense."

"It makes perfect sense—if Ben wasn't the murderer. If he was, he wouldn't be there with them. He just wouldn't."

Jack shakes his head. "That's a big leap, Abby. You told me yourself that everyone thinks it was him."

"Don't you see, Jack? It's the only thing that does make sense."

He sighs, crosses his arms over his chest and challenges, "Okay, then what's the deal with the marbles? How do they tie in with all this?"

"I can see that one of the little boys in the mirror is playing with marbles. I think they're using them to get my attention. They're saying, 'Here we are—pay attention to us. We're trying to tell you something—that Ben was innocent. Now do something about it.' "

Jack looks deeply doubtful. "As I said, I don't believe in ghosts." Then his expression lightens. "But I believe in marbles. I'd like to take a look at them. Where are they?"

"In a jar on the counter." Relieved that Jack is at least taking seriously my word about the marbles, I jump up to grab the pickle jar--then stand rooted to the floor in shock. "Damn, damn, damn!" I point to the empty counter. "Do you see any marbles there?"

"No," he says cautiously, "do you?"

"Obviously not, but they can't have just disappeared!" In disbelief, I look around the kitchen, but the jar is not there. "The marbles were real; one was clear with a spiral down the center. I've never seen one like it before, so I couldn't have dreamed it up."

Jack's eyes meet mine. "I don't know what to say, Abby."

"Say you believe me, Jack. I know it's a lot to ask. After all, you've only known me a few days."

"Well," he says slowly, "I believe that YOU believe what you're telling me."

There's nothing more either of us can say. After Jack goes back to work in the bathroom, I return to the living room, hoping the family scene is there. It is, and immediately I see the marbles, laid out in a circle on the table.

So, were the marbles I found real—or not? Is the scene in the mirror real—or not? Are my "mental issues" causing me to have some kind of crazy delusion? Or am I just plain crazy?

Feeling as if the earth is trembling beneath my feet, I continue painting. Rolling swaths of "chocolate mist" across ugly beige is somewhat therapeutic, but my mind isn't really on the task.

When my paint tray is empty, I clean up and tell Jack I'm leaving early. Whether by coincidence or not, he's ready to leave, too. He says (in a very business-like manner, with no references to ghosts or marbles) that the news in the bathroom isn't good. It needs a new sub-floor for sure. Well, it's kind of hard to have a bathroom without a sub-floor.

As he pulls on his jacket, Jack adds that he has other things to do tomorrow, so he won't be here. His hard eyes rest on me as he opens the front door. I smile briefly and get a searching look in return, but at least he's not running for his pickup.

Sprinkles of rain dot the sidewalk, and we pause for a moment in the porch, savoring the smell of wet earth and new leaves. The shrubs along the garage are sporting delicate green flags, and a ragged row of red and yellow tulips by the road are almost ready to pop open.

Jack points out a patch of little purple flowers he says are crocuses. He adds gruffly, "Look, I've been thinking. You need to tell your sister the same stuff you told me."

"Why?"

"She should know what you think is going on. After all, it's her house."

"Well, they're my marbles, though I seem to have lost them." Caught by surprise at my own words, I laugh. "Lost my marbles— get it? I've literally lost my marbles."

Jack doesn't seem to think it's funny. "Abby, I'm reserving judgment on what you told me. After what happened in this house, well, maybe some weird stuff is going on out here. Maybe."

Jack's pickup roars away in one direction, while I go in the other. The rain lets up after a brief shower, and I think back over what Jack said. His words about it being "her house" sent a surprising jolt of anger through me. Because they're mine: My marbles. My ghosts. My house.

# CHAPTER 25

On the way home, I stop to buy a pot of pink hyacinths, then drive to the town cemetery. The rain has cleared and, in the west, low on the horizon, spears of bright sunshine are poking through the clouds. Tall pines cast long shadows as I walk over the damp grass to the black marble tombstone of Mom and Dad.

This is a duty visit. I don't think of them as being here, in this grave, but in a sunny "forever" place, together and probably bickering over some trifling heavenly issue. They were sweet, loving parents. I'll always miss them. The hyacinths make a splash of bright color on the sodden ground, the promise of a spring they'll never see.

I wipe the tears from my eyes. "I wish you both were still here," I mumble to myself and wonder how many other people have uttered those words in this place.

My thoughts turn to the Millers. Somewhere in this cemetery (I can't remember where) is the Miller family plot. I picture Ed Miller standing over the graves of his wife and children. I start wandering around without much hope, but feel compelled to try to find them and pay my respects.

I've never heard where Ben Stockton is buried. Sadly, if I'm supposed to prove that Ben wasn't the killer, there's nothing I can do about it. I wouldn't know where to begin. *What a ridiculous idea,* I scold myself. *Me playing detective.*

Annoyed with myself for going off on flights of fancy, I turn to head back to my car when a glint of light catches my eyes. Not far from where I'm standing something small reflects the sun that's broken free of the clouds. Walking over, my heart thumps in my throat. I know what it's going to be as soon as I'm close enough to read the gravestones the object rests between: David and Dennis Miller. Nearby are the graves of Audrey and her parents.

I clutch the marble in my hand. It's bigger than the others—a shooter, I think they're called. This seems to have some kind of meaning. Maybe the boys' way of telling me they're real, and I'm not nuts. I slip the marble into a pocket to show Jack later. "Thank you," I murmur.

It sounds strange (well, the whole thing sounds strange) but I'm becoming protective of the "ghosts." And if the Miller house is somehow their sanctuary, I'd like to keep it that way. They deserve whatever peace they can find after the horrible way they died. It's sad that the house, which has seen so much tragedy, is vulnerable to someone with a heart of stone like Tom Trimble.

Clearly, Tom wants the place destroyed—just as he destroyed the Stocktons' home, and I think he'll figure out a way of doing it, sooner or later. Really, besides installing cameras and dogs and an armed guard, how can I protect it from him?

There's a truck parked along the edge of the cemetery. Some workers are putting up the final panels of black wrought-iron fence to enclose a new section. Sad to say, Mt. Prospect's live population seems to be shrinking, while the dead one keeps growing.

Though the wrought-iron is ornamental, it's clearly not that spindly sort of fencing you see around flower gardens. This is stalwart stuff, with each post-hole filled with cement.

An idea begins to take shape as I watch. I bet if they dug the holes twice as deep and filled them with twice the cement, the fence would be even stronger.

I introduce myself to the man in charge, who says his name is Phil. When he asks how he can help me, I tell him that I want a fence built around my house that will look nice, like the cemetery fence, but be strong enough to protect it from varmints.

Phil looks puzzled. "From what kind of varmints—deer?"

I'm thinking Trimble varmints, but I can't very well say that. "No, from vandals, actually—it's out in the country and empty right now. There have been some threats, and I think a fence would take care of that."

"Sure; when we get this job done, I can fit you in." He pulls a pad of paper and pencil from his pocket. "Tell me what you need."

I can do better than that. I draw a picture, and add that we've just had the place surveyed. "The surveyor's stakes are still there." I tell him I want the house and yard enclosed but not the garage and driveway.

Phil thinks deeply and scribbles on the paper. "I'll send my guys out to measure tomorrow. I can get the supplies and be ready to go in a couple of days."

After some hesitation, I tell him my worry about pickups and chains. Phil assures me that trying to pull down the fence with a pickup would be a tough job. "What about a Cadillac Escalade XZT?" I ask.

Phil grins. "This fence would chew up a Caddy and spit out the pieces. You'd need some freakin' big equipment to rip out this baby." I can't restrain a smile of satisfaction. Then he adds, "If you'd like to have some landscaping done after the fence is up, just give me a call. My cousin's in the landscaping business."

I drive back into the country and turn in the driveway of the Miller place. In a month, this house will be surrounded by an eight-foot wrought-iron fence, black and sturdy, with deep cement footings.

The only gate will be a small one, able to admit a single person, but not a vehicle.

And beside the gate will be a sign with simple words, something in the memory of the Millers and Ben. Vernelle will have a fit—though not as big as Tom Trimble's.

# CHAPTER 26

A vehicle follows me onto Vernelle's street, though I don't pay much attention until it pulls in beside me. It's a white SUV with a bank of lights across the top. On the side, it says "Grant County Sherriff."

I remain in the car, trying to think what law I could possibly have broken—speeding? Ignoring stop signs? Believing in ghosts?

A man in a brown uniform unfolds himself from the cop car. I recognize Deputy Sheriff Marv Baxter; he's been in the county sheriff's department forever.

I open the window with a smile. "Good evening, is there something I can do for you?" My smiley face probably looks more like a mug shot, since (as most innocent people do) I figure I must be guilty of something.

He comes around the side of the car and leans down, a casual hand on my door frame. Everything about Marv is tall and narrow, even his head beneath his brown hat. He has a toothy, friendly grin. "Miz Bennett, I heard you were back in town. How're things going for you?"

I tell him I'm fine and launch into my now-familiar story about helping Vernelle with the house, though I expect he's heard all about it. If Marv doesn't know what's going on around town, his wife usually does.

Marv nods. "Sheriff Simmons is away right now—asked me to keep an eye on Vernelle's place while he's gone. Empty houses can be targets for all kinds of mischief, especially that one. Noticed any problems out there lately?"

My very hesitation clues Marv in. His eyes narrow quizzically. "Something you want to mention, Miz Bennett?"

"It's not what you'd think. The only person who's caused me any trouble is Tom Trimble. He's mad that Vernelle won't sell the house to him so he can tear it down. In fact, he stopped by and said some stuff—I think you could call them 'veiled threats.' Luckily, this guy who's doing some carpentry work for us—Jack Allender— was there and got rid of him for me."

"Did he now?" Marv unbends from his stance and pushes back his hat. "I know that guy. I wouldn't tangle with him, either." His eyes crinkle. "They say he used to a teacher."

"Well, he's doing a fantastic job of helping me fix the old place up," I say, giving credit where credit is due and hoping to curb some of the rumors that are probably flying around town about Jack.

"Good. Glad to hear it." Marv gives another nod, then changes the subject. "But the thing I don't understand is the great Mr. Trimble's interest in the place. You wouldn't think someone like him would care about an old house like that, would you?"

"No, I don't exactly get it myself," I admit. "Of course, he always refers to what happened there. He says once the house is gone, people will forget. Then there's Dickie Schwarz, who'd like to buy the house and turn it into a tourist attraction. She's about as bad."

Marv rolls his eyes. "Don't you let your sister sell her house to Tom or Dickie and that bunch of history loonies she runs around with. For a while they wanted some kind of hail-stone museum downtown—hail-stone, for God's sake. It's not even a puddle of water anymore—they only have a picture." Then he gets serious again.

"Sounds like you're caught in the middle. Do you even know what went on there that night?"

His question surprises me. "I thought I did, but now I wonder. Could I come by your office sometime and look over the files?"

Marv looks caught off guard by the request. Then he shakes his head regretfully. "Much as I'd like to, I can't let you into the actual files. There are things that to this day haven't been released to the public. Why don't you read the old articles in the newspaper office first? Those murders were big news back in the day. If there's still something you want to know, I'll see if I can help you out.

"And if Tom threatens you again—veiled or otherwise—you call me, okay? Sheriff Simmons won't back down for anybody, even Tom Trimble. But Tom's opinion carries a lot of weight with the 'good old boys in town'," (he adds finger quotes) "plus he has a lot of them in his pocket, financially or otherwise." Here he shrugs, as if it's just a fact of life he has to deal with. "Now, most people in town have learned not to cross Tom, but one of the few people who'll butt heads with him is Ambrosia Swann. Remember her?"

"Of course. Everybody in town knows Ambrosia."

"Well, Burdett Swann had a little thing going with Sylvie Trimble a while back—where he got the nerve is beyond me. Anyway, Tom got wind of it and tried to put the squeeze on Burdett's real-estate business—refused to give loans, that kind of thing. Old Ambrosia warmed up the presses and went after Tom like gang-busters." Marv smiles reminiscently. "The Trimbles have money, but Ambrosia has more money *and* a newspaper. Everybody in town knew what was going on. For weeks, Ambrosia's editorials about banker bandits were more entertaining than the funnies."

I'd forgotten what it was like to live in such a small town—how everyone knows everyone else's business. In this case though, I wonder why Marv is telling me all this.

"Finally, Tom gave Burdett a pass, and Burdett backed off his pursuit of Sylvie. My point is that if Tom is after you about that old

Miller place, get Ambrosia on your side. They both have their fingers in a lot of pies all over town, and they watch each other like hawks. She'd figure something out."

As I absorb the idea, Marv backs away from my car and winks. "Haven't got any more tickets since the last ones I handed out, have you?"

I laugh. "*Me*? Come on, that was Vernelle!"

Marv gives a salute and another of his toothy smiles, then gets into his SUV and drives off, leaving me to wonder exactly what the hell that was all about.

I wait until Vernelle is mellowing with a glass of after-dinner wine before I tell her about the fence. I figure she'll be angry, but she surprises me by giggling (maybe it's the wine). "Oh, my God! Abigail Leigh Bennett, what possessed you to do that?"

"Because I wouldn't put it past our friend Trimble to do something to the house, whether he owns it or not. He's threatened to often enough."

Vernelle twirls her glass and watches the little purple whirlpool thoughtfully. "Well, I hate to tell you this, but a fence isn't going to stop him from tossing a freaking match through a window some dark night."

There's that scary thought again—Tom and a match. "I know, but even if the house is gone, the fence will remind him of it every time he drives past."

She puts her glass down. "Abby, are you sure about this? That fence will cost a shitload of money!"

"More than the mortgage Tom Trimble was so angry about," I admit. "And that's not counting Phil's cousin's landscaping. But, yeah, I'm sure."

# CHAPTER 27

Friday morning I plan to spend painting. The weather, dark and gloomy again, matches my mood. The house seems lonely without Jack—or even Marge. My ghostly friends have apparently deserted me, too. Some friends they turned out to be.

Morosely, I'm thinking about painting when my phone rings.

It's Vernelle inviting me for lunch at the Main Street Café. When she hears how enthused I am, she laughs and asks if I know the Friday Special is her second favorite: hot turkey sandwiches with slices of real turkey, not that canned stuff, and mashed potatoes with real gravy, not that yellow shit out of a jar you get at most places. Vernelle might be a good cook, but she'd never make it as a food writer.

There's no point in getting all the paint stuff out; I'll just have to quit in a couple of hours, so I head for home. Since I'm meeting Vernelle, I change my painting T-shirt and jeans for a better T-shirt and jeans, then run a few errands until it's time for lunch.

When I enter the café, the first person I see across the room is Tom Trimble. He's with Sylvie this time instead of his cronies. With her pale blue suit, her perfect coiffure and make-up, Sylvie looks as if she's either going to, or coming from, a Women's Tea, if there is such a thing in Mt. Prospect anymore. In front of her is a plate with a single dab of cottage cheese on a peach half. It's probably the only diet item on the menu—and it looks like half an order.

Her pale hands flash with diamond rings as she picks at her "meal." Tom does all the talking. When Sylvie smiles, it's the fakest smile I've ever seen, turning off and on like a light.

Vernelle's in the same booth as last time, and Burdett Swann is with her. Her smile is tinged with embarrassment. "You remember Burdett, don't you? He invited me to join him. I hope you don't mind?"

Even in the awkward booth, Burdett rises a little and extends his hand, his usual greeting for a "lady." What can I do? I have to smile and say it's nice to see him again, too, as I slide into the booth beside Vernelle. With his thick silver hair and clear blue eyes, Burdett's as attractive as I remembered. He's also wearing the only sport coat and tie in the place; I suppose realtors have some kind of standard to uphold in a small town like this.

I take a quick sip of water to cover my annoyance. I'm betting that Burdett has a reason for inviting Vernelle—and now me—to join him.

Vernelle beams. "I ordered Specials for us both." It's what Burdett already has in front of him. The huge pile of turkey and golden gravy does look appetizing, though Burdett hasn't touched his food. Instead, he sends Vernelle the kind of raised-eyebrow look that clearly expects her to say something.

She takes the cue and jumps in. "Abby, Burdett has been telling me that he has a client interested in buying the Miller place."

Bingo. I try to keep my voice neutral. "I thought you didn't want to sell."

Vernelle takes on a defensive tone. "I wasn't thinking of it, but he's brought up a couple of good points. The first, which I have to agree with, is that you're putting so much work into the house—not to mention money—that it would be a shame if the next renter trashed the place, and we have to start all over."

At that moment, the waitress slides two giant platters (enough to share with Sylvie, that's for sure) onto the table, which gives me time to think. As I unwrap my fork from its roll of napkin, I choose my words carefully. "You know I haven't minded the work, Sis. In fact, I've really enjoyed it. What's the other point?"

Her eyes light with enthusiasm. "I could use the money from the house to open a coffee shop—you know, lattes and smoothies in the morning, and lunches at noon. Burdett has been on the look-out for a good location for me, and now there's a vacant store that's just what I want. You know I never intended to be Clarence's secretary forever, and what's been going on there lately has made me think it's time for a change."

Vernelle's cheeks are pink with excitement, and she looks at me expectantly. I put aside my own selfish doubts. "That's a wonderful idea, Sis, it really is. You'd do great."

Burdett breaks in smoothly. "Mt. Prospect doesn't have anything like a coffee shop. I think it has a good chance of succeeding. Now as I've said, I have some people interested in the Miller place." His mouth tightens. "Oh, here comes one of them now."

It's Dickie! I barely hold back a curse.

She pauses by our booth and smiles brightly, her flickery eyes taking in the scene. She shifts a big take-out container from one hand to the other. "What a coincidence! I don't usually come here, but hot lunch at school is chicken again. If it isn't chicken fingers, it's chicken nuggets or chicken drummies. Today, it's chicken dunkers, and I just couldn't take it."

When no one says anything (I at least have my mouth closed as opposed to Vernelle), Dickie goes on. "So, Burdett, have you talked to the girls about selling the old Miller place to the Historical Society?"

Burdett smiles one of those smiles that never quite make it to the eyes. "Well, Dickie, we hadn't got that far, but you're not the only one interested, you know."

"Really?" Dickie's surprise is almost comical. "I can't imagine anyone else would want it with a history like that."

I kick Vernelle's leg under the table. She jumps and gives me a frown, but says, "Dickie, you know I said I'd never sell my house to the Historical Society, so I can't imagine why you talked to Burdett."

Dickie's smile is triumphant. "Well, we didn't have much money before. Now we've got a donor who's willing to put up the big bucks. He thinks the place is an important historical site that should be preserved for posterity."

It's not hard to hear the quotation marks dotting that phrase. Purely out of curiosity, I ask, "So, now what are your plans for this important historical site?"

"Oh my goodness, we've revised them completely! We'll tear down the house and build a museum with interactive exhibits about Mt. Prospect. For example, we'll have a life-sized manikin of Audrey Miller wearing a pioneer dress; when you push a button, she'll recite the history—"

I interrupt her. "The murders happened in the sixties, Dickie."

Dickie starts to look cranky. "Well, we can't very well put her in a miniskirt if she's going to tell the history of the Millers and other early pioneers in Mt. Prospect, can we? You did know they were early pioneers in the area—didn't you?"

After one look at Vernelle's face, I say hurriedly, "Who's this big donor?"

Suddenly cautious, Dickie leans down and says confidentially, "He prefers to remain anonymous." But her eyes flicker meaningfully towards Tom.

Vernelle's smile is venomous. "I won't sell the house to your Society. Not ever. So you'd better head back to school before your hot turkey sandwich turns into a cold pile of shit."

After Dickie whirls around and stomps out the door, there's a moment of tense silence at our table. Burdett shakes his head. "God, I'm sorry about that. Dickie can be such a pain. But there is another interested party, a nice little old couple looking for a cottage in a rural area—"

"I'll buy the house." The words pop out of my mouth before I have time to think.

They both stare at me. Vernelle says, "You don't have to do that, Abby. There'll be other opportunities to start my restaurant."

"No, I think you're right—this is a good time. And I'll need a house soon anyways—I can't very well live with you for the rest of my life. Perhaps Burdett would be willing to give us an estimate of what the place is worth."

Vernelle looks uneasy. "I'll have to think this through." She turns to Burdett. "I'll let you know, okay?"

He nods as Tom and Sylvie sweep by. Tom's features are frozen into an arctic smile, and Burdett's expression turns cold enough to chill the entire room. And Sylvie? Even her fake smile is gone, leaving her face a blank mask. I wonder what drug can do that— certainly not the ones I'm taking.

Once the Trimbles are out the door, Burdett lets out his breath and turns on his realtor's smile. "I wasn't aware that Dickie had already talked to you, and I apologize again. Let me make this up to you with dinner at the Italian Garden. They have a wonderful special tonight—I believe it's even a step or two above a hot turkey sandwich."

Vernelle shakes her head. "I'm busy, but Abby can go. She absolutely loves the Italian Garden."

I open my mouth to protest but sense it's a losing battle. I smile and agree, feeling a little sorry for the handsome Burdett. I've spent the whole meal with the bad side of my face toward him. I'll bet he hopes the restaurant's lighting will be dimmer than usual tonight—much dimmer.

# CHAPTER 28

It's a relief to get back to the house and start painting, even though I'm still hungry; none of us had much appetite for cold turkey sandwiches. Plus Vernelle was still upset after Burdett left. She wouldn't even talk to me about my offer to buy this house. I'd never intended to buy it—hadn't thought about it, but that's the only way I can really protect my ghosts in the mirror.

I put down my roller and stand in front of the fireplace, curious to see whether there's anything new in the mirror. Maybe the dampness of the last few days is affecting it. One of the dark spots in the corner is definitely larger, about the size of a quarter, with a man-in-the-moon look to it.

Though even that comparison is a stretch, it's kind of creepy, and I'm glad when Marge shows up and starts talking—loudly—as she works in the kitchen. "I'm going to scrub out this here fridge this afternoon, Miz Bennett. Your daddy bought it for Miss Bryant just before he died. That sister of yours shouldn't get rid of it—there's not a thing wrong that a good scrubbing won't fix. If you really don't want it, I can give it to Ike's nephew. He don't have a thing—lives from paycheck to paycheck in that old trailer of his. All he's got is one of those little fridges, like rich kids have at college these days."

As she goes on, the sounds of thumping and banging are soon joined by the sound of water running. "Now the stove, that's another matter. Looks like them folks tried to fry an egg on the bottom of the oven. Even the self-cleaning cycle won't take care of that kind of mess. Ike's nephew wouldn't want it anyway. He don't cook with anything but a microwave. How a body can eat food that's cooked with little waves is beyond me."

When I don't answer, Marge comes into the living room, wiping her hands on her apron. She surveys my handiwork. "That paint's kinda dark, ain't it? I always like a nice green, myself. Or gray. They say gray is the new neutral. I saw on *The Today Show* where a lady said she's decorating a big fancy house in 50 shades of gray. What do you think of that?"

"Maybe it's supposed to be erotic," I offer.

Marge blinks and looks deeply suspicious. She's obviously never heard of the books.

I continue hurriedly, "I think I'd get depressed with all that gray. Ike's nephew is welcome to the refrigerator. I was just going to have Tuffy and Ace haul it and the stove to the dump tomorrow. After I'm done with the downstairs bedroom, I'm going to paint that pink room upstairs—maybe a 'nice green.' Isn't it funny that Miss Bryant would have a pink bedroom?"

Marge puts her hands on her wide, aproned hips. "Oh, Miss Bryant never slept upstairs. She never used those rooms, except the one as a spare bedroom for company—not that she ever needed it. The 'hippos' hardly ever stayed over. She never touched the pink room, either. She always said it was that girl's room—the one that was murdered—Audrey, I think her name was."

After dropping this bombshell, Marge waddles back into the kitchen, and I'm left staring after her. On impulse, I drop my paintbrush and rush up the stairs. When I flip on the switch, light floods the pink room. Why didn't it occur to me that this room was Audrey's? I'm beginning to distrust my imagination, but I swear the room has a different feel now that I know it was hers. She must have spent hours up here, maybe sitting at the window, dreaming of her future—a future that was stolen from her.

I walk around, looking for I-don't-know-what, but nothing of Audrey remains. It's bare; even the last family that lived here didn't leave more than a few bits of paper behind. There's one small closet. It contains a short rod for hanging clothes and a couple of iron hooks on the side for other things. Apparently, people didn't have so much "stuff" back in those days.

Above the rod are three shelves. They're high, and the top two would have been out of easy reach. Without much hope, I bring the stepladder from downstairs into the closet. The bottom shelf is empty of everything except dust; so is the one above it. But on the very top shelf, way back in the corner, I can see a couple items made of glass. By reaching my arm as far as possible, I can grab hold of pieces of a miniature dish set. With rising excitement, I slip them into my pocket.

In the kitchen, Marge is still scrubbing the refrigerator, muttering under her breath about "cheap plastic shelves." I ask if she knows what happened to the jar of marbles that was on the counter.

She frowns. "You left that jar in my way. I was afraid I'd knock it over and have broken glass and marbles everywhere." She opens a cabinet and pulls the pickle jar out to show me. "I put it out of the way. Though why a grown woman like yourself would collect marbles is beyond me."

I add the giant shooter marble from my pocket and put the jar back where Marge had it stored. "Thanks. My boys will love them."

Marge's head jerks over to look at me, but she says nothing. I realize this is the first time I've mentioned Hunter and Grayson to her. But in a small town like this, I'd assumed she'd heard. She gives me a weak smile—not fake like Tom's wife—just weak. Maybe she doesn't think I have much of a chance of getting them back.

"I'd best get to work," she says before turning back to the fridge.

I spend the remainder of the afternoon painting feverishly until the living room is done. After a couple of remarks about how deeply disappointed she is that her new can opener was made in a country she's never heard of, Marge takes her leave.

After she's gone, I take the jar of marbles into the living room and set it on the mantel. Beside it, I put the two objects from my pocket--a miniature bowl and its tiny lid—the lost sugar bowl from my set of doll dishes. The dishes must have originally belonged to Audrey. For some reason, long forgotten, Grandpa Miller passed them along to me when he cleaned out the house.

As I stare at the fragile bits of glass, I can almost hear Audrey's voice: "Now that you know my brother's marbles are real, here's something from me that's real, too—a little sugar bowl. My sugar bowl. Your sugar bowl."

It takes my breath away.

# CHAPTER 29

I'm not in the mood to have dinner with Burdett Swann, and I can't imagine what possessed him to include me in the invitation.

Still, it was a nice gesture to make up for the Dickie fiasco, so I put on a silvery-green Sophie outfit, fix my hair, and even dab on some mascara. I was going to add perfume when I realized that I don't have any. But maybe it's better that way; wouldn't wearing perfume send a signal of pathetic eagerness—which I don't feel?

Burdett drives a big silver Lexus, the perfect accessory for him. But it looks like Brad's, so his fancy car doesn't score any points with me. Since there's half an hour before the reservations, he takes me on a quick tour of the town, and I begin to relax. Burdett's tone is just right—generic-attentive instead of date-attentive. I try to swivel on the seat so my bad side is in the shadows—no need to ruin the man's appetite.

Burdett points out the houses that are listed with him. In fact, he knows something about almost every house in town. When I ask where he lives, Burdett turns down a street lined with big houses—not Victorian, but ones from the early 1900's set on generous lots. He stops in front of a three-story brick that's tidy with pristine white trim, but not necessarily homey. There isn't a flower to be seen, though six small evergreen shrubs are spaced evenly across its front.

"Wow, you live in that all by yourself?"

Burdett shakes his head. "No, this is Mother's house. I live in an apartment over the garage in back, which I've fixed up to suit me. I have my privacy and can still help Mother if she needs it, though she never does. Ambrosia's eighty-six, you know. I've tried to talk her into moving into something smaller, but she'll never do it."

He gazes out the window into the sunset and there's a combination of admiration and frustration in his expression when he continues, "Her doctor has told her she needs a plan for the future, like assisted living or a nursing home. She says her "plan" is to be carried out of the house feet-first. My instructions are to make sure she leaves the neighborhood in style. I'm supposed to call a limo, not an ambulance, when the time comes."

From the tone of Burdett's voice, he's not kidding.

We both consider the house. "Colonial Revival, 1918," he says. "Brick exterior, semi-circular front porch with four white pillars, and a balcony on the second level. Three dormers in the roof. Two sun-rooms, formal dining room with French doors, original kitchen with updated amenities. Master suite with walk-in closet and full bath. Maid's quarters on third floor—well, I could go on and on."

"It would make quite a listing," I suggest a little daringly.

Burdett has an easy smile. "Don't think I haven't thought about it."

Dinner at the Italian Garden pretty much follows the pattern of the first time I was here. Good food, quiet music, whispered conversations—probably about the two of us. Burdett is clearly at ease and has another glass of red wine after we finish dinner. I didn't have a clue what we'd find to talk about, but I shouldn't have wondered. With a realtor's ready smile and skillful small-talk, Burdett steers the conversation to people that we both know, or have in the past, including some who were in high school when I was.

The people he doesn't mention are more telling: Ambrosia, Dickie, Vernelle, Sylvie, Tom—it's like a table set for absent diners. Still, I enjoy the meal more than I'd expected.

On the way out, I'm surprised to catch a glimpse of Jack. Seated by himself in an odd corner (almost hidden by the fake plants), he gives a casual wave and a wink as we walk by. I grin and wave back.

Burdett glances at me curiously. "May I ask how you know that guy?"

"He's a carpenter I hired to do some odd jobs at Vernelle's house. His name's Jack Allender."

"I've seen him around a few times. He looks pretty rough. If he gives you any trouble, let me know. A guy like that might try to take advantage of someone in your situation."

I don't have an answer because there are so many annoying phrases in his warning that I can't sort them all out.

As we drive home, I try to reassure myself that this was just the "apology" dinner Burdett said it was. But maybe I'm wrong. When we get to Vernelle's house, Burdett pulls into the driveway and turns to me. "Abby, I want to tell you how much I admire you for coming back to Mt. Prospect and—"

I cut him off, saying there's nothing about me to admire. "I'm just here to get my life together." They're words I've said so often that they come out automatically.

He shakes his head. "Vernelle's a tough cookie, but I can tell you're not." He takes my left hand, rubbing it gently.

"After what happened in California, you need someone to take care of you. You should be taking it easy, not slaving away in that old house. It's bad enough you have that Allender guy around. God knows what else might happen out there." He pauses then adds, "I'd like us to be friends, Abby. And I'd like to take you out again."

I pull my hand away. "I don't think that's going to happen."

Burdett frowns. "There's a lot I can offer. If it's the age thing—"

"It's nothing to do with our ages, Burdett. I've enjoyed this evening, and I appreciate your concern. But I'm just not ready to date anyone yet." And while I'm not at all attracted to the guy, I'm being completely honest about not wanting the complications of a relationship—especially one built on pity. Besides, all my energy needs to go toward proving I'm ready to be a mom to my boys again.

He starts to say something else, but stops and shrugs. After an awkward pause, I jump out of the car and shut the door.

Why am I not surprised when Vernelle ambushes me the minute I step into the house?

She's wiping her hands on a dishtowel, eyebrows raised. "Well?" she asks. "How was dinner with MP's leading bachelor?"

"It was a nice dinner, but that's all," I say firmly. "Why is it that Burdett isn't married?"

She shrugs. "He's dated a few women since I've been in town, but it never seems to go anywhere permanent. I don't think Ambrosia's the problem. Maybe he just hasn't found the right woman yet."

I put my hand on the stair rail. "As far as I'm concerned, he can keep on looking." I head upstairs, suddenly too tired to talk. I can feel Vernelle's puzzled glance following me.

I may be wrong, but I think I have Burdett figured out. At the restaurant, he quite deliberately sat on my left side when the waiter pulled out the chair on my right. I could often feel his gaze rest on me throughout the meal—not curious or repelled but pitying. To my surprise, part of me is offended.

Perhaps he looked at Sylvie in just that way. My guess is that Burdett likes to rescue hurt things and take care of them: put them in a little box in a nest of cotton like Vernelle and I used to do when we found birds with broken wings. Only the birds never got better that way; they never flew on their own again.

# CHAPTER 30

Saturday morning rolls around. Jack is due back today, ready to "tear into the bathroom." I watch him dash from the pickup, head ducked against the rain. It has turned into an ugly, wet spring. It might have been gloomy yesterday, but Mother Nature has brought out the big guns today. The garage is obscured by a gray curtain of rain, and there's water gushing from the downspouts onto the grass by the back door.

After making trips to the hardware store and lumberyard before coming over, Jack's threatening to charge me for gas. That could add up to a lot of money considering his big old Silverado. On the other hand, he hasn't asked for a dime for all the work he's done. Maybe he just works for food.

As Jack hangs up his coat, I offer to pay him whatever he thinks is fair. After our last conversation, I'm feeling a little awkward.

He just shrugs and says, "We can settle up once the work's all done."

I take that as a good sign—at least he's not quitting on me. I work up the nerve to mention that the marble jar had simply been put in a cabinet and even get it to prove the marbles are real.

He shrugs again. "Okay. You really have found a lot of marbles left around the property. Not sure how that proves there are ghosts. By the way, have you talked to your sister yet?"

CORINNE MALCOLM IBELING / R.I.PARTRIDGE 167

With a sudden sense of foreboding, I mumble, "Not yet. But I will."

I decide to change the subject, and the pouring rain reminds me of Jack's advice about having the roof checked. It might be a sieve for all I know. "I was just about to check the upstairs for leaks." I rush up the stairs as well as I can with a bum leg, all the while feeling self-conscious that Jack is watching me. But when I glance back, he hasn't followed me from the kitchen.

I can plainly hear the pounding rain, but there's no water dripping anywhere. Then the word "attic" pops into my head; what if it's like Niagara Falls up there?

The doors in the hallway open into the bathroom, the bedrooms, and a small linen closet—but not an attic. After peering at the ceilings and in closets for a non-existent trap door or something, I finally head downstairs, defeated. What kind of idiot can't find a door to an attic?

The geezers, who have been away at other jobs for a few days, are now in the kitchen, ready to load the stove for its final journey to "appliance heaven." It's the last thing to go, they tell me.

The garage is now empty, too, except for an old lawn mower and a couple of cans of gas, which they're leaving in case the next tenant can use them. As Tuffy says, "Miss Bryant was a real tyrant when it come to mowing grass, but she always threw in an extra buck or two for the gas."

On impulse, I ask Tuffy and Ace if they know where the attic door is. They look at each other as if it's a trick question. Ace hunches his shoulders, but Tuffy says warily, "We was never upstairs, but there has to be a door." They are too polite to say "duh!" to me, but their faces make their opinions plenty clear.

Still, the geezers troop willingly upstairs, their heavy work boots clunking on the treads. After checking the same doors I did, they stand in the hall in their blue bibs, looking, as Tuffy says, "flummoxed." Ace literally scratches his bald head for a moment—and then leaves to fetch their flashlights.

Now they are on the hunt, but at first they don't have any more luck than I did. Then Ace flashes his light deep into a bedroom closet and says, "Well, looky there." I take a peek; if there's a door, it's invisible. But Tuffy points out how the ceiling of the long closet slopes down to the floor at the far end. "Ergo, must be a stairway up there somewheres." I've rarely heard anyone say, "Ergo," and I'm impressed just with that.

The geezers return to the linen closet and examine it more closely. Behind the door is a unit of shallow shelves that fills the space. It's made of unpainted wood and is clearly not original to the house. Muttering something about two "danged odd hinges," they pull on the shelves which creak slowly out, revealing a steep stairway. "Well, I'll be a son-of-a-gun," Ace says, staring into the darkness above.

Tuffy adds, "That's the damnest thing I've ever seen."

It's the damnedest thing I've ever seen, too. I can't thank the geezers enough, though they don't look as thrilled as I am. No wonder; Tuffy growls, "Gawd, I hope you don't find nothing you want up there. I ain't no mountain goat."

The dust on the steps indicates that neither Miss Bryant nor Tuffy's mountain goat has been up to the attic for years—maybe never. With some ceremony, Ace hands me his flashlight and gestures up the narrow stairway.

When my head reaches above floor level, I can see that the attic consists of one small square room. It smells of dampness and old wood—but not mice, thank goodness. The windows at each of the two peaks are covered with ragged lace curtains. In the dimness, I can see old furniture and boxes, piled helter-skelter in the middle of the room.

I am "flummoxed" myself, and back down the stairway. Then I brush the dirt from my hands and pull out my cell phone to call Vernelle. This is something she won't want to miss.

*\*\**

Vernelle gives a loud squawk and says she'll be out in five minutes flat, which must mean she plans to fly as usual. It's a very long five minutes. When she finally shows up, she's with Garrett in his pickup. I wonder if that's because Vernelle anticipates taking something home—or if Garrett is afraid to ride with her. Maybe both.

Jack follows them upstairs. He's as curious as the rest of us to see what's in the attic. Vernelle leads the way up. When she reaches the top, I expect a loud expletive of some kind, but there's total silence. For one of the few times in her life, Vernelle is speechless.

As we all crowd into the attic, Tuffy spots a bulb dangling from the ceiling and pulls an old, frayed cord. Light floods the attic. Okay, it doesn't exactly flood the attic; it just adds another dim glow to that of the two little windows, but at least we can see.

Rain is still drumming on the roof, and occasional lightning flashes in the little windows. On the good side, there aren't any drips bopping our heads or dead bats hanging around. On the not-so-good side, the furniture and boxes are covered with the dust and dirt of nearly sixty years.

"My God," Vernelle mutters, "this all must've belonged to the Millers—the murdered Millers."

Garrett and the geezers take only a quick look around. When I mention that there's coffee and Vernelle's brownies in the kitchen, they disappear down the stairs.

Still dazed, Vernelle begins pulling things from the pile and setting them aside. I spot a marble on the floor, partly under a big box. When Jack lifts the box for me, the marble goes rolling across the floor to a corner of the room. Jack has a strange look on his face as his eyes follow it.

The marble stops by three cardboard boxes. I kneel down beside them, opening them one by one. The first two boxes contain boys' things: Lincoln Logs; a ranch set with cowboys, horses, and a tin ranch house; and two old metal Flintstones lunch boxes.

At the bottom of one box is a brown leather bag, now stiff with age. It's filled with marbles. With a sense of relief, I add the one I just found. When I look up, Jack is staring at the bag of marbles incredulously. Then he shakes his head—and smiles ruefully at me. Now it's clear that at least he does believe in marbles—maybe even that they're some kind of message.

The remaining box is smaller but heavier. On top are some old report cards and a crushed brown corsage. At the bottom are textbooks and a high school yearbook. Every one of the books has "Audrey Lynn Miller" written inside the front cover. It's a shock, really, those carefully formed letters with fancy little curlicues on the capitals. All of a sudden, Audrey isn't just a shadow in a mirror anymore.

I stare sadly at the pile of possessions now strewn on the dusty floor around me. They're like the ghosts themselves—remnants of four shattered lives.

When Grandpa Miller inherited this property, he didn't want to auction off the contents of the "murder house," so people figured that he'd burned it all. Obviously, that's not what happened. Instead, he hid most of it away up here. Why? I guess we'll never know.

I replace the boxes containing Dennis and Davie's things, but decide to take Audrey's home. I'd like to look through the yearbook if nothing else.

Jack leaves to take Audrey's box to my car and Vernelle stands up and dusts off her hands. By her feet is one tea-pot, cream-colored with a big blue flower and green leaves on the side. "That's all you want?" I ask in surprise.

"Yeah." She looks around uncertainly. "There are a few bits of furniture I'd like, but it doesn't seem right to paint them black and perch them here and there around my house. I'll leave them here, where they belong." She picks up the teapot. "I want this, though. Mom had one a lot like it. I'll give them both a place of honor when I finally open my bistro."

Ah, so it's a "bistro" now. Interesting.

# CHAPTER 31

After dinner, I thumb through the old yearbook with its padded cover of maroon and gold. I stop at the sophomore pictures. There's Audrey, with fine features and light hair, lips curved into a faint smile. Though her face is still round and girlish, she would have been a beauty in a few years, no doubt of that.

Ben was a junior. He looks darker in his picture, with a narrow face and a for-the-camera smile. Maybe pictures don't reveal much about character, but it's almost incomprehensible that such an ordinary-looking kid could have become a monster.

Vernelle plops herself down next to me on the couch, and I pass her the yearbook. She laughs as soon as she sees the cover. "Hey, look at that! It's called The Torch just like it was when we were in high school! Nobody could ever figure out what the hell a torch had to do with our mascot, the Bulldogs."

She flips through the pages, while I turn to Audrey's textbooks. As a sophomore, Audrey was taking English, biology, geometry, and world history. As I leaf absently through her English textbook, a note falls out. No surprise. Isn't writing notes what high school girls did before cell phones?

I'm chuckling as I begin to read, but my amusement soon fades. On the note are two different sets of handwriting--neither very neat. My eyes follow the scribbles down the page:

*He said more stuff to me today, dirty stuff, even after what I told him yesterday!*

*Aud, you've got to tell somebody about JT—counselor?*

*Ha—counselor never does anything!* ('Anything' is heavily underscored.) *Anyway, I can't. Ben would fight him. So would my Dad & get fired! I don't know what to do. I can't stay home all the time—Mom already wonders what's going on.*

*You've got to tell somebody.*

This is not the silly, girly gossip I was expecting. I reread the note a couple more times, then turn the paper over. A graded assignment with Audrey's name is on the other side; the handwriting is clearly the same as part of the note. While the other girl didn't add her name or initials, she must have been a friend of Audrey's.

I pass the note to Vernelle. "Sis, look at this."

Vernelle scans it and looks up, aghast. "My God! Do you really think Audrey was being stalked by this JT?"

"That's my guess. She sounds terrified of him."

"I'd have been pissed! She should have got some big football player to beat the shit out of him. But things were different back then. The kid had to be going to the school, so let's see if we can figure out who he was."

I lean close to Vernelle as we search the index for the JT's. Only two boys have those initials. Jerry Thompson looks like a geek and he's smiling broadly, at least as much as he can with big steel braces. Then there's Jim Tisdale. Now, Jim isn't particularly smiling, but since his nickname is "Skip," I'd have a hard time tagging him as a stalker of sophomore girls.

That idea didn't go anywhere, so we page through the other pictures and come upon one of a senior boy, which practically jumps off the page. His name is Terence Trimble, and he has Tom Trimble's attractive features stretched slightly askew onto a round face. His mouth is drooped into a leer, and he's looking at the camera with a steady, menacing glare.

Vernelle's face scrunches up in disgust. "He's scarier than all the other Trimbles combined, which is saying a lot. Just looking at him gives me the creeps—I'll bet the photographer was glad to get the hell out of Dodge that day."

"Do you think he belongs on the Trimble family tree?"

"He must be related to Tom, but I don't know how—maybe he's a dead branch or something. He sure looks like the perfect candidate for the pervert in Audrey's note, though. Are you positive about the initials?"

I examine the note again, and admit to her there's no doubt—Audrey's scary admirer is clearly JT, not TT. So Terence, for all his nasty appearance, can't be the one.

Vernelle shakes her head. "My money's still on the Trimble."

"Come on," I protest. "You can't judge someone by his picture."

"I don't care if he looked like a choirboy. A Trimble's a Trimble."

Vernelle can be awfully stubborn sometimes.

She's still flipping through the pages of the yearbook when she gives a sudden gasp.

"What is it?" I ask, hoping for a JT that we missed.

Vernelle looks down at a picture, then back at me. "Abby, if you'd had a '60's hairdo when you were sixteen—and a sweeter expression, of course—you'd have looked just like Audrey." Besides both having blond hair, there's a definite family resemblance. She stares down at the picture again. "Holy shit!"

I think back to the image in the mirror and admit to myself that we do look a bit alike, but not all that much. Vernelle can also be awfully dramatic sometimes.

# CHAPTER 32

Since it's Sunday, Vernelle and Garrett took off to Cedar Rapids for an antiques show. They invited me, but I said it would be a good day to take it easy. In reality, I feel kind of lost. Or maybe "unsettled" is a better word.

Before she left, Vernelle commented idly over breakfast, "That was odd about Audrey's note, wasn't it? It's almost as if you were meant to find it."

Unsettled, as I said.

The calendar has flipped over to April, and the weather has changed from gloomy and rainy to warm and sunny. Church bells peal in the distance. On impulse, I change into one of my more muted Sophie outfits and head for the Methodist Church. Why doesn't it surprise me that Tom Trimble's big SUV is there, sitting smugly in the parking lot?

The service has already started, so I sneak into the vestibule where the ushers used to hang out. They were known for dozing in comfortable chairs or talking about sports instead of listening to the sermon. Sure enough, there are four of them (two women now—a radical change there), and they give me brief smiles and nods when I slide onto a chair.

My family spent many happy hours at this church. One of my favorite memories concerns Vernelle, on a Communion Sunday when we were both little. For some reason, Mom had planned to leave early. When she whispered very quietly that it was time for us to go, Vernelle said in her piercing five-year-old voice, "But Mommy, they haven't served the drinks yet!" People are probably still chuckling over that one.

Glass windows and closed double doors separate the vestibule from the sanctuary. When the congregation rises for a song, I can see Tom and Sylvie.

Speakers in the vestibule broadcast the service loud and clear. I was hoping for a sermon entitled "How to Ignore Ghosts in a Mirror," but no such luck. Still, the Doxology and familiar hymns are a comfort, even after all these years. I offer a prayer for my sons, then wonder what Tom prays for—if he prays at all.

I'm about to duck out, when a sign over another door catches my attention: "LIBRARY: All welcome." Strange that I'd never noticed the church had a library before. Maybe this is new. I enter the walk-in-closet-sized room with floor to ceiling bookcases unsure what subject to look under. I'm still hoping to find something that applies to the bizarre situation I've ended up in. I find a few books on The Holy Ghost—or Holy Spirit. Interesting, but not what I need.

Suddenly an old black book with gold writing on the spine catches my attention. *Christians and the Spirit World.* I go to the table with the ledger and sign out the book, glad not to have to explain my interest in the book to anyone. Only church gossip spreads faster than small town gossip. As I hurry out, I see Tom holding court with many of Mt. Prospect's leading citizens. Thankfully he doesn't notice me.

Back at Vernelle's, I thumb through the book and am immediately disappointed. It's about spiritual warfare and how to get rid of evil spirits. The Millers aren't evil, and I've become convinced that Ben was innocent. Of course, according to movies and TV shows, ghosts usually hang around until some issue is resolved. But how am I supposed to resolve a wrong committed decades ago?

I consider what to do with my day. Since I'm not up to playing detective, I should spend at least some of it painting. There's still a lot to do, and it's weighing heavily on me. After the past week, I'm tired, both in body and mind. I change into my "painting clothes"— a particular pair of jeans and a tee shirt I've sacrificed to the project.

As I head out, it occurs to me that if the ghosts in the mirror want to be so busy, they could at least do some painting instead of just causing me headaches. At least, the fencing guys are supposed to come next week. With the house Trimble-proofed, maybe I can finally relax.

The gravel roads are soggy, but the ditches are suddenly alive with red-winged blackbirds perched among green weeds. By the back door, the "daffs" (as Marge calls them) are fading away, but tulips are in full bloom. Trees and shrubs have leafed out in shades of bright green or cerise, and the air is balmy.

Once inside the house, I lock the door (post-Trimble) and drift listlessly around the living room. I start to congratulate myself that at least I've finished painting this far. Then I see in the bright light of day, patches of nasty beige peeking through the chocolate mist. It's not an attractive look.

With resignation, I open a can of paint and kneel on the floor, lethargically stirring what's left. The paint roller is nearby, but somehow I can't "get up the gumption" (as Tuffy would say—it's scary that I'm starting to mimic him) to start painting. I slide to the floor, lean against the wall, and contemplate my day with a sigh.

The truth is, for the first time, I dread being in the house. I want the happy scene in the mirror to stay just as it was. But even from here, I can see the black spot on the bottom is bigger—much bigger—than it was a couple of days ago. Something unsettling is going on, but I can't begin to guess what.

Somehow Audrey's note ties in with all this, I'm sure of it. But how? Tomorrow, I have to go to the newspaper office. Maybe one of the articles will mention a "JT" involved in the investigation of the murders—it's the only new clue I have. What if JT killed Audrey—but if so, why did he let Ben Stockton live? It doesn't make sense.

My thoughts are interrupted by the sound of a vehicle. I can see Jack climbing out of his pickup, so I unlock the door and resume my spot on the floor. He stops in the doorway when he sees me. "Hey, Abby! Paint fumes getting to you?"

I grab a paintbrush and throw it at him. He catches it and grins. "Really, what's going on—besides the fact that the door was unlocked?"

"I unlocked it just for you—and I wouldn't have if I'd known you were going to insult me. What's going on is I thought I was done in here, but now I see spots of that ugly beige. And I just can't get motivated to do anything about it."

Jack tips up his sunglasses and strolls around the room, peering now and then at a patch on the wall. "I see what you mean." He turns to me. "You got one of those little bitty rollers?"

"I do, and a matching little bitty tray somewhere in that pile. Never used either one of them."

"You stay there, and I'll finish up for you."

And he does. In about fifteen minutes, the walls are a uniform chocolate. Somehow it's annoying that Jack didn't get a drip or a drop of paint on anything else, including himself.

When he's finished cleaning up, Jack settles down on the floor beside me, knees up with his hands clasped across them. His shoulder just touches mine. "Abby, about those marbles...Sorry I—"

I interrupt him with a smile. "It's okay. Honestly." I don't add that I have other things on my mind today.

Jack looks relieved. "After I got home yesterday, I had a talk with Spencer about you."

"Spencer? I suppose that's your rural mailman who roams the backroads spreading gossip."

"Spencer roams the backroads, all right, but that's because he's a dog. And I value his opinion more than the mailman's."

"I'm not sure that's better, but go ahead." How could I have forgotten the dog who likes Italian Garden steak?

"We, Spencer and I, feel it's too nice outside for you to be stuck in here painting, or" —and here he looks at me pointedly— "not painting. We think you need a break. How about I show you around my place?"

"Well, I was really planning to start on another room today."

Jack looks surprised—and gratifyingly disappointed. "Okay, if that's what you want. I guess."

"Jack, you're supposed to say, 'Hey, Abby, Spencer will be broken-hearted if you don't come along with me.'"

Jack grins. "He might be more than that. He's been out in my pickup all this time."

# CHAPTER 33

Spencer is a big dog, as brown and slick as a bar of Hershey's chocolate. He gives a sharp yip when we come out of the house but looks perfectly happy to ride in the back of the pickup. At least, I won't have to share the seat with him.

Jack's place is at the end of a long gravel drive that curves through thick woods. It doesn't look like much—a pale gray-green double-garage appears bigger than the attached house. Jack stops the truck in front, and Spencer lopes off on business of his own while we follow a shady stone walkway to the front door.

In a flowerpot by the step are some pansies. Grandma Miller always had them in her flower beds, which is the only reason I know what they are. Jack pauses. "My sister-in-law Amy gave me that pot. She thought it would spruce up the entrance. Do you think those plants look healthy?"

I lean down and touch one leaf. "Well, they're spindly and yellow." I cup my hand around my ear and lean closer. "Plus, they're crying, 'Please help us!' so I'd say not."

He looks morose. "What d'you think is wrong with them?"

I troll my scanty plant knowledge. "I'm pretty sure most plants need sunshine—and occasional watering."

"That might be part of the problem—Spencer takes care of the occasional watering."

As I consider the pathetic plants, I notice a hook attached to the rough wood siding by the door. "Why don't you hang the pot up there? That would definitely spoil Spencer's aim."

Jack's brow clears. "Great idea, Abby—I always appreciate a woman who's pretty *and* practical."

As Jack turns to unlock the door, a warm glow washes over me. Even though he must have been kidding, who'd have thought Jack would even hint that I'm pretty?

The front door opens into a large tiled foyer that's almost a balcony. From behind a railing we can look down on the room below and then up to the slanted ceiling that soars above. It's a big room, but wood paneling on the walls and a rough stone fireplace give it a warm, lodgy feeling. Fortunately for my taste, there aren't any deer heads or stuffed birds staring down from the walls.

The door to the right leads to the garage, while we follow steps on the left down to the living room. The furniture is simple: a brown leather couch, a TV, and a red-plaid rocking chair on one side of the fireplace and a small dining table and chairs on the other.

Jack explains that there's a bedroom and bath off the living room and a small kitchen off the dining area. Since the house is built into the hillside, the only windows face the woods, but they're large and flood the room with sunshine.

I would never have guessed, from the outside, that Jack's place would look like this. "What a fantastic house, Jack!"

I can tell that's he's pleased. "The nice thing is that it's cool in the summer and warm in the winter. There's third level below—that's where my woodworking shop is. I made some of the pieces in here. My favorite is this dining table." He runs his hand along the edge. Just from his touch, I can see that he loves the wood.

There's a tiny design on the back of one of the chairs, and I bend down for a closer look. Jack says, "It's an inlaid lily made of abalone shell. There's a furniture maker in England who carves a tiny mouse into each piece of furniture—that's where I came up with the idea."

"It's beautiful," I marvel. "I've never seen anything like it."

"Yeah, it's a reminder of the promise I made to Lily."

But he doesn't explain his promise, and I don't want to ask.

Jack opens the French doors to the deck, which is high off the ground because of the way the house is built. The air is warm, here in the dappled sunshine. It's almost like being in a tree house. A few branches even droop over the railing, and there are blooms on some, delicate splotches of pink and white against a green background. Several lawn chairs are grouped around a small table, and I settle into one with well-worn red cushions. I'm guessing that Jack spends a lot of time out here—I would.

Jack follows with a pitcher, glasses, and cookies that he sets on the table. "I figured I owe you some food. There's lemonade and some Oreos—I'll bet even Vernelle can't make Oreos."

From somewhere below us, barking erupts. "Geez, I hope he hasn't cornered a skunk again." Jack leans over the rail and whistles. Spencer comes bounding up the steep wooden steps, his tail lashing dangerously near the pitcher of lemonade.

Surprisingly, Spencer lays his head on my knee and looks up, his brown eyes soulful. Jack chuckles and sits down. "Spence, you old devil." Spencer gives him what I can only call a reproving look before plopping down at his feet. "Spence must like you; he doesn't usually like women. Not that I've brought very many here—just a couple as a matter of fact. Hardly any, really, and not lately."

I burst out laughing as I take a handful of cookies. "Jack, your personal life is you own business."

Jack's eyes crinkle up nicely when he smiles. "The women were mostly relatives, anyway." Then he adds sheepishly. "I might as well just shut the hell up, right?"

I can't disagree with that.

It's peaceful here on the deck with lemonade and cookies near at hand. Jack isn't one of those fidgety people. There's a stillness—maybe a contentedness—about him that calms my spirit. With a sigh, I lean back into the cushions and munch on my Oreos.

Spencer has gone to sleep, and I ask idly what breed he is.

"Just a mutt—chocolate lab crossed with some kind of hunting dog. That's my best guess." Jack regards him disapprovingly. "He doesn't do much except lay around and eat—that's when he's not barking at the deer or wild turkeys or anything else that moves."

I think back to my old life. "We were planning to get the boys a dog. I wonder if they have one now."

Jack reaches over and pats his dog's head. "Yeah, Lily would have loved Spencer."

I slosh the ice cubes around and stare down into my empty glass of lemonade. "Losing a child—I don't see how you can get over it."

"You never get over it. Life just goes on."

"You seem to be doing pretty well." It's more a question than a statement.

"It takes a while." Jack looks off into the distance, and I wonder what he's seeing. "The guilt was the worst thing. Steph hadn't wanted us to go to Iowa City that day, because of the weather. But it really didn't sound like much, and I already had a substitute and lesson plans all lined up. You know what that's like."

"I remember." There were teachers who'd drag themselves to school looking like death warmed over instead of calling in sick, just so they wouldn't have to do lesson plans for a sub.

Jack nods. "So it was my decision to go, and Steph blamed me for the accident, though not as much as I blamed myself. But as time went on, Steph coped with Lily's death much better than I did. Somehow, she was able to grieve openly, with her parents and family, with her girlfriends. At first, I felt too guilty to even feel grief."

I wonder if that's similar to what's going on with me. Is my guilt at not being able to be a mother to my boys for the last year affecting me? Am I filling the void left from not seeing Hunter and Greyson with those boys in the mirror?

I scold myself for being so wrapped up in my own situation, while Jack is sharing his story with me and refocus myself on what he's saying.

"Steph wanted us to get on with life. She went back to work, started going out with her friends again, while I spent my time in therapy, watching my teaching career go to hell. She said she wanted her life back, with a husband and another child. I couldn't give that to her. Finally, Steph said she was tired of living with ghosts—and that included me.

"I knew she was right, and that's when I moved out. After the divorce went through, Steph married a dentist from her office. She has her little girls now. She sends me pictures sometimes."

"How did you end up here?" I ask curiously.

He shrugs. "For months, I lived in this black hole of guilt. Not an hour went by—and that included most nights—that I didn't blame myself for Lily's death. My main gig was wishing I could turn back the clock—if only we'd left five minutes earlier, Lily would still be alive. If only I hadn't stopped for that cup of coffee, if only we'd cancelled the appointment that day as Steph wanted, if only . . ."

He pauses thoughtfully before continuing, "As I said, I wallowed in guilt. I'd killed my only child and destroyed my marriage and my career. I didn't see much point in living, but gradually, a sense of reason came back. I knew Lily wouldn't have wanted me to feel like that. I figured I needed to start over, so I came here, by chance as much as anything else.

"I bought this place—it was just a couple of rooms perched on a hillside then—and I've made it into a house I love. I started working with my hands again, designing and selling furniture. And Spencer?"

Jack leans over and gives the dog a good pat. "He just appeared one day, dirty and skinny, so I've had him ever since. I'm not saying things are perfect now, but I'm getting along. I still regret the accident, but it's at a level I can live with."

Jack's honesty strikes a chord in me. "I know what you mean about 'if-onlys.' If only I hadn't rushed away and left the boys that day, maybe I would have noticed the fire. Or if I'd taken them with me, we wouldn't be separated like this now. If only, if only . . . .

"You know, some of the "ologists"—that's what I called the various psychologists I dealt with—didn't want me to leave the hospital. They said I wasn't facing reality, that I wanted things back the way they were, and that could never be again."

Jack's eyes search my face. "Are you facing reality now?"

I avoid answering directly. "Coming back to Mt. Prospect has been good for me, but I have to start making plans for when the house is done."

"What do you want to do?"

"First, find a job. I've already eliminated teaching—I'd scare the kids!" I take another bite of cookie, considering. "And being a model for Victoria's Secret is probably out, too, though I'll bet I could start a lawsuit that would scare them silly."

Jack laughs. "One time, we passed a Victoria's Secret in the mall, and Lily asked why those girls had their pictures taken in their underwear."

"What did you say?"

"What could I say? I told her to ask her mother." We look at each other and laugh. "Lily was funny that way—she noticed a lot of things you thought she wouldn't. I remember one time, when it was snowing outside, she picked up one of those snow-globes with a winter scene in it and asked me, 'Daddy, what if the world is really a snow-globe? What if it is, and God shakes it sometimes to make it snow?' When I think of that accident, I think that maybe God shook our snow globe."

"You blame God for what happened?" Because I'd never thought that way about the fire, not once.

"No, I just mean that sometimes, when we least expect it, our world is shaken to pieces. I guess for me, it's finally coming together again." Jack reaches over and gently takes my hand. "I hope it comes together soon for you, too, Abby."

I look down at the strong brown hand holding mine. "I still have a ways to go, Jack." I think of my boys so far away, Vernelle's house still not done, the five ghosts that haunt my days, and whisper, "I hope I won't disappoint everyone."

His hand squeezes mine. "The only way I'll be disappointed is if you don't eat those last two Oreos. Spence will eat dead rabbits, but for some reason he won't touch an Oreo."

\*\*\*

After a companionable silence, Jack points to the expanse of trees that follow the downward slope of the hill. "If you look through that gap, you can get a good view of your house. Then at the bottom of the hill, there's a nice little creek—I think you'd enjoy seeing it." I brush the crumbs from the last two cookies off my lap and follow Jack down the stairs. He adds, "The hill's pretty steep, so watch your step."

Steep is right! The hill slopes so sharply it's hard for me to keep my balance, especially since my left leg decides to be tricky. If Jack hadn't kindly taken my hand, I'd probably be rolling all the way down.

As we approach the creek, I can see that it's running bank-full from all the rain. Nearby is a grassy area with a firepit and a couple of old plastic lawn chairs. Jack drops onto one and pats the other. "The ground by the creek is muddy, but it's okay here."

I sit down beside him. The creek is small but fierce, gurgling over and around rocks. Its water is clear except for the old leaves and little sticks that swirl in the eddies and over the miniature falls.

Jack scrunches down in the chair and puts his hands behind his head, watching the creek. How could I ever have thought he wasn't attractive? There's something to be said for smooth and handsome, like Brad, but I decide rough and muscular is a lot nicer. Then there's his thick, dark hair, even his clipped beard. . .

Jack turns his head and smiles. "You look beautiful there in the sun, Abby."

His comment catches me by surprise, and something must have changed in my face, because Jack's eyes get that hard look in them.

I say defensively, "Beautiful! Well, it's not true, is it? I mean, half my face is ugly."

"Half isn't, so am I supposed to pity you?"

"Jack, you know I hate pity!"

"Do you? You sure looked like you were having a pity party at the lumberyard the first time I met you."

"Maybe I was." It's not hard to remember how mortified I felt by Drew's reaction to my face. "Is that why you offered to help?"

"It was not. I offered to help because of that asshole Drew."

I can't help smirking a little. "I figured Drew out, but you scared me at first—I thought you looked like a serial killer."

"A serial killer? What the hell!" Jack sits up and looks at me indignantly, rubbing his chin. "Just because I have a beard?"

"It was more your dark glasses and baseball cap—they looked like a disguise." I decide not to mention his scowl that day.

"Okay, then—maybe I did have a slight Uni-bomber look. And I repeat, you look beautiful today, sitting there in the sunshine. Amy might not have a clue about pansies, but you know what she told me once?" I can't imagine. " 'Compliments are like gifts. Just accept them and say thank-you.'"

His words bring a smile to my face. "All right, then. Thank-you, Jack."

"See, that wasn't so hard, was it?" He folds his arms across his broad chest and leans back, staring at me with raised brows.

"What?" Then it dawns on me. "Oh—okay, Jack. You've been just an amazing help to me at the house, and I appreciate it very much! There—is that a good enough compliment?"

"I don't care about the house. I'm waiting to hear you say you think I'm better-looking than that silver fox you were out with the other night."

" 'Silver fox?' Oh, you mean Burdett Swann! You're right—you're much better looking than he is. How's that?"

"The sincerity level was a little low, but I'll take it."

# CHAPTER 34

My car is still at the Miller place, so Jack takes me back there and follows me into the house. He immediately spots the jar of marbles on the mantel by the mirror. He takes out the big shooter I'd found at the cemetery, turning it between his fingers. "This is old, for sure. I remember my grand-dad having some like it."

"That's the one I found by the grave of the Miller boys. And look at this," I add, pointing to the tiny sugar bowl beside it. "It matches a set of dishes I had when I was little. My Grandpa cleaned this house out when Ed Miller died and must have thought the doll dishes would make a good present for me. I found the sugar bowl in the pink room—Audrey's room—just yesterday."

Jack drops the marble back into the jar as if it would burn his fingers. "So, you still think these haunted marbles and doll dishes are some kind of message?" The skepticism in his voice is hard to ignore. "Abby, that's not exactly dealing with reality."

"I know it sounds crazy, but it's true. Sometimes I wish it wasn't." I can hear the stubbornness in my voice, but that's how I feel.

"Have you told Vernelle about this yet?"

"She knows I don't think Ben was the murderer, but I haven't told her about the mirror. Tomorrow I'm going to the newspaper office to look through the old articles. I want to know exactly what happened here the night of the murders, before I say anything."

He gives me a hard look. "You're getting way too involved in this murder stuff. I'm surprised you're not afraid to be here."

"I don't feel personally threatened, and I love being here," I say defensively. "At least, I did until—"

Jack's eyebrows rise. "Until what, Abby?"

I stare into the mirror. The scene is misty today, the people barely discernible. The black spot I point to has grown to the size of a silver dollar. "Does this look like a face to you?"

"About as much as the man in the moon looks like a face," Jack says, echoing what I thought. He frowns. "But the spot is definitely bigger now than it was."

Right then, the mirror shimmers into clarity. For the first time, I can see what the other little boy is doing.

Jack looks curiously from me to the mirror. "What's going on?"

"It's the usual scene, except the little boy—not the one with the marbles, the other one—has a small knife in his hand." I'm a little breathless. "He's carving—whittling? —something made of whitish wood—an airplane maybe?"

Jack actually squints at the mirror. "Years ago, they used to sell kits to make model airplanes out of balsa wood. It was real light and easy to carve—" He stops abruptly. "Listen to me—I can't believe I'm going along with this! And I don't see a thing in that mirror that shouldn't be there."

My tone changes from stubborn to defiant. "Well, I can, and it used to be a peaceful scene. Now that black spot is getting bigger, and a creepy face is starting to form. I don't like what's going on."

We're standing eye to eye. Jack's expression has grown stern, and he puts his hands on my shoulders. "I'm about to say something I'll regret. But let's assume—just for the moment—that your ghostly pals are for real. If the mirror is changing now, maybe you shouldn't be here—maybe you're the one causing the changes. And if that mirror is some kind of doorway to the great beyond, maybe you should just break the damned thing before something really bad happens."

\*\*\*

When I get home, Vernelle doesn't seem to have much news about her day, though she says she and Garrett had a good time. She's still subdued as I chatter on about my afternoon with Jack at his place, avoiding all mention of the Miller house or the mirror.

Vernelle starts making a casserole for dinner, clattering pots and pans loud enough to make me jump. I sit at the kitchen table, chopping some carrots for her, and tell her the geezers are coming by to collect their checks tomorrow. I want to do something special, so I've decided to buy them a big sack of 7-Up and Twinkies. Marge is a tougher proposition altogether. After some discussion, Vernelle volunteers (somewhat absently) to make some chocolate chip cookies for her.

She puts the casserole in the oven, then sits down and folds her hands in front of her on the table. I can sense something serious is coming. For a moment I wonder if she and Garrett broke up, but she'd look a lot worse than this.

Vernelle licks her lips, a habit she's always had when she's very nervous. "Brad called just before you got home."

At the sound of his name, my heart starts to pound. "Did he mention the boys?"

"No, he didn't."

"I wish he'd call *me*. Then I could ask about them myself."

"Maybe that's why he doesn't call you." She stops and bites her lip. "Abby, there's no easy way to say this. Chloe had a baby—a little girl. She was born yesterday. Brad wanted you to know."

A pain shoots through me, sharp and sudden as a cut finger. "Oh." Then I remember Jack's reaction to his ex-wife's girls. I swallow the lump in my throat. "I'll try to be happy for them."

After an awkward silence, I add, "Did you get Brad's number? I've been trying to call, just to talk to the boys, but his number isn't in service anymore, and the airline won't give me his new one. Even the letters I've sent to his parents have been returned—they've moved and left no forwarding address. I just want to hear their voices, you know?"

There's a long hesitation. Vernelle's eyes tear up, but then she sighs and gives me a supportive smile. "I know." She places a comforting hand on mine. "But the number was blocked, and I didn't think to ask." At my disappointed expression she adds, "There must be some way of getting it, though. I'll try."

A tear slides down my cheek. "Thanks. I just want a chance to tell them I love them. That's not too much to expect, is it?"

Vernelle looks away, and silence fills the kitchen like a tomb until she finally answers. "No. Of course not. But—" she cuts herself off.

When she doesn't continue, I rush to tell her, "Now that I'm planning to live in the house, I want to ask the boys what color they want their rooms painted. Hunter always likes green the best, and Grayson likes blue. I need to stop by the hardware and get some paint chips."

Vernelle's face is pale and drawn. The subject of the boys obviously makes her uncomfortable. I don't want her to have to say it, so I do. "Of course, I need to prove that I'm really recovered and up to it before they can come here. But it gives me something to work toward."

Vernelle nods eagerly. "Yes. You concentrate on yourself for a while. Give it a little more time."

I sense this isn't really the time to bring up the ghosts, so I say, "And I promise I'll get an appointment with one of the Iowa City psychiatrists, I was referred to. I kept putting it off, but I'm ready now."

Vernelle lets out a pent-up breath in relief. It's obviously been hard for her to wait for me to get to this point. My words seem to be taking a huge weight off her shoulders, so I take a deep breath and go on. "I know I'm not the same person I was before the fire. Brad used to call me Little Miss Sunshine—not in a nice tone, of course—because I was always so happy. But the fire and my time in the hospital changed all that—operations, handfuls of pills, therapies, the "ologists." Then of course, my face. For months, they wouldn't allow a mirror in my room. I couldn't even see to comb my hair, at least what was left of it. Everyday was a new nightmare."

Vernelle is staring at me, her eyes wide. She doesn't even glance at the oven, where the casserole is no doubt bubbling away.

I reach for her hand and continue. "Then you asked me to come home, Vernelle. You and Jack and my work on the house—and even the geezers—have all helped me get back to the old Abby. I'm not there yet, but I will be. Like the Woman at the Airport told me, I am strong. I am the one who has to make it happen."

Vernelle comes around the table and gives me an awkward hug, then kisses the top of my head the way our parents used to do. I can feel her body shake as if she's holding back a good cry. There's no way I'm going to tell her about the ghosts now. It'll have to wait. She's obviously worried enough about me.

Her next words take me by surprise and make me laugh. "Screw Brad and his bimbo, anyway. I hope getting pregnant made her blow up like an elephant. See how much he likes her then."

# CHAPTER 35

I pull up in front of the *Mt. Prospect Chronicle* first thing Monday morning. The outer office probably looks just as it did thirty or forty years ago. It's bare and business-like with one long counter—no chairs, no dusty plants, no comfy couches. Customers are clearly expected to take care of their business and leave.

The owner/publisher/editor, a tall woman with faded red hair and patrician features, probably doesn't look that different either. Ambrosia Swann is one of those women whose face somehow escapes the ravages of time. And I can't imagine that she ever had children. Maybe Burdett just sprang forth from her pen.

Though I introduce myself, Ambrosia clearly knows who I am. Thank goodness she doesn't comment about my ill-fated "date" with her son; my guess is that she doesn't care. After I tell her why I'm here, Ambrosia looks at me as she would one of her minions who's left a comma out of a compound sentence. But for me, that steely-eyed stare is better than the pity I often encounter.

Since I don't turn tail and run, Ambrosia agrees to let me read the articles about the murders. She says, "I keep them in a special file and don't give them to just anybody." At my curious expression, she explains, "I caught Dickie Schwarz trying to steal an article."

She's not the least bit shy about telling me this. Then again, everyone knows that Ambrosia Swann isn't shy about saying anything.

She puts me in her personal office and tosses a thick file on the desk. "It's all there," she says and closes the door. I open the manila file to find the first screaming headlines and the pictures of the murder scene—exteriors only. There are interviews with officials, with shocked family and friends as they tried to make sense of a tragic, senseless, act committed in their peaceful town. For the first few days, words must have poured like a molten stream from the reporters' Smith-Coronas to the hot press in the back room of the *Chronicle*.

The first article in the folder is padded with convoluted "official-ese" from Grant County Sheriff Bill Wendt, but the basic facts are there: Sheriff Wendt and his deputy were called to the rural Ed Miller home on the evening of April 15, 1965 by an ambulance crew. When they arrived, they found the bodies of Mrs. Ed (Nancy) Miller and her three children. A fifth person present at the crime scene was taken into custody for questioning and remained in the county jail. No arrests had been made.

Well, there's not much to disagree with in that story, except to wonder how the ambulance got there before the sheriff. In the next article, Sheriff Wendt added a few details: Ben Stockton, aged 17 of rural Mt. Prospect, was taken into custody at the scene of the Miller murders with blood on his clothing. A pen-knife with his initials on the handle was also covered with blood. It was presumed that sometime around eight o'clock, Mrs. Ed (Nancy) Miller and the three Miller children, Audrey, Dennis, and David, were killed by the suspect. The Sheriff noted, much as an after-thought, that though Ben denied killing the Millers, the County Attorney was considering a charge against him of willful murder.

Yellowed with age, the next article was almost as tragic as the first. It was a statement released by the sheriff's office saying that Ben Stockton had been found dead in his jail cell, the apparent victim of a "remorseful" suicide. Sheriff Wendt went on "to reassure" the citizens of Mt. Prospect that they could rest easy. Sad though it was, the murder of the Miller family was now resolved with his (the murderer's) suicide.

While the sheriff expressed his sympathy for the Miller family, he never once mentioned the Stocktons. You could almost hear the smug satisfaction that the investigation had been concluded so swiftly. Justice had been served.

All that was Sheriff Wendt's version; it wasn't so easy to find Ben's. In fact, there was just one story, with the byline of a reporter named Harry Steadman. Surprisingly, he'd cornered the sheriff and hit him with a barrage of questions concerning Ben.

From the sheriff's disjointed ramblings (it's hard to sort out the "said subject" from the "said suspect"), Mr. Steadman had somehow managed to glean a few details about Ben's story. When he was questioned, Ben had denied knowing anything about the murders. He had stated that he and Audrey were working on a school report that night at her home. He'd forgotten something they needed, so he biked back to his house to get it.

When he returned, Ben found the bodies and called an ambulance. (bingo!) He couldn't tell the sheriff much else; he hadn't seen or heard anything unusual. He claimed the blood on his clothing was from holding Audrey as she was dying. He couldn't explain the blood on the pen-knife but didn't deny that it was his.

Mr. Steadman also noted that, according to the sheriff, Ben's parents couldn't vouch for his movements that night since they were in town buying groceries. So much for Ben's alibi, such as it was. But he'd never denied being at the Miller place. He just denied being the murderer.

The case was basically closed upon Ben's death, and the story faded from the newspaper pages. I imagine everyone wanted to forget the whole thing, which couldn't have been easy. The town was probably flooded with reporters when the story was picked up around the state. Four grisly murders and a dramatic jail cell suicide are more interesting than a stupid hailstone. I do have to agree with Dickie about that.

A ragged pile of articles is all that's left to sort through. A few are the obituaries of various people concerned with the case. Other articles appeared on the anniversaries of the murder—a rehash of what happened that night, memories of the townspeople, personal testimonies about the Millers, that sort of thing. But never any new developments.

There was one interesting article, though—a blistering editorial, also by Harry Steadman, questioning Sheriff Wendt's handling of the case. Specifically, he asked why Ben wasn't being watched. A seventeen-year-old held overnight as the only suspect in four gruesome murders should not have been left alone. Someone should have been with him. Was Ben really guilty, Mr. Steadman had the nerve to ask—or had his life turned into a nightmare he could no longer endure?

\*\*\*

With a sigh, I put the articles back in order and close the file. Truly, I think anyone would agree that the physical evidence almost overwhelmingly pointed to Ben as the murderer. On the other hand, if he was telling the truth, someone else could have gotten into the house while he was gone and killed the family. And how about a motive? None of the articles even hinted at one. Maybe Ben's story was so simple because it was true.

I just wish he'd mentioned seeing JT hanging around—with a knife.

When I return to the outer office, I lay the folder on the counter. Ambrosia is standing beside it working on a pile of ads. "I suppose you want to know what I thought about it back then," she says stiffly.

"Were you working here?" I ask in surprise. I hadn't noticed her name on any of the articles.

"Before I bought the paper, I was a reporter for the *Chronicle*." She reaches for a handy box of paperclips. "Well, 'reporter' is a pretty loose term. Didn't you wonder why my byline was never on an actual murder story? Harry Steadman was the owner, and he wouldn't have let me touch a real news story with a ten-foot pole. Instead, I did the society page—club meetings, weddings, news around the town. You know—'Mr. and Mrs. Jim Smith motored last Wednesday to Iowa City to visit the Joneses'—that sort of drivel."

The paperclips rattle as she absently toys with the box. "Anyway, back to Ben. I knew him, a little. He used to come in and sweep after school. He seemed very ordinary—I don't remember that he ever mentioned Audrey, but he talked about sports and school with the pressmen and some of the other guys."

I tap the file folder with one finger. "Did you have any sense that he could have been the killer these stories say he was?"

She shakes her head. "I didn't think he had it in him to murder anybody. A lot of people around town agreed—for a while. Then Ed Miller started shooting off his mouth about never liking Ben. He wanted to get even with someone for what happened to his family. You couldn't blame the man for that. But having done the follow-up articles, I still have doubts that Ben Stockton killed anyone. Though the sheriff was dead certain at the time."

I can't resist asking what she thought of the sheriff.

Her mouth purses sourly. "Did you notice that Bill Wendt was always described as the 'long-time county sheriff'? Well, Buddy Wendt was an old, incompetent drunk. Of course," she adds, pausing reflectively, "there's something to be said for experience. The sheriff we have now is barely old enough to shave.

"Anyway," she resumes in her usual confident tone, "there were a few rumors around town that Buddy didn't know where to begin on a case like that. Any crime-scene stuff he and his deputies did was pretty shoddy. CSI guys would faint if an investigation was run like that today."

She looks away from me for a moment. "But the most unconscionable thing was that the sheriff left Ben locked up all alone that night. Supposedly the parents weren't even allowed to see their son. Then Ben's suicide—*if* it was suicide—sure took the heat off old Buddy."

The words, "*if* it was suicide," ring in my ears. The story just keeps getting more tragic. But at least I've found an ally. "What if you were shown new evidence that Ben wasn't the murderer? What then?"

She drops the box of paper clips onto the counter and gives me a hard stare. "Do you have that kind of evidence?"

"Not yet, but I have what I'd call a pretty good clue."

Ambrosia's green eyes narrow. "You show me that evidence, and I'll tell you the 'what then' part."

# CHAPTER 36

When I'm back in the car, with the latest issue of the *Chronicle* under my arm, I think about the articles in the file. Mostly, I'm disappointed that there was no mention of JT anywhere. If ghosts can leave marbles and doll dishes as messages, why can't they scribble a name across the mirror? How hard could that be?

With some frustration, I drive to my next stop, the grocery store. It's kind of a culture shock, going from a murder case to pushing a grocery cart around—especially one with a crazy front wheel that makes an annoying clicking sound. But I need the treats for the geezers, and Vernelle's low on baking supplies, so here I am.

Vernelle's handwriting consists of dots and squiggles, but she's so organized that her list of food follows the order of the aisles. When I turn into the baking aisle, I immediately hear a familiar, high-pitched voice. Dickie Schwarz is in front of the cake mixes, talking loudly to an older lady.

Dickie spots me before I can whirl my clicky cart around. "Why, Abby! Imagine meeting you here." She gestures for me to join them, and I do as she says, feeling like a puppet on a string.

Her quick, birdlike eyes glance over everything in my cart. I wouldn't be surprised if she sorted my groceries to get a better view. She gives a faint whistle of surprise. "You must be shopping for

Vernelle. I can't afford real butter—I always have to buy the fake stuff for my classes at school."

A quavery voice says, "Is that why you're here now, Dickie? I wondered why you weren't in school."

The speaker is a tiny stick of a lady who's leaning on her cart for support; her wrinkled face is oddly familiar. It's one of those moments when you freeze, knowing there's a name buried deep in your gray cells that you should remember.

Dickie's shrill voice rattles on. "Can you believe it? I have to give up my free hour to shop for one of my classes. We're starting our 'Miniature Meatloaf' unit, where the kids make little meatloaves and decorate them with tomato sauce like cupcakes. The kids love it, and it's a skill they can carry over into their adult life."

I try to focus on Dickie's words, but suddenly my brain kicks in. "Mrs. Mayes! How wonderful to see you!" Mrs. Mayes was one of my high school teachers.

She peers up at my face. It's obvious that her eyesight isn't what it was when she could spot a sophomore whispering in the back row while correcting papers at her desk.

"THIS IS ABBY MILLER, MRS. MAYES. REMEMBER HER?" For some reason, Dickie has decided that since Mrs. Mayes wears thick glasses, her hearing must be bad. "I HAVE TO GET BACK TO SCHOOL NOW."

I wait until Dickie is safely gone. "It's Abby Bennett now, Mrs. Mayes. I had you for tenth grade English. You were my favorite teacher."

She smiles gently. "Thank you, dear. What are you doing in town? Visiting your sister?"

I am taken aback for a moment. Apparently, Mrs. Mayes isn't up on all the town gossip. "I live here now. I'm helping Vernelle fix up the old Miller place so she can rent it out. You know, the house where Miss Bryant lived."

"Of course!" Her face lights up. "I often visited Miss Bryant. Did you know I grew up on a farm just across the fields? I knew the Miller family very well. I still think of them now and then, though I try to remember the happy times."

Now, that's interesting. "I've always been curious about what they were like. We're related, you know, though I don't remember anyone talking about them much."

"I suppose not, after what happened. I'd enjoy visiting with you about them. Would you like to join me for tea this afternoon? I live at the Pheasant Creek Independent Living Apartments." (She stresses the 'independent' part) "The afternoons go by so slowly— all my neighbors take long naps in the afternoon, and I get horribly bored. Would three o'clock suit you?"

Well, who'd have thought Mrs. Mayes would be such a steamroller in the invitation department? Still, she could be a font of information, so I agree. We finalize the time and place before we finish shopping.

When I'm in the car, a column on the front page of the folded *Chronicle* catches my eye: "Ambrosial Moments" by Ambrosia Swann, Editor. It's a thoughtful little piece about those harbingers of spring—the robins.

I love their gait—run a few steps, stop, peer this way and that with beady eyes and then run again. The robins remind me of property owners who, having left town for the cold winter months, are back, inspecting Mt. Prospect to make sure we're ready for them. And I want to tell them, "Oh yes, my feathered friends, after a hard winter of scooping snow and scraping ice, we are more than ready for robins, for warm sunshine, daffodils and tulips. We are ready for spring.

And at the bottom of the column: "To my readers with long memories: take a moment to remember that on a beautiful April evening nearly sixty years ago, Evil stole into our town and took five innocent lives."

\*\*\*

After dropping off the groceries, I head for the Miller house—a route I literally could drive with my eyes closed by now. Beside the back door, there are sawhorses and a power saw of some kind. Pausing after cutting a piece of plywood, Jack rubs the sweat off his forehead with one wrist and gives me a wry smile. It's hot out here in the sun, and Jack looks kind of hot himself in his T-shirt and jeans.

He informs me that he's decided to install the subfloor in the bathroom for us. "Nothing to it," he says. "It's just a jig-saw puzzle made of plywood. Then Vernelle can get the floor tiled by someone else. I don't have time to take on that job."

Jack quits willingly for lunch. Vernelle has switched from sandwiches and soup to a "lighter" menu. Today it's Italian meatballs smothered with pizza sauce and mozzarella cheese on hoagie rolls, to be heated in the microwave. Little Tupperware containers hold sliced fruit and vegetables.

Jack takes a bite of his sandwich and heaves a deep sigh. "Garrett's going to blow up like a balloon from eating Vernelle's food after they get married."

I have to agree. "I'll put in a word with Vernelle. Maybe you can help plan her menu when she opens her bistro."

Jack doesn't give much more than a grunt. He's obviously more interested in real food than a hypothetical bistro menu.

As we munch our way through today's lunch, I tell Jack what I learned at the *Chronicle*, especially about the pen-knife with initials and blood on it. "It's exactly what the one little boy in the mirror was using to whittle with, remember?"

He frowns. "Are you sure the article said 'penknife'? Not a pocket- or a jackknife? A penknife is fairly small. I think they were used to sharpen quill pens in the past—don't know where I got that idea, but it sounds reasonable. I'd have a hard time believing anyone could kill four people with a penknife."

I snag a long string of mozzarella from my chin and pop it into my mouth. "Again, I think the scene in the mirror indicates that it wasn't the murder weapon." Even ghosts wouldn't play around with a murder weapon, I want to add—but wisely don't.

"Either way, there was blood on it," Jack says objectively, "but whose? Maybe that little kid cut himself whittling."

"And maybe the killer was smart enough to leave the pen-knife there as a clue."

Mouth full, Jack nods, and by mutual, unspoken agreement, we switch the topic of our conversation to the house. Jack will be done with the bathroom soon, and I plan to concentrate on painting the bedrooms. It's odd to think that the house will be finished before summer arrives.

Still, the murders are never far from my mind. As Jack stands up to clear the table, I tell him, "I'm going into town around three to chat with an old teacher of mine who knew the Millers." I see Jack's look. "It's just something I have to do, though I admit sometimes I think about these murders too much."

Before I can say anything else, Jack leans down and kisses me long and hard on the lips. "There," he says with satisfaction as he draws back, "that'll give you something else to think about."

He goes out the door, leaving me speechless. But I liked the kiss—I liked it a lot.

It takes me a while to switch from the dreamy state of a fifteen-year-old after her first kiss to that of a dedicated painter.

I decide to paint the pink bedroom upstairs next—time to change that horrendous shade to "Subtle Sand." It takes me a few trips to move all the paint stuff upstairs because I keep forgetting what I'm doing.

I'm heading for the stairs with my last load when I notice the mirror. Except for the black blob in the corner, it's in fine form with the usual scene like a full-color family portrait.

For the first time I pay more attention to Ben, his fine features, the sweet smile as he faces Audrey. Of course he hadn't committed suicide out of guilt. Instead, he was caught in the anguish of being blamed for Audrey's horrible death—and facing life without her.

On an impulse, I go to the mirror. I look from it to the items on the mantel. I touch the jar of marbles and the sugar bowl. "Hey," I say to the people in the mirror, "remember me, your cousin Abby? I'm back. I finally understand what you've been trying to tell me.

"And Ben, I know that you're innocent. I'll do everything I can to make sure every single person in Mt. Prospect knows it, too. I promise." I pause, then add as I turn away, "Just so you know."

Then, it's back to painting.

Not much gets done because of interruptions.

First, Vernelle and Garrett turn up. Vernelle found some curtains at a resale place and thinks they'll be perfect for the living room once they're hemmed. This means that Garrett has to stand on the stepladder holding the curtains up against the window. Vernelle alternately critiques the curtains ("not bad") and Garrett (as whispered to me, "Yummy!"). Honestly, it's a relief when they leave.

Then the geezers come for their final checks. They grin as they thank me for the sacks of Twinkies and 7-Up. I hate to say good-bye and promise to call them when I need someone for odd jobs. They've been a comfort to have around, and each gives me a hug on the way out. Who'd have thought?

When she arrives, Marge is happy with her final check but doubtful about the chocolate chip cookies. Once again, she reminds me that she doesn't eat snacks. But she graciously accepts the fragrant sack, saying she'll give them to her sister-in-law, Agnes.

When I tell Jack about it on my way out, he gives a big guffaw and bets the cookies won't make it into town. He's probably right. He also gives me a wink that makes me turn red. Maybe he's still thinking about that kiss; I know I am.

# CHAPTER 37

Mrs. Mayes' assisted living apartment is in a long brick building that looks more like a nice motel. Saying she'll meet me in the sitting room, Mrs. Mayes buzzes me into the foyer. I'm not sure if they're trying to keep the rabble-rousers inside the building or out.

The empty foyer is as quiet as a cemetery, though maybe that's not a good comparison in these circumstances. From what I can see, the dark furniture, cushy taupe carpets, and elaborate flower arrangements give the dining and sitting rooms a kind of funeral splendor—getting a head start, so to speak.

Mrs. Mayes doesn't seem to mind. Ensconced in a maroon wing chair in the sitting room, she looks even tinier than before. In fact, her feet don't quite touch the floor. With her white permed curls and powdery complexion, Mrs. Mayes reminds me of a diminutive elderly queen. But her greeting is genuinely friendly, and she pats a nearby chair as if in anticipation of a cozy chat.

A blond woman in a flowered smock brings in a tray loaded with a teapot, cups, and fancy cookies, which she places in easy reach. Mrs. Mayes introduces her as Jody Davis, an aide, and adds in a loud whisper, "They like to keep us happy here with good food." Ms. Davis, who looks like she can keep old people in line without having to resort to food rewards, gives her a fond smile and pats her arm as she leaves.

Mrs. Mayes doesn't waste any time getting back into the teacher mode. "Do you still like *Pride and Prejudice*?" she asks as she pours out the tea and passes the cookies.

I laugh with surprise. "I do. I reread it every few years. I've read Jane Austen's other novels, too, but I like *Pride and Prejudice* best."

She sighs. "I think you were the only sophomore girl I could talk into reading it. Another girl said she'd read it, but she also said she'd just finished *Moby Dick*, so I had my doubts." There's no segue to the next topic; I almost drop my cup when Mrs. Mayes adds, "So, what is it you want to know about the Millers, dear?"

Somehow I manage not to slosh my tea into my lap. "I've seen them—in pictures, that is—but I'd like a better sense of what they were really like as people."

"They enjoyed being together. They were a happy family." Her milky blue eyes waver sadly. "That makes what happened so unbelievable. But the murders didn't seem to bother Alice—Miss Bryant—after she moved there. Loved the old house, she did. She claimed she was never lonesome, but I often wondered. She did get a little odd toward the end."

She pauses thoughtfully, and I want to ask her if she ever mentioned seeing people in the mirror, but decide it wouldn't be polite. Mrs. Mayes lets out a long sad sigh before continuing. "Anyway, Alice and I taught together for years. She was older, an established teacher by the time I got a job at the high school, but we became good friends."

She peers at the cookies. Apparently, her eyesight is good enough to pick out the fancy macaroons. "But about the Millers. As I said, I grew up on a farm across the field. I was older than Audrey, but I had two younger brothers who loved playing with the twins. My brothers went there often during the summer, and I'd walk them home.

"Audrey was quiet, but nice. I usually stayed an hour or so, and we'd play records or look through her movie magazines. Her mother, Nancy, was busy with things like gardening or sewing clothes for Audrey. She was a sweet person."

"I've always heard that about her. What was Ed like?"

"No one in town liked him much. He had an awfully hot temper. But he was usually working at the bank when we were around. He was real tight with the Trimbles, you know. I do remember that he was very attractive—tall and blond, like all the Millers. You could see where Audrey got her good looks—you, too, dear. There's definitely a family resemblance."

I tell Mrs. Mayes that I've heard about the resemblance, and ask if she had Audrey as a student.

"Oh my, no—I'm not that old! But Alice had her in class and was very upset. As a teacher, you just don't think one of your students would ever kill another one."

"So even the teachers believed Ben was the killer?"

Mrs. Mayes shrugs. "Most people just accepted it. As I remember, the Stocktons lived in a dilapidated old farmhouse down the road from Audrey's folks. The dad was an alcoholic, but the mom managed to hold things together. It was that kind of family.

"Ben was an only child. I never heard anything bad about him, until that terrible murder. And he hanged himself, didn't he? I was away at college by then, but of course I came home for the funerals. It was a relief to everyone when it was all over."

I lean a little closer to her. "Mrs. Mayes, did you ever hear of a boy at school named Terence Trimble? He would have been a senior when Audrey was a sophomore."

Her lips draw back from her cup in distaste. "Oh my, yes. Though I don't think he ever graduated. The other students didn't like him much, but being a Trimble, he always had plenty of money and a fancy car. Some gravitate to that kind of person."

Ms. Davis comes bustling in again, refilling the cookie plate and adding hot water to the teapot. Mrs. Mayes thanks her and goes on, while the aide straightens the already neat room. "According to Alice, Terence was the worst kind of bully. Back then, it was physical stuff, not comments on Facebook or something like now. He mostly picked on younger and smaller students when no one was looking. He'd terrorize them in the halls, but he was worse down in the locker-rooms—no cameras in those days."

"Couldn't anyone—say the principal—do anything about it?"

"They didn't do much about bullying back then, though I'm sure some people tried. It was up to the older boys, the seniors, to straighten out anyone who acted like that. But even those big senior boys were afraid of Terence."

She starts to chuckle. "Alice told about one time when Terence finally got his comeuppance. It seems that some of his usual victims collected manure—human manure, that is—in a paper bag and squished it in one of the books in Terence's locker!"

"Good heavens!" My voice is a good deal louder than I'd meant, and Jody knocks over something then apologizes for the noise. I'd forgotten she was even in the room.

I turn back to Mrs. Mayes. "That must have smelled awful! I'll bet the kids got a good laugh out of it, though."

Mrs. Mayes shakes her head vehemently. "Not at all. It happened before the first bell, and the students were standing around, but not one cracked a smile. Terence gave out a roar like an angry bull—those were Alice's exact words—and looked ready to attack, but everyone just watched in dead silence until he ran off to the principal's office."

I slide my empty cup back onto the tray. "I guess the kids finally did get even then, but it's funny—I don't remember ever hearing anything like that."

"It happened long before your time, dear, though it's still a legend in the teacher's lounge, believe me. No one was ever punished. Alice said Audrey and her friends were watching, but they wouldn't have done anything like that. Ben either. And then, of course, the murders happened a day or two later, so the story faded quickly."

"Still," I venture, "Terence must have been the laughing stock of the school for a while."

She frowns. "Well, not that Alice ever said. Anyway, the teachers were the only ones who called him Terence. He'd beat up any student who called him that."

"Really? And what did the kids call him?"

"Why Junior, of course. He was always known as Junior."

*Junior. Junior Trimble. J.T!*

\*\*\*

It shouldn't have been hard to locate my silver car among all the beige Buicks in the parking lot, but my head was spinning too fast to see or think clearly. I locate it and lean against it, thinking back over my visit with Mrs. Mayes. She dispensed a lot more than tea and cookies. Along with a wealth of other information, she'd confirmed that Terence Trimble is our mysterious JT. (I can hear Vernelle crowing already.)

And when I'd asked her, almost as an afterthought, whether Junior ever did anything to the girls at school, she'd answered, "Well, Alice did mention that he 'bothered' the girls sometimes, whatever that means. I think 'creepy' was the term she used for him."

I'm suddenly reminded of the face in the yearbook. "Creepy" is the term I'd definitely use for Junior—and I'm not sixteen.

# CHAPTER 38

Vernelle is home early. She's interested to hear what Mrs. Mayes had to say and comments, "I knew it was that freaky Trimble!" But it's obvious she has other things on her mind.

When she suggests that we enjoy what's left of the spring afternoon, I follow her outside to the patio. We brush the dead leaves from the bench so we can sit down, and I try to erase all the thoughts crowding my mind (Jack's kiss, Junior, Jack's kiss) in order to concentrate on what Vernelle's saying.

"Burdett called me again today. He wants my decision on the building we talked about—the one that would be perfect for my bistro. I can let it go—there'll be another along sometime—but I wanted to see what you think first." Vernelle's hands are clutched together in her lap, and she looks at me expectantly.

I decide a business-like approach is best. "Have you looked this building over? Some of those downtown buildings are old. You don't want to buy a money pit, Sis."

Vernelle relaxes enough to smile. "Garrett and I and a builder he knows went over it pretty thoroughly. It was a bar for years— remember Squeaky's Tap? —they served sandwiches and shit, so the basics are there. The owners are even throwing in the contents of the building, tables and chairs and shit like that. With a little elbow grease, it'll be perfect."

"The sale of the house would pay for the building?"

Her eyes are shining. "It would cover most of it, Abby, depending. And Garrett said he could help—"

I pull my jacket more closely around me; the April breeze is still cool. "I'll leave that between you two. Come up with the price you want for the house, and I'll write you a check. The Bank of Brad will be happy to finance your new business. Maybe you could name it "Brad's Place."

She's laughing as she hugs me. "Not a chance."

Vernelle's excited chatter fills the evening, but she's already in bed when there's a knock at the back door—a strange occurrence for this time of night. I'm pretty sure it's not the UPS guy, so I flip on the porch light and peer cautiously out.

Standing back in the shadows is a woman. It takes me a moment to recognize the aide from the assisted living facility. "Jody! I didn't hear a car," I say as I open the door.

Jody takes a step forward. "I left it down the block. It wouldn't be worth my job if anyone saw me here." I open the door wider, and she shakes her head. "No, I can't come in, but I brought you something. I heard you talking to Mrs. Mayes this afternoon. You wouldn't guess it, but I'm related to the Trimbles—a second cousin once removed or something."

She pauses and looks around before going on. "My mother was a close friend of Junior's sister, Margaret—Maggie, everyone called her. She moved out to California, but she gave my mother her diary before she left. She thought somebody ought to have it, just not her. It brought back too many bad memories.

"When I heard what you were saying, I thought you might be interested in the truth. So I copied off some of the pages. It doesn't matter what you do with them—publish them in the *New York Times* for all I care. Just don't tell Tom Trimble where you got them."

I can see the folded pages in her hand. "It never occurred to me that someone would have kept a diary!"

She shrugs. "Maggie wrote down what happened at their house the night of the murders, and she kept it a secret. Old man Trimble threatened to put her mother into an insane asylum if they ever breathed a word about what they knew. He would have, too. He was a real bastard. But it bothered Maggie that people thought the boyfriend was the murderer. He wasn't—you'll see." She thrusts the papers into my hands and disappears into the night.

I close the door and sit down at the kitchen table. For a moment, the words on the paper waver before my eyes. Then I find the right date, April 15th and begin to read the shaky handwriting. According to the diary, Margaret and her mother were in the kitchen when Junior burst through the back door, holding a knife in one hand. His clothes were soaked in blood. When he described what he'd done to Audrey and her family, "he was like a monster," she writes, "a horrible monster, waving the bloody knife at us and laughing."

Margaret and her mother were afraid of Terence, but they wanted to call the sheriff. Tom Senior had other ideas. He ordered the women upstairs, and (Margaret guessed) made Terence, aka Junior, clean up while he got rid of the bloody clothes—and the knife.

Later, on an upstairs extension, Margaret listened as Tom Senior talked to a doctor somewhere in Missouri. Then throughout the night, she and her mother huddled together as crying and yelling went on downstairs as Terence and his father argued. The next morning, they were both gone.

I turn to the last entry in the diary, "I don't think I'm ever going to see my brother again."

Was she sorry—or relieved? I can't tell. But the last three words on the page hit me hard, "That poor family."

# CHAPTER 39

In the morning, as Vernelle gets ready for work, we discuss the diary pages. Before I show them to Ambrosia, Vernelle's advice is to consult with the sheriff's office first. So I make the call and schedule an appointment with Marv.

Later, I enter the Sheriff's Department, which is located in the basement of the Grant County Court House. Marv spots me as I tentatively enter and ushers me back into his office. Well, it's not much of an office, more of a desk crowded with what looks like old computer parts. He pulls a chair out for me and then sits in a swivel chair behind his desk.

I gesture toward the outer office. "I didn't see anyone around who looks too young to shave—that's how Ambrosia Swann described your sheriff."

"Del's not back yet from his vacation in Arizona." A grin spreads across Marv's face. "Don't pay no mind to Ambrosia. She's not particularly fond of our young sheriff. He crossed her once and lived to tell about it—but that's a whole 'nother story.

"I'm guessing you're not here to talk about Del. Since you've been to the newspaper, I expect you want more information about our famous murders."

I admit that I do and ask again for a quick look into the old files as there are still a couple of things that puzzle me.

Marv leans back in his chair and shakes his head with a great show of regret. "Now we already discussed that, Miz Bennett. But since I've always had an interest in the Miller case, I guess I'm probably the official expert on it these days. Exactly what puzzles you?"

"The murder weapon. The only one mentioned in the articles was a small pen-knife. Was that it?"

"Sheriff Wendt thought so—an opinion not universally shared, I've gotta add. He never found another weapon, probably didn't look much, but the autopsy indicated those knife wounds were never made by a little ol' penknife. They were too deep and wide. Good question, Abby. What else?"

"Ambrosia said the sheriff didn't conduct a very thorough investigation. I think the words she used for him were 'old' and 'incompetent.' What's your take on that? It's a pretty serious accusation."

"Well," he continues with his wide grin, "Ambrosia never had a good word to say about Buddy. He might've been old, but he wasn't incompetent. In fact, he was pretty sharp.

"But Buddy's biggest sin was laziness—and Hamm's Beer, maybe. Why waste time dusting for prints or looking around outside when you've got the murderer at the crime scene? And with his initials on the murder weapon—it doesn't get much better than that! Buddy and his deputies—they were mostly his redneck relatives—didn't do a whole lot more than take a few pictures out there that night. A real good lawyer, with a jury from another county, could have got that kid off scot-free. What else do you want to know?"

I take a deep breath. "Marv, I might as well just come out and tell you. I don't believe Ben Stockton murdered the family. And I have some pretty convincing proof to back me up."

I don't expect Marv to fall off his chair, but he sits up straight and his grin disappears in a flash. "My first question is 'What kind of proof?' and the second is, 'Why do you care?' "

If I told Marv about the ghosts in the mirror, I'd be the one in a cell—a padded one. Instead, I prevaricate just a little. "I don't like to see someone—even a dead someone—blamed for something he didn't do. I've got copies of my 'proof' with me in this file."

He reaches out an impatient hand. "Jesus, why didn't you say so?"

I pass him Audrey's note and the diary pages and watch as he scans them. Then he tosses them on his desk. "Hell. Where'd you get this stuff after all these years?"

"The note I found in a textbook of Audrey's. A Trimble relative gave me the copies of Margaret's diary." He nods, and I can tell by his face he knows immediately who that relative is. "Do you have trouble believing Junior was the murderer?"

"Nope. There've always been rumors." Marv is more willing to talk now. "In fact, Junior's name did come up in the investigation, such as it was, after the Stockton kid's death. I guess he was involved in some pretty nasty stuff at the high school—something to do with the Miller girl—like her note says. But Junior was already gone. It's true that old man Trimble took him to a psychiatric hospital in Kansas City. And as you can guess, the family all swore he'd been home the night of the murders."

He strokes his long narrow chin considering. I wait to see if he'll tell me anything more, which he does. "Now, Sheriff Wendt was a poker buddy of Tom Senior's, but he wasn't real fond of the kid.

There'd already been some complaints that Junior's old man had managed to hush up. I remember hearing that Junior partly buried a neighbor's cat one time and then ran over its head with a lawn mower. That should have been a red flag for anybody.

"But as you can tell from the diary, Tom Senior wasn't taking any chances. He had a fancy doctor looking after Junior, and he had a fancy lawyer lined up just in case. The kid was tucked away somewhere, and nobody could get at him—unless they had some kind of evidence, which they didn't."

I gather up the note and diary pages. "So Junior's father covered up the murders of four people. That's beyond belief! What happened to Junior? Did he ever come back to Mt. Prospect?"

Marv gives a snort. "His sister was right when she thought she'd never see Junior again. Terence didn't even make it to his next birthday. He died of appendicitis down there at the clinic. I suspect if it hadn't been that, it would have been something else. Junior was too dangerous for old Tom Senior to deal with."

He pauses and gestures toward my "proof." "That's the first new evidence to come out in sixty years. I'd like it for the file. Then when Sheriff Simmons gets back—"

I'm reluctant to hand over my evidence to just sit in a cold case file, never to be looked at again. But Marv offers to make copies of everything for me. While he runs copies on a machine that looks like it's from the nineties, I ask, "Do you think the case could be reopened? I'd like to find a way of proving Ben innocent."

Marv shakes his head. "There's not much use even trying, since everyone concerned is dead. And there's no physical evidence from the murder scene that would even place Junior there that night."

"What if I took my proof to a judge?" I put the copies of the note and diary pages back in my file.

"It would be the District Attorney. But it don't matter. The courts are so clogged with live-people cases, I doubt they'd take on any dead-people ones. No, if you really want people to know the truth, I think your best bet is Ambrosia. The anniversary of the murders is coming up, and it would make one hell of a story."

I consider the idea for a moment, but worry about the consequences. No matter how distantly related—I figure Terence was Tom's uncle or some such thing—he was a Trimble. And the Tom Trimble who now thinks he runs this town because he owns the bank isn't likely to take any besmirching of the family name without retaliation. Finally, I confide my thoughts to Marv. "I'd be worried for Ambrosia. Tom won't let something like this go by."

Marv shrugs his narrow shoulders. "The worst he could do would be to pull the bank's advertising from Ambrosia's paper. Maybe lean on a few of the town businesses to do the same, but that wouldn't stop her. She's about the only person in this town who can stand up to Tom."

I sigh with disappointment. It all feels so anti-climactic. "I guess, I'll go over there and let her make copies of all this."

He sets his hands on his hips and shakes his head slowly. "You want my advice, pretend you're a lawyer. Build up a case for the Stockton kid's innocence and Junior's guilt. Then go to Ambrosia. She'll go for it, I guarantee."

"I suppose you're right; I'll try. But I really wanted some kind of legal ruling." Then I brighten. "But, even if all this fails, Ben is still innocent. I guess he doesn't need a lawyer in heaven to prove that."

Marv smirks. "Hon, take my word for it—there aren't any lawyers in heaven."

# CHAPTER 40

After talking to Marv, I stop by the newspaper office to discuss the possibilities of *The Chronicle* running an article about what I've discovered. Unfortunately, Ambrosia is out of town for a couple of days—a huge let down. Trying to keep my voice coolly professional, I leave her a message, then head out to the house. It's afternoon by the time I'm ready to continue my anti-ugly pink-quest, and the first look is discouraging.

I didn't get much painting done yesterday, and it's clear that the walls should have been primed first (I'm learning the lingo) because the pink shows maddeningly through everywhere. It simply won't go away. For sure the room will need two coats; I'm just hoping it won't need three.

I dip my roller into the paint and have managed one half-hearted swipe when a loud "harrumph" interrupts my pity party. I whirl around to see Jack leaning against the doorframe, watching me sympathetically. "I've seen people in a dentist's waiting room with more enthusiasm than you've got there."

"Hey, Jack." I grin, thinking I'd be a lot more enthused if I could just paint *him*. "I am pretty tired of painting," I admit, making another half-hearted swipe, "but I've got to get this room finished. This pink is just awful."

He glances at the wall I'm working on. "They shouldn't sell Pepto-Bismol by the gallon. Anyway, I stopped by to let you know that I'm done with the bathroom. I'd stay here to help you, but I have to meet a client about a new table in a few minutes."

I nod, and Jack clears his throat again. "What are you doing Friday night?"

I look at him questioningly.

"Give me a break here, Abby. A date, I'm asking you out on a date! Would you rather go to an art exhibit at the university in Iowa City or to a barbeque place that has a band?"

This cheers me immediately, and I jump up to join him in the doorway. "I'd like to do them both! How about if we go to the art exhibit first and then eat at the barbeque place?"

Jack laughs. "I've never seen you move that fast."

He leans over to kiss me, but I still have my paint roller in one hand. "Watch out—I'll get paint on you!"

"A little paint never hurt anybody."

After another kiss or two (maybe more), I follow Jack down to say good-bye. In the living room, the mirror draws our attention like a magnet. I gasp. Jack lets loose an expletive I've never heard come out of his mouth, even when he dropped a sheet of plywood on his foot. The "face" at the bottom of the mirror has grown bigger and creepier—if that's possible. Even without the yearbook page, I'd know who it is.

"Junior," I whisper.

Jack glances from the mirror to me. "What's going on besides that ugly face? Can you see anything else in there?"

I reach out and touch the cool glass. "Yeah, the others don't look any different. But I've never seen the mirror like this before. It's scary—it's like Junior's gaining some kind of power."

Jack glances at his watch.

"You go ahead to see your client," I tell him. When he hesitates, I add, "I'll be fine, really. It's just a mirror."

"I still say you should destroy it," Jack grumbles. When I tell him I couldn't do that, he suggests, "Then get rid of it. Have Ace and Tuffy haul it away."

"I'll think about it," I say to appease him. His concern makes me feel good and I confess, "It's not spirits I'm worried about. If Tom Trimble gets wind that I've got evidence implicating a relative of his..." I throw my hands up to indicate that I have no idea what he might do.

Jack puts his hands on my shoulders. "Make sure you lock the door after me. And you have your phone with my number, right?"

"It's always in my pocket."

I watch as he drives away. Then, giving a last puzzled glance at the mirror, I run back upstairs. With renewed enthusiasm, I load a roller of "Subtle Sand" and start painting. It's easy to forget about the mirror for now. A date—Jack has actually asked me out on a date! My first for real date in—what—ten years? Eleven?

I'm thinking about what I'm going to wear (What do I have that's dressy enough for an art exhibit but casual enough for a barbeque?) when I have a feeling that someone is watching me. I slowly put the roller down and look around the room, though I know there can't be anyone else in the house. Then out of the corner of my eye, I catch a glimpse of movement in the doorway.

It's not much more than a swish of air or maybe a shadow, but my hands go instantly clammy. With a pounding heart, I shove the roller and paint-brush into plastic bags, slam the lid on the paint can, and leave the room—fast.

There's no one in the hallway, but the door to another bedroom is partly open, and again I have the feeling that someone—or something—is watching me. It can't be, of course it can't be, but I don't have the nerve to look inside the room to make sure.

With a last glance behind me, I run down the stairs and out the front door. When I reach my car, I make the mistake of looking back at the house. Are those eyes staring at me from one of the upstairs windows? Or is it just my imagination at work again?

I'm taking deep breaths to calm myself when I hear a vehicle on the road. I turn to see Tom Trimble's SUV pull into the drive, blocking my car in. With the presence of someone filming a movie scene, Tom steps slowly out of his big Escalade. He has on a black cowboy hat and fancy snakeskin boots, which seems only fitting.

"Howdy, Ms. Bennett, looks like you've been busy tarting up your little house again. In a hurry to leave, are you?"

I glance at my watch. "I was supposed to meet Jack here five minutes ago."

He looks down the road. "Doesn't look like your redneck buddy is going to make it."

"Jack just went to the lumber yard; he'll be back any minute."

Tom relaxes, leaning against his door and watching me. His eyes are cold and nearly colorless, like puddles of frozen ditchwater. "Don't worry about me. I'm here on a friendly little visit, on the way to one of my farms where I have a pond. I like to take a weed eater to trim off the brush around it this time of year. When it's dry enough, I'll make a nice little pile and burn it. I always have a can of gasoline with me just in case. I like fires." His voice pauses momentarily.

When I don't answer, he gestures down the road to where the Stockton place once stood. "When that murdering scum-bag's family moved years ago, my daddy bought the house and burned it to ashes. These old houses burn real easy, you know. Then, you take a backhoe to what's left and bury it. Now we raise corn on that ground, and you'd never know it was ever there."

I stubbornly refuse to react.

"I hear you're getting real friendly with Burdett and Ambrosia Swann. I'm here to suggest you don't cook up a bunch of lies about what happened out here and go spreading them around town."

This is too much, seeing him stand there cool as you please after what Trimble Senior did all those years ago. "I don't have to cook up lies. Your family has let years pass with people still blaming Ben Stockton for what Junior did. People deserve to know the truth, and I'm going to find a way to let the whole town know what really happened."

I regret the words as soon as they come out. I've said too much. Though his expression hasn't changed, there is murder in his eyes— apparently that's not just a phrase.

"Ben's dead, and people don't deserve shit." Tom's voice is icy. He considers me like you would when looking at a nasty bug you're about to step on. "But I'm real curious to know why you think Junior had anything to do with those murders."

I refuse to answer.

Tom's big body tenses, and his voice changes. "Has Jody Davis been spreading lies again? She likes to tell people she's related to us Trimbles, but her whole family's trash. If she's involved in this, I'll make sure that crummy job of hers at the old folks home is history."

"I found a note of Audrey's." My coldness matches his. "She said that Junior was threatening her. It doesn't take much of a leap to figure out he's the killer. I hear he was a real mental case. Did you know he once mowed off a cat's head? That's one uncle you can be real proud of," I say, taking my best guess at their relationship.

Tom's features twist into a sneer. "You don't know what you're talking about. Junior was my older brother, not my uncle. He wasn't even really named after my daddy. He was just big and fat and strutted around trying to look like my daddy, so that's what everyone called him—Junior Trimble.

"After Junior died, my daddy wanted to make sure he had another son to carry on his name. I don't suppose Ma was very happy to participate, though."

Tom rubs his chin thoughtfully. "You have to understand what our name means in this town. We own the bank and a lot of property, but it's not just that. People look up to us—they respect the Trimble name. And you're trying to drag it through mud—for nothing that matters!"

Tom looks at the house for a moment and then turns back to me. "I was real sorry to hear what happened to you out in California. About your boys, too."

"Don't you dare say anything about my sons!" White hot rage I had no idea was bottled up inside me explodes. First, he threatens Jody's job. Now he's threatening my efforts to get my boys back. I call him a series of names Vernelle would be shocked to hear come from my mouth.

Tom's eyes go wide. He raises his hands and looks at me as if I've gone crazy. "Didn't mean to get you so upset, little lady. I mean you got burned pretty bad yourself, didn't you?"

His gentle tone doesn't quite mask the threat. I should let it go, because people like him just get meaner when they're challenged. Instead, I hold up my left hand, with its mottled, puckered skin and stump of a little finger. And I turn my left side toward him and push back my hair.

"Yes, I got burned, Mr. Trimble. Do you want me to go through that again, so my right side matches my left? Because I want you to know that fire doesn't scare me anymore. It's taken almost everything away from me already. But if you set this house, or me, on fire, I will come back to get you. I know you go to the Methodist Church. You'd better sit in the front pew, because that's the only place you'll be safe from me and the hellfire I've already been through."

Tom stares at me for a long moment. If he is searching for words, they're not coming easily to him. "You bitch," he finally hisses and turns back to his SUV.

After his vehicle swings out of the driveway and down the road, I lean limply against my car. I've never lost my temper like that. Worse, much of what I told Tom is a lie. I can hardly see a lit match without feeling the searing flames eating at me, scorching my body and melting my clothing into the very pores of my skin. I expect that on some deep level, Tom Trimble knows it. *What was I thinking?*

# CHAPTER 41

As soon as I walk in the door, I can tell that Vernelle has some important news. She's practically bursting with anticipation. She waits until I sit down at the table with a glass of milk and a blueberry muffin and then can contain herself no longer.

Garrett has asked her to visit his parents in Dubuque for the weekend. They'll leave after Vernelle gets off work Friday. Even more impressive, this is all relayed without a single word that would make a Sunday school teacher blush. An engagement can't be far off.

Hearing her chatter on excitedly about Garrett and his family, there's no way I can ruin her starry-eyed bliss by telling her about Tom's latest "visit." I haven't seen her this happy in years. Besides, to be honest, I haven't really processed everything myself. It occurs to me she might not like me bringing the evidence I have to Ambrosia for publication in the local paper. She'll probably worry that I can't handle the stress.

Surprisingly, I don't want to tell her about my date with Jack, either. It's a little secret that I hug to myself as she decides to spend the evening having a bake-fest. It's a way to use up her excess energy—and she has a lot of it. There are at least three new muffin recipes she wants to try. She'll save the best ones for Garrett's parents. No doubt it'll be love at first sight—or bite.

***

The next morning, I tell Vernelle that I'm taking a couple of days off from painting as there are some things I need to catch up on. She doesn't see the need to paint anymore anyway since I'm going to buy the house from her. ("You'll want different colors, Abby. You know you will!") My reply is that I can't very well leave a room only halfway done. It's the principle of the thing.

But I do need a couple of days to regroup, so to speak. Plus, there's important business to take care of. After Tom's unnerving visit last night—not to mention his threat—I have to make sure Ben Stockton's name is truly cleared, not just for me, but for Mt. Prospect.

As soon as Vernelle leaves, I give the *Chronicle* a call to find out when Ambrosia will be back. "Tomorrow for sure," they tell me, so I leave another message for her asking to set up a meeting time.

Then, I settle myself in the den and fire up Vernelle's old computer. It seems to work pretty well, in spite of having a hard-drive crammed (no doubt) with recipes.

To give myself some inspiration, I place on the desk the teapot that matches the sugar bowl I found in the house. Then I spread out my "proof" and get to work.

I'm not a reporter, but I guess I'll have to become one. I'll write the article from the viewpoint of a Miller family member who wanted to solve the mystery of what really happened that night. It becomes the story of two young men, one accused of the murders sixty years ago, and the one who cold-bloodedly carried them out . . .

My fingers fly across the keys. The hours pass as I relate the facts as I discovered them: Audrey's note in the textbook in the attic, Mrs. Mayes' information about Junior, and Maggie's diary pages. The origin of the diary pages is a little tricky as I can't give Jody's name, but their authenticity won't be much in doubt when Ambrosia reads them.

Using facts from the newspaper articles, I want to tell how the events that night must have unfolded—not as the sheriff thought—but as they really happened. Then my fingers hesitate. It feels as if Audrey is looking over my shoulder, so it's difficult to put words describing those moments of terror on the black-and-white computer screen. But it's Ben's story, too, and since he can't write the words about his innocence, I have to do it for him.

After the article is finished, I spend more time revising and editing—good thing I'm not a reporter with a deadline. When I hear Vernelle's car pulling into the garage, I save, print and close down the computer. I plan to tell her everything and ask her to proofread my attempt at a newspaper article, but catch a typo in the first paragraph. *Damn, how can that be?*

On second thought, maybe now isn't the best time anyway. I don't want her worrying about how Tom Trimble is going to react while she's visiting Garrett's parents. Let her enjoy the weekend. We can talk about everything, including my article, when she gets back. Maybe I'm shielding Vernelle a little too much. But isn't that what big sisters are supposed to do?

# CHAPTER 42

The next day, Vernelle leaves the house mumbling about what all she has to get done before she can leave tomorrow. Since I seem to hear the words "pedicure" and "hair stylist," it's pretty certain that Clarence is at the c-a-s-i-n-o again.

I proofread what I wrote, make corrections and print out copies for both Ambrosia and Marv. After dropping off a copy for Marv, who's out on patrol at the moment, I head for the *Chronicle*.

Ambrosia is waiting for me. I don't know her well enough to read her expression as I sit across from her and take out my file. Perhaps it's partly anticipation, partly doubt. I feel like a student handing in a final exam to a tough professor. Maybe she won't like what I wrote; maybe she won't even think it's worth printing.

I push the file across to Ambrosia. She shoves on a pair of glasses with frames as red as her hair and starts reading. Time slows. I can hear the clock ticking, traffic going by, the sounds of the printing office behind us. Then she looks over the diary pages and Audrey's note.

Ambrosia looks up. "My God," is all she says for a moment. "Junior." She stares out the window for a long time before she turns back to me. "Despite the rumors, I never expected anything like this. Does Tom know?"

"He knows about Audrey's note. I think he suspects there's more than that. He definitely knows I think Junior was the murderer. He's also apparently heard that I've been here at the paper. He threatened me about making any of this public."

She nods, her eyes taking on a steely color. "He would." She tosses the file back to me, and I stare at her in dismay. Ambrosia goes on briskly. "If I publish this—after I do some checking of my own— will you be ready for the consequences? I'm not sure what they'll be, but for Tom, the Trimble name is everything. Look what he and his father, the Great Thomas Trimble Senior, have already done to keep this secret."

I think of my ghosts in the mirror and release a shaky breath. "I'm sure I want to go ahead with this. The story should be told— the true story. How about you?"

For the first time, Ambrosia smiles. "Don't worry about me," she says. "The anniversary of the murders is coming up, and this will be a scoop—one hell of a scoop."

\*\*\*

On Friday morning, Vernelle's packed and gone before my morning Cheerios have a chance to get soggy. With my new resolve (and principles) still going strong, I'm on my way to the house on an April day so bright I have to put on sunglasses. Now it's easy to think that feeling of being watched the other day was my imagination. It's just an empty old house in the country—with a weird mirror.

And the pink room is just a pink room that needs to be painted—and I'm loaded for bear. I carry the big cooler through the house and up the stairs (I'll have muscles like a weight-lifter before long), then make sure all the doors and windows are locked. No use making it easy for Tom to sneak in and catch me by surprise.

As I return to Audrey's room, I find myself closing all the doors along the hall. Maybe I'm more creeped out than I want to admit. I shut myself in with enough food and water (Vernelle's parting gift) that I won't have to leave until I'm done. Two gallons of paint and new rollers crouch in the corner. Loaded for bear, as I said.

Once I get started, I paint like a wild woman. By late afternoon, I've painted twice around the room—in some places, three times. I take one last swipe at a pinkish patch in a corner and stop, exhausted. Clouds are filling the sky, and the sunshine is gone. The darkness of a spring evening is closing in early. I need to get out of here and get ready for my date. It makes me smile just to think of it.

I'm starting to pack up when I hear a snuffling noise on the other side of the door. I rest the roller on the paint tray and turn to look. There's something moving along the crack under the door. Could a dog or animal have somehow gotten in? The noise, though not loud, scares me. Whatever's out there seems to know I'm in here. There's no way to lock the door. I brace my hand against it and try to think what to do.

That's when the whispering starts, and a tremor of terror runs through me. At first, there's just gibberish; then I distinctly hear the word "Audrey" in a breathy whisper.

In a panic, I lean back hard against the door, bracing my feet. Trying to sound brave, I call out, "Tom? If that's you, you're trespassing. I'm calling the sheriff."

The voice keeps whispering, "Audrey." It sounds nothing like Tom. As a matter of fact, it doesn't sound human.

The light switch is easy to reach, and I flip it off and on as fast as I can about a million times. Is Jack outside? Is it dark enough that he can see my desperate SOS? I dig my phone out of my pocket and hit his number, hoping he can get here quick.

Jack's voice comes across loud and clear. "What the hell's going on, Abby?"

"I'm at the Miller house. I need you to get me out of here!"

"Okay, okay. Calm down. I saw the lights. I'm on my way."

I swallow and try to speak more calmly. "I'm upstairs in the pink room, but there's something in the hall! For God's sake, Jack, be careful."

"I will," he says. "I've got a gun."

The whispering is mixed with weird sounds I can't identify. The prickle at the back of my neck is more than fear. It's the feeling of sensing evil. All I can think to do is pray that it can't enter the room.

I know Jack will be here in minutes, but his gun is probably useless against whatever—or whoever—is in this house. Time slows. I'm absolutely terrified and breathe a second prayer; this one to make Jack get here faster.

The whispered "Audrey" is repeated over and over, so that the words run together. Finally, with a firmness I'm far from feeling, I call out, "Is that you, Junior? Audrey isn't in here—she's hasn't been for a long time. And you've got it all wrong. I'm not Audrey. I'm Abby Bennett!"

"It" quiets for a moment, as if listening.

"I'm Abby," I repeat. But then the snuffling resumes—higher this time, up along the side of the door and then down toward the door-knob. There's a slight vibration that makes my skin crawl and stomach churn.

The crash of breaking glass downstairs shatters what's left of my composure, and I let out a scream. Footsteps come pounding up the stairs, hesitate for a moment, then head toward me. I move out of the way just before Jack bursts through the door, gun in hand. I slam the door shut behind him.

"Are you okay?" Jack shoves the gun into his jacket pocket and folds me into his arms. I can only nod. Jack's arms are tight around me, and the hall is quiet now. "Sorry, I had to break a window to get in. What's going on?"

I lean into Jack's chest and manage to control my breathing. Maybe Jack scared "it" away. "I was almost done painting up here when something started making noises out in the hall. I got scared—I'm still scared."

Jack pulls back and puts his hand on my cheek reassuringly. "Abby, the doors were locked, and there's nothing in the hall—nothing at all."

"Someone's out there," I whisper. "Someone who wants to get to me." I break away from Jack—just a little—to keep an eye on the door.

Jack frowns. "You mean, like one of your ghosts? Come on, it's getting dark and your imagination is playing tricks on you. I'll search the house if you want before we leave, but there's nothing there."

Then the snuffling begins again, and the doorknob behind us rattles. Jack whirls around and stares at it incredulously. "Jesus Christ!"

Whispered words seep under the door like a trail of fog: "AudreyAudreyAudrey."

I can tell Jack hears it because he sucks in his breath. Then we follow with our eyes as the snuffling goes back and forth along the crack under the door, a little louder each time.

The doorknob rattles again. Jack takes my hand and whispers, "Stay with me, Abby, we're getting out of here."

I pull back. "I can't go out that door, Jack. I can't!"

He looks around the room. "Well, we can't go out the window, that's for sure." Then Jack steps forward, grabbing the doorknob with one hand and hanging onto me with the other. At first, Jack can't turn the knob, but when he does, the door flies open with a bang. He pulls me out of the room and down the stairs.

Through half-closed eyes, I concentrate on not tripping. No way am I going to look around and meet a pair of glaring eyes.

Suddenly we're outside on the driveway. Without a wasted motion, Jack opens the door of his pickup and shoves me inside. When I turn to say something to him, he shakes his head. "Not now. Fasten your seatbelt."

He puts the truck into gear and doesn't even bother to back up. Instead, he guns the motor and makes a big loop right across the yard and back onto the road. It's not until we're a mile down the road that he stops the truck.

Jack turns toward me, and his dark eyes burn into mine. "What the freaking hell was that?"

"It's Junior," I whisper. "He was the killer, and he's not just in the mirror anymore. Somehow he got loose."

Jack doesn't even question my words. "He thinks you're Audrey?"

I clasp my hands together to stop them from shaking. "It must be something like that."

"My God." There's a moment of silence. "Abby, you've got to get rid of that house."

"I don't know what to do. We have it almost fixed up." I turn toward him. "I couldn't have done it without you."

"I wish I hadn't set foot in there," Jack mutters.

"Oh." I feel like crying. "I suppose you wish you hadn't met me that day at the lumberyard, either. That's how you got caught up in all this."

Jack takes my hand. "I regret a lot of things in my life, hon, but I don't regret that. Anyway, you've got to tell Vernelle what's been going on—tonight."

His warm hand is like an anchor in all this craziness, and I hold it tightly. "I can't. She's not home. She and Garrett are visiting his parents. And Jack, as much as I was looking forward to our date tonight," I start reluctantly, "I don't think...that is, I—"

"It's okay, Abby. There'll be other nights." Jack doesn't speak for a moment, considering. "Anyway, you shouldn't be alone after what just happened. You can stay the night at my place. It won't be Greasy Steve's Barbeque, but I'll rustle up a pizza or something."

"I think Junior wanted into that room because he thought Audrey was there. Maybe he's hoping for the thrill of reliving that night. But it's not like he can track me down," I say, hoping it's true. "I appreciate the offer, but I'll be fine."

The truth is, I don't really feel all that safe even though the book I checked out from the church library said spirits often attach themselves to a location. Apparently, Junior's spirit had found its way back to the site of his murder.

Jack takes a deep breath. "Abby, you might not be afraid to be home alone tonight. But after what just happened in that house, I think I am."

# CHAPTER 43

We're sitting on Jack's leather couch watching a movie. The overnight bag that I'd packed at Vernelle's is by the door, and the remains of a frozen pizza dot the paper plates on the table nearby. Spencer lies on the rug at our feet, snoozing his way through doggy dreams.

It's a comfy, domestic scene, but I couldn't tell you what the movie is about or what the pizza tasted like. Though Jack seems engrossed in the action-adventure flick, I can't keep my mind from being pulled—maybe "yanked" is a better word—back to my ghost house.

How and why did Junior get loose? Jack says that my being there has somehow changed the dynamics of the house, and I think he's right. Junior now seems to have the strength to do something—besides terrifying me I can't begin to guess what, though.

On a more selfish level, my dream of living in the house is gone. It's not remotely practical. Junior and I cannot coexist. In fact, no one can live there anymore, not with Junior's evil presence. Maybe I can talk Tom into renting the house for his brother. Just thinking how he'd react makes me smile.

Jack asks me what I'm grinning about. I'm not grinning, though I can see that the movie is one of those ridiculous James Bond action-thrillers. I just shake my head. His arm is comfortingly around me, as his attention is drawn back to an unlikely scene where Bond is jumping from one flying helicopter to another. I'd like to see how brave he'd be in my ghost house. Now *that's* scary.

After the movie's over, I shower and get ready for bed. It's by mutual agreement that I'll be sleeping in Jack's bedroom, and he'll be on the couch. If anything is going to happen between us, it won't be tonight. I can blame Junior for that, too.

Jack's bed is big and comfortable, and although he changed the sheets, I can breathe his scent from the pillow. I'm glad I'm here and not alone at Vernelle's. That horrible time with Junior is finally fading from my mind. *Christians and the Spirit World* sits in my overnight bag, but it will wait until tomorrow. Tonight, I just want to sleep. I'm so exhausted I'm sure to sleep peacefully tonight.

So I'm totally unprepared to find Jack gently shaking my shoulder. "Abby, Abby, wake up! You're screaming." When I open my eyes, the bedside lamp is on, and Jack is kneeling beside me. "Hey, it's okay—you're here at my place."

I take a shaky breath and sit up, but my heart is still pounding. "Sorry. It's just a dream I have every few weeks—my fire dream. I'm trapped in the house with flames all around me. And you know how dreams are—it seemed so real!" In my mind, I can hear the roar of the fire and the crackling of burning wood all around me." My heart starts pounding even harder; my hands become clammy.

Jack squeezes my shoulder. "You okay?"

I try to smile a little. "Yeah. I don't usually scream. Sorry."

"Don't apologize."

I shiver and catch his hand. "Can you stay with me the rest of the night? Please?" I see his hesitation. "With me, in bed? I need you, Jack." I need a warm body beside me, an alive body beside me, someone to stop that dream.

Jack nods and squeezes my hand. Then he turns off the light and climbs into bed, wrapping his strong arms around me. His body is warm and solid, his breath soft against my face. Maybe his kiss started out as a goodnight kiss, but it turns into something else. The frightening dream recedes, and it's not long before my heart is pounding for another reason, and my senses are full of Jack Allender.

After Jack's regular breaths tell me he's asleep, I lie there in the comforting dark, still in his arms. It's pitch black in the room. I am reassured, because I know in this darkness, Jack wasn't able to see that parts my body he was touching and kissing are red and scarred. So he wasn't shocked. I smile into the darkness. I hate to tell you, Brad, but you weren't much of a lover. Chloe can have you. I'll take Jack anytime.

And then I open my eyes.

Moonlight is streaming through the window right across the bed. Across me. It could as well be a searchlight. I make a sharp movement that causes Jack to stir. "It's okay, love," he murmurs, holding me tighter. "I'm still here. Go back to sleep."

# CHAPTER 44

It's bright daylight when I stumble out of the bedroom. Jack is sitting at the table and gives me a broad grin. There's no way I can't smile back. When I get near him, he pulls me onto his lap and kisses me.

"That's nice," I murmur.

He gestures toward the table. "I didn't want to leave you here while I ran into town, so maybe that will make up for the fact that I don't have any breakfast stuff around except coffee and cereal."

"Cereal's fine. I've eaten plenty of it in my day." I stop abruptly, thinking of little hands fishing spoonfuls of Fruit Loops from their bowls. It hits me that all my plans to have Hunter and Grayson in my new home are ruined. "I'm not all that hungry anyway."

"No surprise there. You had a rough night."

I don't want to talk about the house. For just a little while I want to stay in our morning-after couple's moment. So, I smile, give him a poke in the side, and say with obvious humor, "That's not what I'd call it."

His eyes crinkle. "No, it was better than an art exhibit, for sure."

I move to the chair next to him not caring that my left side is facing him. "Better than Greasy Steve's?"

He nods. "Even better than Greasy Steve's."

Jack passes me the cereal and milk then pours himself a cup of coffee. "But *that's* not what I referring to, and you know it. That was some weird ass stuff that happened, yesterday. What are you going to do?"

My good mood bursts like a balloon. Here I was just starting to believe that I could prove I was a fit mother. That I wasn't mentally unfit. And now here I am dealing with a freaking haunted house. What are the odds?

I fix my bowl of cereal, to give myself a chance to come up with an answer to Jack's question. What am I going to do? I'd rather stay here with Jack, and forget about the whole thing just for today. But I feel compelled to go back to Audrey's room to check on Junior. Maybe he's gone. And if he's not, I have to figure out a way to get rid of him.

"I guess I'd better get the window fixed," I say, still trying to avoid the subject.

"I'll fix the window, Abby." He sounds a bit exasperated and casts a suspicious eye my way. "What else do you have planned for today?"

"Well, I need to get my car," I continue firmly.

His eyes are watchful as he takes a sip of coffee. "Fine. I'll take you over to get your car—but don't go inside. After last night, I have to admit there's something evil in there. You shouldn't step foot in that place again."

"Oh Jack, what am I going to do? That was supposed to be my home."

"Sell it and buy another house. You certainly can't live there," he says matter-of-factly.

"I can't. That just wouldn't be right."

He rubs his face, then picks back up his mug of steaming black coffee and takes a sip. "Yeah, I guess there's no guarantee that *thing* in the house will just go away if you're gone."

I think back to Marge's comment about Miss Bryant seeing faces in the mirror. "That *thing* is called Junior, and I need to figure out just what's going on in that house in order to find a away to get rid of him." I chase a last errant bran flake around the bowl. "Just drop me off. I'll only be a minute; you don't even need to wait."

"Like hell." Jack growls, "I'm not letting you go in there alone. I'll go with your later, if you're going to insist on going inside."

A warm glow spreads through me, knowing Jack has assigned himself the role of my protector. He certainly was yesterday. "Fine. Just let me get my car, and I'll go talk to someone at the church about doing an exorcism."

Jack looks shocked. "Are you serious?"

"You have any better ideas?"

"Yeah, get rid of the damn mirror."

"I'm not sure that would help at this point, especially after last night. Besides, what about the Miller family?"

He shakes his head. I'm sure he's about to tell me they aren't my problem. But seeing the resolve in my face, he changes tactics. "Then just sell the house. Maybe without you there, Junior will go back to wherever he came from."

"That might work," I say noncommittally. "But if it doesn't, I should at least have a back-up plan, so I'll stop by the Methodist Church today."

Jack finishes off his coffee before he answers. "I thought only Catholics did exorcisms."

"Well, I have to start somewhere," I point out. "And the Trimbles have always been Methodists, so I'll start there."

This seems reasonable enough to me, but Jack mutters something under his breath as he pours himself another cup of coffee.

That reminds me of the book, *Christians and the Spirit World* I'd checked out. I retrieve it from my bag and show it to him. Still looking doubtful, he says, "Might be worth a try. I'll drop you off to get your car on my way into town to pick up the load of wood and supplies I ordered. You can go talk to whoever, and then we'll meet back here. Shouldn't take me long." He nudges Spencer with his foot. "I'm just hoping I can get it all into my pickup. Otherwise, I'll have to leave you at the lumberyard, old buddy." Spencer sits up but doesn't look very concerned.

Glad that's settled, I run my hand over the smooth, beautiful wood of the table. "Remember when you told me you'd made a promise to Lily? I've always wondered what it was." Then I add hurriedly, "You don't have to tell me if you don't want to."

"No, that's okay. I was going to tell you sometime." Jack takes a deep breath. "The truth is, I was the reason Lily died that day in the accident. It was my fault we were on the Interstate. So I promised her that I'd save someone else's life to make up, at least a little, for hers, that's all."

"That's a wonderful promise, Jack, but—" I pause, not knowing how to go on.

"I know what you were going to say, something like, 'How has that worked out for you?' Well, it hasn't exactly, but I was serious. When I moved here, I talked to a guy about becoming an EMT in town. They always need people. They let me go through some of the training, but that was when walking was still tricky for me. I think they were afraid I'd be some kind of liability. Now that I'm a lot better, I'm going to check it out again. As I said, I made Lily a promise, and it's one I mean to keep."

# CHAPTER 45

The little white cottage looks the same as usual on this sunny April day. Nothing hints at the bizarre events of yesterday. Even so, Jack insists that I just take my car and go. He even waits until I've pulled away before he leaves. After about a mile, he turns down the road toward the lumberyard, while I head for church.

I haven't gone very far when I hit the brakes. Here I am headed for the church, and I forgot the damn book. (Oops, sorry, *Christians in the Spiritual World.*) It takes me just a few minutes to turn around and head back to Jack's. His "secret" key in the pansy pot lets me in so I can grab the book I left on the table.

Back in the car, I glance through the book. It says that ghosts can be linked to a specific place where it has strong ties. Tell me something I don't know. Then it goes on to say the ghost can also be linked to a specific person, like Junior is to Audrey. And it can transfer that link from one person to another if the ghost becomes strong enough. That idea scares the hell out of me. As I hurriedly flip through more pages, I can almost feel Junior reading over my shoulder.

I find the chapter on getting rid of evil spirits. The first section heading I see is "Purification Through Fire." *Well, that's so not going to happen.* I skip to the next section that mainly says you need to get a knowledgeable member of the clergy involved. Okay, so what am

I going to tell this pastor who I don't even know? What if he just thinks I'm nuts?

What I need is proof, to build a case, just like the one I built for Ambrosia. But what kind of proof could I offer? A picture of a black spot on the mirror? A recording (if I can get one) of Junior? It sounds so simple. Too bad I hadn't thought to record the sounds Junior was making yesterday. I check my phone. Sure enough it has an app for that. A plan forms, but I'm not sure I'm brave enough to carry it out. Clearly, I have to give this whole idea of exorcism more thought; no wonder Jack was so doubtful. The possibility of Tom hearing about my claims of ghosts haunting the Old Miller place sends shivers down my back.

With new resolution, I head toward town and Vernelle's to do some on-line sleuthing. Maybe I'll find some ideas for gathering evidence. But as I pass the Miller house there are curtains on the windows. Curtains that weren't there a few minutes ago. I'm sure I would have noticed. My foot slams on the brakes of its own volition.

*Just a quick peek to see what's going on in there,* I tell myself as I pull into the driveway. I catch my breath, say a quick prayer, get out of the car and step onto the front porch. Maybe I really didn't notice the curtains before. Maybe Vernelle. . . ?

But no. I peer through a crack between the curtains. Inside the house is the family as I first saw them—not in the mirror, but gathered around the table in the living room and cast in the glow of the fire: Nancy with her needlework, the twins with their toys, and Audrey and Ben, clasping hands beneath a pile of papers and books. They all appear contented and peaceful. There's even a pot of yellow daffodils in the center of the table, adding to the happy scene.

With shaking hands, I unlock the door and step into the room. The family looks real enough to touch, but something is different now. They're all looking directly at me—Nancy with her motherly smile and the two little boys with shy grins. Audrey, whose fine features and blond hair are so like mine, regards me for a long, breathless moment. But then it's Ben who draws my attention. His shoulders relax, and he gives me a smile and a nod that feels like a thank you.

Outside noises recede, and in the hush of a few seconds, the ghosts—my ghosts—fade away until they're gone. Not just not there anymore, but gone. The house is empty. And I'm sure of that because left lying on the floor is a single daffodil.

The mirror, too, has changed, back to the way it used to be—a spotty old mirror reflecting an empty room. I lay the daffodil on the mantel where it seems to belong. I feel happy in a sad way, if that's possible—happy that Ben and the Miller family finally found release from this tragic place. I want to think it's because they know someone is finally going to tell the world that Ben was innocent. Truly, I believe that's why they were here in the first place.

Still wary, I slip upstairs. I have a desperate hope that Junior followed the others away from the house—though not likely to the same place they're going.

With some trepidation, I step through the open door to Audrey's room. It feels empty—at least there are no movements, no whispers. I want to believe all my problems have been miraculously solved and Junior has been banished from this house—my house. The light is dim on this side of the house, and the room is in shadow until I turn on the light. The pink is gone, but there's something new on the Subtle Sand walls: dots and splotches and streaks running down the walls, all red as blood.

I gasp in shock and turn slowly around.

By the closet, in the messy crimson print of an angry kindergartener, are the numbers "4-15."

Somehow I get up the courage to ask, "Did you kill Audrey here, in this room? Is that why you came back—to relive it? But I'm Abby, not Audrey, Junior. There's nothing for you here anymore."

Silence. I continue. "They left. Don't you understand that? Audrey and Ben and the others. They're all gone. It's just you here now, alone." More silence. "Your brother would like to destroy this house, Junior. Did you know that? He doesn't care about you. You should leave. You should find somewhere else to go before it's too late." My voice fades to a whisper. "Somewhere far away—"

Suddenly, the room is no longer empty. There's a sense of presence, of cruel eyes watching and waiting. A reddish mist fills the corners of the room with a strange metallic smell, like blood.

My whole body starts to shake, and my left leg nearly gives way as I stare around me in revulsion. Then the whispering starts. Only this time the words are "Abby, Abby, Abby" and I know it's not a memory but a threat. Tomorrow is April fifteenth, the same date as the murders.

Backing out the door, I hiss, "You're not going to get *me*, Junior. I'm getting rid of *you*." Nothing seems to follow me as I head down the stairs. Now, clearly, it's just Junior and me in this house. But how do I get rid of him? Is there such a thing as a quick exorcism? Unfortunately, I'm pretty sure I don't have the time to find out.

When I reach the bottom of the stairs, the door above me slams shut.

I'm drawn to the silvery glass of the mirror. "I know you're gone," I whisper to the ghosts in desperation, "but I wish you could tell me how to make Junior leave. I can't take the chance of being here with him —no one can." I shiver as I hear something moving around upstairs, something big. Junior, furiously slopping more red on the walls?

As the steps above creak, a shadow spreads across the bottom of the mirror, peaked, like a roof. Little curls of gray rise above it. I know where I've seen that picture before. It's burned into my mind.

"Fire?" I'm not sure whether I say the word, or it's whispered from the mirror. And now the words, "Fire house."

I close my eyes and lean against the mantel. The words—
nightmare words to me—come again: "Fire house." There's got to
be another way. I think about Jack's words calling the mirror a
doorway to the beyond. Since the Milliers are free, I don't hesitate.
I grab the long extension handle for painting and swing it like a bat
at the mirror. It cracks and splinters like an elaborate spiderweb.

I close my eyes and breathe a sigh of relief. But when I open my
eyes, the reddish mist is snaking down the stairs. Junior can't be far
behind. I should have broken the mirror sooner. Now it's too late.
Junior has obviously crossed over and no longer needs the mirror.

"Fire house." The soft words repeat. Burn the house? I cannot
possibly do that! But the voices insist, "Fire house fire house fire
house" until they finally become a wordless murmur.

"This is all my fault," I whisper to myself. "I'm the reason
Junior's here. He never had the power to do anything like this until
I came along…" And if I don't do something quick, he might be able
to attach himself to me and follow me out of here. Somehow I know
this as sure as if Junior had whispered in my ears.

Fire.

I used to help Dad burn leaves in the fall; it's not that hard to
start a fire. But in here? How can I start a fire inside the house?

That's when the geezers' words come back to me: there are cans
of gas in the garage. Still I waver. There has to be another way. I can't
burn this house down; it was supposed to be my fresh start. It was
supposed to be home to me and my boys. Besides, the mere thought
of a fire makes me weak at the knees.

Then another thought pops into my head: Vernelle has
insurance on this place. If I burn it down, I could I go to jail for
arson. But what if Vernelle doesn't collect the money? Is that still
arson? Because if I'm caught for arson, I'll never get my boys back.
Never.

But it's either burn down this house or leave Junior in charge. Already the peace of the little house is gone. Junior is taking over. The reddish mist is forming into long tendrils around the room that remind me of hands, of bloodied hands. . . .

Somehow I push that thought aside and force myself to make a plan. I'll have to say the fire was an accident. I'll make up some story that will make me sound incredibly stupid. You can't go to jail for doing something incredibly stupid, can you?

There are matches and a pile of old newspapers in the kitchen.

Suppose I start a fire in the fireplace to burn up the old newspapers. And when I leave, maybe the fire spreads to the other piles of newspapers and then to some brushes I left to soak in a can of gasoline. "I didn't mean for that to happen," I'll say, crying into a giant snowy handkerchief, "It was a stupid accident."

I do not have a snowy handkerchief, but one way or another, I will set this house on fire. I'm going to burn Junior out before he becomes strong enough to leave this place.

Before I lose my nerve, I collect the stuff I need from the kitchen and the container of gasoline from the garage. With shaky hands, I set a couple of cans filled with brushes and gas near the fireplace and put crumpled piles of newspaper around them and on the mantel. Then I make a trail of newspapers leading behind the wall in the dining room. I know that fumes can be dangerous, so I will light the paper from there.

From the red container, I dribble gas onto the paper. By now, the smell of gasoline is almost overpowering. I'm holding a bunch of matches in my hand when I pause. What kind of madness is this??? I remember the flames and the heat and smell of burning flesh when our house was burning down around me. I remember the blanket of smoke that choked my throat until I couldn't breathe.

My heart starts pounding, and a sheen of sweat forms across my forehead: I can't do this.

Then with a sudden impulse, I toss a lighted match onto the paper and watch as the flames race in a yellow-orange ribbon toward the fireplace. For a moment, I'm afraid that the fire will burn out (or only burn the fireplace), but it gains energy as it goes. Then with a sudden WHOOSH, the whole fireplace and the area in front of it is burning.

But something else is going on in the mirror. As the bright flames lick upward to touch the glass, a huge blotch appears. It's Junior's face, completely distorted in the fractured mirror. His eyes are black slits, and his mouth's a giant hole as if he's screaming in terror. Maybe he's trying to escape, to follow the others from the mirror, but it's too late. Thankfully, he must still be tethered to the mirror.

I can't look anymore. I back up and cover my eyes. I can hear a giant crack! when the mirror splits apart and shatters into a thousand pieces. When I open my eyes, the pieces of splintered glass are lying across the burning carpet, and Junior is gone.

But so is the house. I put an arm across my face to shield it from the heat and back up further. I need to leave. I'll call 911 when I get to my car, but I don't think anything can save the house now.

# CHAPTER 46

"What the hell?"

I whirl, expecting to find Jack behind me, but it's Tom Trimble, standing in the kitchen doorway, a satisfied smirk on his face. "Little lady, I sure never thought you'd have the guts for an insurance scam."

He's the last person I want to see. "It's not a scam. I'm burning this house down to get rid of your murdering brother!" I take a few steps back, though I can't go far now. "Get out, Tom."

Tom's cold eyes sweep across the living room. "That's crazy! Junior died in a nut house years ago!" By now, the far end of the room is engulfed in flames. Even the wood of the stairway is starting to curl and spit. "I've told you all along this place should be burned to the ground. I'm just disappointed that you took the pleasure of doing it away from me." His features harden. "I want that note—and anything else you've got about my family."

"Why are you so worried?" I ask impatiently. "This is all about Junior, not you." We need to get out of here. The smoke is making my eyes water and my throat burn.

"You don't get it." Tom shakes his head. He's still smiling, but it's not a pleasant smile. "Junior might've had something wrong with him, but he was still a Trimble. I don't want my family name drug through the filth for no reason."

"No reason?" Panic and the acrid smoke make my voice shrill. "Junior killed four innocent people, and if your father had turned Junior in on the night of the murders, Ben Stockton wouldn't have died. Don't you get it? An innocent boy committed suicide because your family was protecting the Trimble name. And what was the point? Why are you above the law?"

As I'm talking, I edge forward toward the kitchen and toward my only escape, but Tom's body fills the doorway. He snarls, "Maybe he didn't commit suicide. Have you ever thought of that? We—and our money—run this town. We do anything it takes to protect our family from trash like you and your sister." He gives me a shove. "Now, Ms. Bennett, I want that note. Then I'll let you leave."

Smoke is roiling all around, and every instinct warns me that we have to leave before it's too late. But what Tom just said still registers. He pretty much admitted his father had Ben killed. I lose control. "Ambrosia already has the note. Marv, too. So it doesn't make any difference anymore! Everyone's going to know!" Behind me, the flames are crackling. I can feel the heat on my back as the fire spreads. "Now for God's sake, let me go!"

Tom's face contorts with fury until he could be Junior's twin. He pulls out a handkerchief and coughs into it. I try to dash passed him but he catches me and pushes me back. "I don't think you gave that note to anyone, you lying bitch." His voice is muffled by the handkerchief and the crackle of the fire, but he makes sure to speak loud enough that I can't miss a word. "You can go—out the front through the fire. I know how much you like fire."

Frantically I look around at the front door, but I can't see it through the smoke and flames. In desperation I run at Tom as hard as I can, arms swinging, fingernails clawing. "What's the matter with you?" I'm screaming now. "We have to get out of here!"

I start choking on the smoke, and wipe my face on my arm. When I look up, I see that Tom has something in his hand and is swinging it at me. I put an arm up to shield myself, then everything goes black.

I wake up groggily, lying on the floor. I'm woozy and my head feels like it's splitting open. There's thick smoke in my throat and in my eyes. I've lost all sense of direction and can't see a way out.

That's when I see Hunter and Grayson, just a few feet away from me. Hunter holds his airplane, and Grayson is clutching his teddy bear. They have their arms around each other, and they're smiling at me.

I reach out to them and try to stand up, but my left leg buckles beneath me, and I fall back. In desperation, I pull my body across the floor, but I can't seem to get any closer. I can still hear the fire behind me, but now I don't care. I just want to get to Hunter and Grayson—I have to get them out of the burning house.

Somehow I manage to get through the kitchen to the doorway and gasp in a breath of fresh air. But the boys are gone. All that's left is a tunnel of white. . .

# CHAPTER 47

The mattress I'm lying on is as hard and lumpy as a log raft. It's a familiar feeling I recognize: I'm in a hospital bed. Sure enough, there's the adjustable side table beside me with its usual glass of water (bent straw included) and a box of Kleenex. Hospitals always have a ready supply of bent straws and Kleenex.

Gauze bandages cover my hands and—my exploring fingers discover—on my face. On my right side, an IV needle is taped painfully into the back of my hand, and my head feels as if it's been hit with a hammer. I close my eyes again and a groan escapes my lips. I'm still in the hospital in California...

A cool hand covers mine, and from the side of the bed, Vernelle says, "Abby, are you awake?"

I open my eyes. Vernelle is smiling at me, but I can read the relief in her face. "Sis," I start to say, but it comes out in a croak, hardly like a word at all. She gives me a sip of water, and the second time it sounds better. "Sis, where am I?"

"In the hospital in Mt. Prospect. They almost sent you to Iowa City, but the doctor decided you'd be okay here."

"I thought you were in Dubuque!"

She rolls her eyes at me. "Are you shitting me? After Jack called me, Garrett drove like hell to get us here."

I hold up my hands. "How bad?" I ask. All I can think is, please no more surgeries.

Vernelle's voice is soothing. "They're not bad at all, mostly scrapes and bruises. Your face isn't bad, either. The doctors were more concerned about the knot on your head." She takes a deep breath. "Abby, what the hell happened to you out there?"

I lick my dry lips. "Tom Trimble. He hit me with something; I'm not sure what, and then he left me lying there, in the fire."

She jumps up. "That bastard! I'll tell Marv. He's just outside."

I grab her arm. Before she leaves, there's something I have to ask my sister. "Vernelle. Are my boys dead?"

"What?"

"Hunter and Grayson—they're dead, aren't they? I didn't believe it before, but now I want to know the truth."

She sinks slowly back into the chair. "Yes. They died in the fire. I'm so sorry, Abby." Her voice has a quaver in it. "Brad told you—everyone told you—but you always insisted they'd gotten out, that their beds were empty when you got to their room. That was because the babysitter let them stay in their sleeping bags in the family room so they could watch a movie. They died peacefully, of smoke inhalation. They just went to sleep and never woke up."

"But I remember Brad saying he'd taken them to New York." It's my last protest.

She's crying now. "Their bodies, Abby. Brad took their bodies for burial in his family's plot. I'll give him that—he didn't want them left alone out in California. When you're better, Jack said he'll take you to New York to visit their graves."

Their graves—it's something I'll have to get used to. "Jack knew they were dead?"

"He asked me a few days ago, but he'd already guessed."

Tears start running down my cheeks. Vernelle squeezes my hand. "I'll give you a moment to pull yourself together. Then you have to talk to Marv. He's outside and wants to know about Tom and all the shit that went on out there."

Vernelle helps me sit up, but I'm still not exactly composed when Marv walks in. Hat in hand and without his usual grin, he stands by the chair that Vernelle vacated. "Miz Bennett, I know you're in a good deal of pain, but I want to know what happened to you this morning, unofficially for now. We'll take your statement when you feel better."

I tell him I'm doing all right and ask what he needs to know. "Just a couple of things, then I'll let Mr. Allender in. He's been pacing the hell out of the tile in the hall."

It makes me feel better, to know Jack's here. "I'll try to remember what I can, but it's kind of mixed up in my mind."

He nods. "Vernelle said Tom Trimble hit you. Is that right?"

"That's almost the last thing I remember. I was getting ready to leave—you know I'd been painting out there—when Tom walked in on me. I don't know what he used, but he definitely hit me with something. It must have knocked me out for a while. He was crazy angry about that stuff I gave to you and Ambrosia about Junior." Without thinking, I place a bandaged hand on my aching head and wince with a sharp pain.

Marv nods again. "So Tom set the house on fire to cover up what he'd done?" He pauses. "Sorry, that was a leading question. Miz Bennett, who started the fire?"

I'm about to blurt out the whole story and tell him everything that happened. Then I think of the Lady at the Airport, Zandra Marx. I am strong, I tell myself.

I manage to look straight into Marv's face. "Knowing my history, do you seriously think I'd burn down my own house—with me in it?"

His eyes study me a moment. They're the color of sherry, and I don't think much gets by him. "It would be real odd," Marv allows, "especially since a coupla' gas cans were found in the wreck of Trimble's SUV."

"He had a wreck? I'm not sure I understand." My head is still spinning from finally accepting the loss of my sons. I can't make sense of what Marv is trying to tell me.

He fidgets with the deputy's hat in his hand while he explains. "After he left your place—witnesses said he was speeding—he went through a stop-sign and got T-boned at the intersection by a truckload of lumber. He didn't have a chance. Jack Allender was following the truck and called it in. Then he saw the smoke and went on to your place."

He leans closer and puts a firm hand on my shoulder. "Allender found you by the back door and carried you out of the house. The EMT guys said you'd be dead if he hadn't got there in time. He has a few little ol' burns, but they don't amount to much." With a final pat on my shoulder, he says, "You get well now, Miz Bennett. It's all over."

I relax with a sigh; I hope he's right. When Marv reaches the door, I ask him to give me a couple of minutes before Jack comes in. As he leaves the room, Marv gives me a snappy salute and a last toothy smile.

The door has barely closed when I grab Vernelle's purse off the chair. She usually carries more cosmetics than an Avon lady. With my free hand, I fish around until I find a comb, mascara, and some lip-gloss. Her tiny mirror helps me (one chunk of my head at a time) comb my hair and give my face some color. The small bandage, placed rakishly across my temple, adds a nice touch.

When the door opens, a man comes into the room, clean-shaven but wearing a baseball cap.

I stare at him uncertainly. "Jack?"

He rubs a hand across his face, smiling sheepishly. "My beard got a little singed, so I shaved it off."

Jack looks nice, but so different that a wave of shyness sweeps over me. When he leans one hand on the bed-rail, I look away. "The house is gone, isn't it? And the ghosts, too, Junior included. He left when the mirror burned; I saw him."

"Abby." Jack leans down and kisses me on the forehead.

I grab his hand like a lifeline. "Jack, Marv said you saved my life."

He gives my hand a quick squeeze. "Honest to God, I thought you were dead. And if you hadn't been just two feet from the door, I'd never have found you." His dark eyes study my face somberly. "When I made that promise to Lily about saving someone's life, I always figured it would be a stranger—not someone I love." His sudden smile is tender. "You've changed my life, too, Abby. I think we saved each other."

# CHAPTER 48

We're standing in front of a fence, Jack and I, on a cool, damp May morning. A heavy mist is swirling around us. The black wrought-iron fence encircles the yard where the house once stood. Over the gate is a sign with gold lettering that reads, "In memory of those who once lingered here."

The burned-out shell of the house is gone, buried by a backhoe one wet afternoon. I had watched, like it was a funeral, and said goodbye to the Millers and my boys as raindrops fell like tears. Vernelle and Garrett and Jack and I planted grass in the scarred patch of dirt where the house used to be, and already there's a faint blur of emerging green.

Now that my hands are fully healed, I take hold of the iron bars and lean my face against them. "Some flowers. I think I'll plant some flowers—roses, maybe—where the daffodils used to grow." Jack nods. "I was going to live here, you know, when Vernelle and Garrett got married. They're making wedding plans now, and I'm so happy for them, but—"

He gives me a sideways glance. "You'd never have wanted to live here, Abby, even if the house hadn't burned down."

"No, not after what happened. I'm glad it's over."

Jack grins. "Or maybe it's not. That was quite a special edition Ambrosia put out. Pictures, too. They say it's being picked up by the *Des Moines Register*."

"It's all more than I ever imagined. Not Ambrosia, though. And she's already got the copyrights sewed up so Dickie can't make a movie or something."

After a moment, Jack says softly, "Abby, you set that fire, didn't you?"

I clutch the bars tighter, remembering. "I had to; I didn't want to, but I had to. How did you know?"

A muscle moves along his jaw. "By the way the fire was burning when I found you. It was pretty obvious it had been started under the mirror. Trimble wouldn't have done that." He tips back his baseball cap and adds in a casual voice, "You can move in with me. Of course, I don't have any spare bedrooms."

"You mean I'll have to bunk with Spencer?"

He shrugs. "We'll figure something out." There's a thoughtful pause, and he adds, "The ring's another matter entirely."

He catches me by surprise. "The ring?"

Jack faces me. There's a softness I'm not used to seeing in his dark eyes. "Yeah, I'm talking marriage here, woman. I was thinking platinum with diamonds around the band and maybe two little blue stones mixed in there somewhere. How does that sound?"

"It sounds wonderful." I stop to wipe the tears from my eyes, but they're tears of joy. Jack's arm goes across my shoulders and pulls me to him. In a shaky voice I add, "What about another little stone, a pink one?"

"Yellow, it would have to be. That was Lily's favorite. She always said yellow was the color of happiness."

"Yellow, then." The mist gathers inside the fence. For a moment, it's almost solid, as if the little white house still stood there. Then it swirls away, leaving behind nothing but emptiness.

Jack and I are turning away when I spot something in the grass at my feet. It's a marble, a sky-blue marble, bright and shiny. I pick it up and hold it in the palm of my hand. The other marbles are gone now, but there's this one. It's a gift, I realize, a gift of goodbye from two little boys who were separated from me by half a century.

I lift my eyes to the gray sky above the trees. There, in the distance, are two other little boys, one with his favorite toy airplane tucked under his arm; the other holding a teddy bear. As I watch with a catch in my breath, Hunter and Grayson smile their sweet smiles and then slowly fade into the mist.

When they're gone, Jack takes my hand, and we walk away from the past and toward our future together.

THE END

# ABOUT THE AUTHORS

This aunt and niece duo have always shared a love of writing. They decided to team up as coauthors and the rest, as they say, is history.

Photo by Lindsay's Photography

Corinne Malcolm Ibeling comes from a long line of Iowans—farmers, coal miners, and even a couple of circus owners. Her experiences living in small-town Iowa serve as inspiration for the settings and characters of her novels. However, her only real-life experience with ghosts was living in an old house where footsteps were occasionally heard at night going up and down the stairs.

Photo by Freeze Frame Photography

R.I.Partridge is a freelance editor who specializes in speculative fiction and mysteries. She's a frequent panelist at science fiction conventions. Her first novel, *Escaping the Dashia*, was released earlier this year. To learn more, go to www.ripartridge.com

# NOTE FROM THE AUTHORS

Word-of-mouth is crucial for any author to succeed. If you enjoyed *Abby's Fire*, please leave a review online—anywhere you are able. Even if it's just a sentence or two. It would make all the difference and would be very much appreciated.

Thanks!
Corinne Malcolm Ibeling & R.I.Partridge

We hope you enjoyed reading this title from:

BLACK❦ROSE
writing™

www.blackrosewriting.com

Subscribe to our mailing list – *The Rosevine* – and receive **FREE** books, daily deals, and stay current with news about upcoming releases and our hottest authors.
Scan the QR code below to sign up.

Already a subscriber? Please accept a sincere thank you for being a fan of Black Rose Writing authors.

View other Black Rose Writing titles at www.blackrosewriting.com/books and use promo code **PRINT** to receive a **20% discount** when purchasing.

Made in the USA
Las Vegas, NV
13 January 2024

84333845R00163